First Dry Rattle

Celia Boyd has written *Young Ravens*, a novel for children set in the Midlands during the Second World War, and *First Fashionings, Social Conditioning in Georgian Children's Fiction* - shortly to be published by *Graficas Books*. She has contributed to *The Cambridge Guide to Children's Books in English*, and has had two articles published in *Signal, Approaches to Children's books*.

As Celia Mason, working for the West Midlands Probation Services, she wrote *Are You Here For The Beer?*, an in-cell, self-help guide for prison inmates, whose criminality stemmed from alcohol abuse. For this she received the Butler Trust Award. She currently writes full time, and is working on the second part of *A Reason from the Stars* series, entitled *A Daring Resolution*.

D1103107

In Memory of Bill

love from Celia

Celia Boyd

First Dry Rattle

*"the first dry rattle of new-dawn steel
changes the world today"*
Kipling: Edgehill Fight

The first book in the series "A Reason from the Stars"

Graficas Books

First published in 2006,
By Graficas Books, Cwmbach, Glasbury-on-Wye

Copyright © Celia Boyd 2006
All rights reserved

Set in Classical Garamond by
Graficas Books

Printed in Great Britain by
Biddles Ltd., Norfolk

ISBN 0 9554834 0 9
ISBN 978 0 9554834 0 0

This book is sold subject to the condition that it shall not, by way
of trade or otherwise, be lent re-sold, hired out, or otherwise
circulated without the publisher's prior consent in any form of
binding or cover other than that in which it is published and
without a similar condition including this condition being im-
posed on the subsequent purchaser.

First Dry Rattle

Being the first of the Thomas Fletcher papers, entitled *A Reason From The Stars*, a first-hand account of the late civil disturbances endured by our unfortunate country, undertaken by royal command in 1668.

"The King Enjoys His Own Again."

"There's neither Swallow, Dove, nor Dade,
Can soar more high or deeper wade;
Nor show a reason from the Stars,
What causeth peace, or Civil Wars."

Matthew Parker d.1656

PREFACE

Extract from a letter from William Cavendish, 3rd Earl of Devonshire to his learned friend, companion and tutor, Thomas Hobbes, at Hardwick Hall in this year of grace 1668.

"...and so the King commends him to you and instructs me to report that should you wish yet again to be the "bear to be baited" by the Court wits (if such they be) order is again given that you shall have free access to His Majesty's gracious self at all times.

An event occurred that put me in mind of your own restoration with the King. Last week his Majesty made his progress with all due pomp towards the Guildhall in the City, there to be feasted by the Mayor and Alderman. The crowds crying out ever "God Save the King" and "Long Live Your Majesty" and such good compliments to their beloved sovereign when His Majesty, espying some man standing tall behind the common sort, a little moppet on his shoulders (the better that she might see her King), His Majesty, I say, on seeing this tall fellow did cause the progress to be stopped and this same fellow to come forward (Just as took place, dear friend, when a few days after the King was restored to us, he espied you at the gate of Little Salisbury House and ordered your approach) To resume – the man comes forward with much show of modesty, and being called up to the very coach door by the King did make his courtesy with much seemliness and pleasure. The happiness at this encounter was reflected in the countenance of his Majesty who said to all privileged to hear: "This good man's dissemblance saved my person from certain death at Rebel Hands." He then bids this good fellow and patriot (who was a churugeon and apothecary from the City of Worcester) to attend him later that even at Whitehall.

This physician had it seemed seen much action in these late Civil Wars (although at no time I think in these Our Islands had Incivility so Tyrannical a sway). He had at 19 after the skirmish at Powick Bridge in Worcestershire suffered a fate so close to that of His Majesty that when they met some nine years later at the Great

Battle of Worcester, there must needs be a close communion. For this Thomas Fletcher's innocent father was hung for a spy by Robert Devereux Earl of Essex in the common market place, and our Gracious Majesty on meeting in this way with Fletcher remembered him of their mutual tragedy.

But there was much merriment also at this later encounter at Whitehall. The service this same fellow performed was one few other citizens could perform for all who saw them side by side remarked well how strangely close in physiognomy and in stature this common surgeon was to His Majesty, although his elder by seven years. It seemed this same resemblance succoured His Majesty by "dissemblance", thus allowing him to avoid the Rebel soldiery intent on his capture after the ill-fated Battle of Worcester.

After his audience with His Majesty when he was dined and feted – his wife, son and daughter likewise – suffice it to report that he left His Majesty's portal, the richer by a knighthood. When His Majesty divulged his intention, he was heard to remark with a degree of assurance that might be judged indiscreet in the Court circle: "*My* grandsire refused this singular honour from your grandsire, sir, when money could have purchased it. But now if it please you to bestow it for service, then it pleases me much to accept." Then did all men present catch their breath, for it did not sort well to speak ill of King James. But His Majesty laughed much and clapping him about the shoulder says: "For a dissembler, true Thomas, you are as bold a man in your words as I could meet in any wood in Worcestershire!" Then they both fell a-laughing as about some private matter. At length without further words 'tis 'Arise, Sir Thomas Fletcher'."

I had speech with this same new Knight after the King's audience had concluded. It is, alas, too infrequent in these days to meet any who had known that rare pleasure of Great Tew discourse and companionship. He had rested there after Edgehill with Edward Holte for two months, and remembered their talk of you. When at last he met you as his patient in Paris, twenty years ago, you spoke with him of Lucius Corley of blessed memory, and said much comfortingly to him of the dreadful end of his innocent father. When he learned that I corresponded with you he begged me to send his affectionate duty. (He jested also that he trusted you will forgive his acceptance of this reward of "knighthood" I found to my shame he was more familiar with *Leviathan* than ever I was).

One further Royal proposition was heeded. Learning that this Fletcher had throughout nine years of unrest, found himself many times as a surgeon on the field of battle, the King demanded that he should commit to the immortality of print his several encounters with discord and death. Upon observing that Thomas had of an instant a "doubting" air at such a notion, the King insisted: "Nay there must be much that you in abstaining from warfare as a physician observed that was cruel and heedless even in the ranks of those who loved my father. Prithee Tom" and here he fell a-laughing again "write your history as I hear the late but not lamented Lord Protector instructed the painter Lely 'With roughness, warts, pimples and all, or I swear I shall not pay a farthing for it'. Do so, Thomas." And so the matter was left.

Ere I conclude I must acquaint you with the news of the new French Ambassador, Monsieur Colbert. He continues to amaze the court with the grandeur of his equipage and costume......."

1

1639

Once whilst committing suicide, I changed my mind.

I related the incident some years later to the great philosopher Thomas Hobbes who listened courteously enough (he had after all demanded to know how I came to the 'doctoring' trade) and then asked graciously: "Ah, but Thomas, which mind did you change?"

My sixteen year old persona, bent on self-slaughter, remembered in the instant before stepping off the joint stool, that the Victor Ludorum crown at Pitchcroft for wrestling and for quarterstaffs was mine for the taking on Wednesday next. My careful preparations - nail in the beam, strong rope fashioned into a noose, noose over the nail - could be hoarded and postponed. But I had reckoned without the crooked treachery of the joint stool.

It fell over. My feet dangled in space. My hands flew above me to the rope in a vain attempt to ease the tension. But my handiwork was good. The noose held for an eternity of choking pain. My feet flailing for a foothold caught on the fallen stool for a tantalizing instant before my frenzied scrabbling and the sloping floor sent it rolling towards the wall. Also to my shame my wayward member set out rampantly for a Parliament all of his own. Burning brands tore my throat and neck apart and my spine stretched and cracked. Then my weight dragged the nail from the beam - or rather through it. As I crashed down, splinters of wood showering around me, the door opened and there was my poor father.

My cheek was pressed to such softness I thought my mother had snatched me to her in heaven, particularly as all I could hear was her name: "Nerys, forgive me. Nerys, sweet wife, forgive me." My father was stroking my hair and weeping over me. My head ached, a very football of pain, and I dribbled and bled, the dryness in my throat causing me to choke with each noisy breath. I realised that my spittle and blood were staining my father's Sunday doublet. With an effort I swallowed and motioned to the pitcher of water that stood on the chest.

My father still weeping brought over the beaker and held it while I tried to drink. My first attempt failed and his gown suffered even more, but then the cool spring water slid down my damaged gullet, bringing some slight relief.

"I've cracked the beam!" I croaked.

"Devil take the beam, boy! You near cracked your neck, numbskull! But can this all be because you cannot stomach the butchery? This is a hard lesson for me, son. Nay, I should have listened." He paused, sighed and hugged me to him.

"You know how I am - how *we* are. Mulish stubborn, the pair of us. I thought your dislike merely youthful fancy and mimsy-pimsy snot in the wind. 'Tis a good trade, lad." He held me away to make his point. "Folks always eat in good times and bad. Here drink again."

I had to keep swallowing which was becoming easier. "You're home from Matins very early," I gasped out.

"And Jesus, Mary and Joseph be praised that a pegging tooth caused me to leave before Doctor Potter got into his sermonising. Listen son. So you cannot abide butchering. Well, well so be it. But a man must live. What I have is yours, son Thomas while I live and after I die. You cannot want to live in idleness." He left me and walked over to the window. "A man must have a calling or the devil in him thrives. What will you do with your life?"

I knew so well what I wanted to be." Father, do you think Ben would have me as an apprentice?"

"We can but ask. I am determined you shan't endure the slaughtering trade. I have thought lately that had I my time again, I might also have chosen not to follow my father even though - Ah Devil take it!"

A spasm of pain crossed my poor father's features. "Cold water, son. It numbs the ache." He closed his eyes as the remedy took effect. "There's nothing for it. Fetch Ben. Tell him it's loosening as he said it would. Tell him it rocks in my jaw."

I had never had toothache, had forgotten that my father had said as we broke our fast, only hours before, "Well I'll go to church, like a Christian, though its with a heavy heart, a nagging tooth and an undutiful son." The agony of pain he had endured in the cold cathedral had driven him home before the Second Collect. Would I have died I wondered if he had not returned to loosen the choking noose as I lay gasping on the floor. My aching lungs could not support much exertion. I tried to run down the empty Sunday streets which but half an hour before I had not thought to see again. I pushed myself along in short bursts down Hounds Lane, skirted All Saints and down Newport Street. As the healing air took effect, I sustained a more constant speed.

I turned aside under the sign, halfway down on my left. "Apothecary. Barber. Chirugeon," knocked loudly on the door but received no reply. Suppose Ben was from home..? I raced down the alley beside the house, shouting, "Ben! Ben, are you there?" There was no answer. Then I remembered Mistress Forest at Grimley insisted that Ben attended her lyings-in and that she was again with child. But then I heard a sleepy voice call, "Through the wicket!"

The gate from the water meadows led directly to the small court behind the shop. Ben was lying on his back beneath an apple tree, the breeze blowing gentle flakes of blossom on to his thin brown chest which he had bared to the Spring's warmth.

As he saw me, he started up. "Tom! Your neck!"

"Oh Mother of God, never mind that. Come now and come prepared. Father says, "Draw it for God's sake!" Will you haste Ben? Bring the pincers. The pain's on him, fit to drive him witless."

Ben went swiftly to his workshop. I followed and in spite of the need for haste, looked round in wonder as I always did. In my heart this seemed a glorious trade. To cure ills, to restore health. Ben should be the happiest man in the world. I watched him select herbs for a poultice and the grim tools needed for drawing teeth. He drew on his shirt and then stood for a moment lost in thought, absent-mindedly scratching his chest.

"Ah Yes!" I said remembering. "And he said to tell you that it rocks somewhat now on its bed."

"Does it so? Then it must be drawn, cousin Thomas. No remedy. The pity is the tooth itself is sound - unrotted and healthy. It's what lurks beneath in the gums that forces action."

"What is beneath it, then?" I asked.

Ben locked the shop and as we were starting back to Fish Street he answered slowly, "I know not. A mess of white pus. A gathering of poison. I believe that had I the skill to disperse that foulness through the blood, Amyas would again sink that tooth into apples or roast beef. As it is the tooth must go, so that the poison can drain off. You must help me." He called over his shoulder as we rounded the corner of Fish Street and entered under the sign of the Hereford Bull.

"Ben, young Ben, I care not how cruel thy pincers so long as I and this accursed tooth part company." My father was sitting in his favourite high backed chair in the kitchen, his large hands grasping its arms. "I swear to you both, I'll be asking leave to borrow my son's rope and nail if this torture goes on."

Ben raised a questioning eyebrow "What rope and nail?"

"Oh, leave that now," I fussed round my father. "Another drink of cold water?"

"This is better," said Ben, producing a phial of colourless liquid. "Swill it round the tooth, good uncle, and swallow or spit out whichever you prefer. Now then Thomas, prepare to hold down your father. There will be great stress between us. You must be steadfast and push down on Amyas' shoulders. Lucky for us it's the lower jaw. Now, good sir, show us the mouth of Hell.

My father opened his mouth. His teeth were good, white and even. He pushed his tongue against the offender. Although it moved fractionally forward, it seemed to me to be innocent, untainted and white.

"Ah, yes!" said Ben calmly. "That is excellent. The poison forces the roots of the tooth apart, I think. Now sir you will know why I advised delay, so that we could be entirely certain of the identity of the offender. More of this Sir if you please." He proffered the colourless phial again, "and wash it around the tooth."

"What is that water?" I asked.

"Water, call you it? It may look pure as water, but it is Hollands Gin, a distillation of juniper berries. Now Tom, be ready to push down as I tell you." Ben had taken off his shirt again and stood in his breeches, pincers in hand. I soon realised the reason why he had prepared himself as if for a wrestling bout. I pushed down on my poor father's shoulders, whilst Ben sought for purchase on the tooth. Sweat started from my forehead, my arms ached. My father's whole weight and strength strained against my hands as Ben pulled upwards.

"It's coming! It's coming!" Ben cried. "We'll rest a moment. Tom, pour more of the Hollands around that part of his jaw."

My poor father groaned as we began again to push and pull. Suddenly Ben jerked back, almost falling. In the pincers was the tooth. I was amazed at the length of its roots. There was a great rush of blood from the wound and a reek of decay that caused Ben to nod his head in satisfaction.

"The charnel-house stench - perfume to my nose," he proclaimed grinning broadly. "That's the cause of the pain. See there!" I could see yellow streaks in the flow of red. "That is poison. Why it forms below teeth I don't know. There must be some herb, some simple that would dissolve it. Devil take it! He's gone! Uncle Amyas! Tom! Cold water! Bathe his face!"

My father had fainted. Blood streamed from his mouth onto his ill-fated Sunday gown.

"As gently as you may. It's a natural conclusion to his suffering. A bowl or a basin for him. Now good Uncle," as my father opened his eyes. "Use this to rinse and spit as the blood flows." He pushed the phial of Hollands gin into Amyas' hands. "Use it, sir. It will make the pain bearable and cleanse the wound."

"How is it with you, father?" I asked softly, and was relieved to see my father force the mouth of hell into a crooked smile.

"Well, son, better than 'twas with thee a short hour ago. Ben will you look to his neck?"

"Yes, what happened?" Ben was searching in his pack. "Ah, here it is. A cooling salve for burns. How did this come about?" He asked again as he applied the ointment.

"Tell him," my father croaked.

"I was set on Damnation. Father prevented it."

"Damnation?" Ben tied a bandage round the sores.

5

"I decided to hang myself. But just as I changed my mind, the stool slipped. Luckily the beam cracked and father came home just in time to loosen the noose. But I have hurt my neck."

"Does that surprise you?" Ben asked me softly. I shook my head. Now that my father had been attended to, the pain throbbed and pulsed unbearably.

"Woodworm!" my father managed to creak out "The simple woodworm saved you son! Ben," he went on "Best name your payments and get back to your maying," as a petal of apple blossom fell from Ben's hair. "Will you take an apprentice?" pointing at me. "Does that suit, Tom?"

The delight in my face was his answer. "Will you consent, Master Doctor?" said my father with formal chivalry.

"With great pleasure and much relief," said Ben. "My practice grows apace. I need a likely young fellow to turn away the young ladies who think I should do nought but make them love potions. Come to me tomorrow, Sir. I'll make a saw-bones of you yet, Cousin Tom."

2

September 1642

There were upward of twenty barrels to fill and the noonday sun beat down on the hillside as strongly as it had done throughout August. Ben insisted that in our medical practice we used the clear water that bubbled up from the Malvern Springs, ("pure as a virgin's thoughts," said my irreverent father), so there I was with Apple, our donkey, who was neither use nor ornament but who would travel everywhere with Hector our excellent Welsh Cob who thought nothing of pulling our heavy cart. As I drank myself after feeding and watering these two good friends, I contemplated the miles to Ledbury I had to.....

Surely that was a scream! I listened. Nothing save the farewell squeaks of swallows as they swooped and dived and the drone of the insects they were seeking. But there it came again! I urged Hector on up the track through the trees, which shadowed the approach to the most northerly village of the Malvern Hills. This was a stone cutters' hamlet under the first of the great quarries cut into the east side of the range.

As we trotted down towards the green area before the inn, surrounded by poor cottages, I saw that four or five youths were stoning a large dog. This was often a means to avoid a rabid bite but unthinkably cruel. I drew my dagger to end the creature's pain. But as we erupted onto this trampled village green, I became aware that it was not a dog. It was a woman.

She was crouching on the rough ground, an open wound on her back and with blood streaming from her brow. Her gown, which I judged had once been brown brocade, scarcely covered her. She had assumed the foetal position, attempting to protect her face and eyes from the young ruffians, who unaware of my appearance continued to pelt her with small rocks.

A whip was attached to the side of our cart, not for our horse but for over-curious cattle. I snatched it up and cracked it. The torturers spun round to face me and one immediately took to his heels. The tallest, thinking to tangle with me, advanced, a rock in his hand. Had faces ever been fortunes, he would have been a pauper. I cracked the whip again, grazing his hand and causing him to drop the rock. His evil young face crumpled and he began to cry like the great coward he was.

I advanced on them, my dagger in my left hand and the whip in my right, which I cracked again for good measure. It curled round the legs of one of the others and he fell heavily. Scrambling up, he felt that flight was now a better option than fight and showed a clean pair of heels with his two fellows, tumbling down the hill towards Leigh Sinton. The great baby who had thought to attack me stood for a few more seconds perhaps expecting help from other sources, but then decided that the giant with the whip and the dagger was not to be gainsayed and followed his cronies falling eastwards down the hillside bawling to the world in general: "He's hurt my hand!"

Almost immediately the Green, shuttered and blinded to the appalling scene but one minute before, suddenly became "a field full of folk." Cottagers came out as if to thank me, but thought better of it and talked excitedly to each other and the inn previously closed and dead was suddenly alive with the innkeeper standing outside, hands on hips contemplating me, and his customers leaning round doors and gawping from windows.

The noise of sudden outraged conversation was quite deafening. An old woman from one of the poorest cottages, a very hovel, went straight to the distraught victim and attempted to comfort her and help her up. But the girl was heaving and retching pitifully as if she wished to bring up the contents of her stomach but had naught there to void. To my surprise I noticed she was clutching a tattered old book.

The innkeeper spoke roughly to the old woman: "Leave her, Martha, for your life. Remember old Kate." Then he shouted at me across the babel which instantly subsided: "Get you gone, sir, if you value your life. That great loon has gone to fetch his father who is the ganger for these men. They won't eat this week.

Dodgeson'll not pay them for their work because that booby was prevented from his purposes."

I could not believe what I was hearing. "You saw ...you knew what they were doing to this poor creature ... and you did nothing! What are you, men or mice!"

"They are mice, young master," said a clear voice behind me. I had not noticed the stocks which stood under the shadow of the hill. A pedlar sat there with blood pouring down his face, his pack of wares scattered in the dust around him. I walked over to him noticing that the stocks were not padlocked in the official manner. A piece of stick was pushed through the catch. This was clearly rough justice of the worst kind.

I tossed away the stick and heaved the upper section off his legs and he staggered up gratefully. He was not a young man and had clearly begun his life in a land where the sun browns human skin. He told me, "they put me here to stone me for their sport. She pleaded with them, and they turned on her."

The stone cutters outside the Inn were still arguing fiercely. There were about twenty of them, strongly built. As I approached one was shouting, "And I say he's right! So Dodgeson has the ear of Sir Roger. Well there are many more of us and I say we approach Sir Roger's other ear. Children, mere children rule the roost. I say we must act and now." Some agreed. The spokesman turned to me, "Sir, please go. Your presence can but inflame matters."

I needed little encouragement. I took Hector's blanket from the cart and wrapped the poor suffering woman in it. "I will take her to the Constable in Great Malvern. Look to hear more of this!" I told them, lifting her into the cart.

They guffawed. One yelled out: "'Tis Dodgeson's brother!"

By now I was past caring. "Surely there are other callings that do not rely on the whims of a cowardly ganger, who withholds the money you have earned by your honest sweat and toil. Or if he withholds your money why do you not withhold your labour?"

They were silent. The spokesman nodded slowly. "You must go, sir. Take her away. Vanish like..." He pointed towards the stocks. The pedlar, his pack and his wares had disappeared.

I put Hector to the Great Malvern track, which hugged the Eastern side of the hills. It seemed politic to put as many miles as possible between myself and the all powerful Master Dodgeson, particularly as I had tried to sow the seeds of revolt in his compliant work-force ...politic but not courageous. Still I had a passenger to consider.

She was clearly shocked and frightened by this sudden abduction. I heard her sobbing quietly but I did not stop until I had the old Britains' Camp behind me, and Colwall away down to our right. I drove the cart into the left side of the track. We could clearly see half a mile down behind us, and would swiftly be aware of any pursuit.

"Now madam," said I, my recent qualification as a Physician burning hot in my memory, "I must treat your wounds or you are like to be in a sorry case from infection."

She whispered softly: "I thank you, sir." I had to pick away pieces of her gown which had become engrained in the broken flesh on her back. It must have sorely hurt her but she said not a word. My clean pieces of rag that Old Jill had boiled in the copper were soon filthy and bloodstained. She watched as I opened my box of tinctures and instruments. I had an excellent infusion of sanicle and marigold flowers and after an initial cleansing of the wound, which was wide but not deep, I applied a poultice of comfrey leaves. The gash on her brow had stopped bleeding - marigold again would lessen any scarring. Her poor arms were scratched and torn with her recent rude contact with Mother Earth. I had essence of lavender for this and handed her another clean rag and encouraged her to apply this infusion as she wished. She smelt the lavender with great pleasure and murmured something I did not hear.

"What was that?" I insisted.

"Sister Hildegarde of Bingen .....lavender was her favourite flower."

"Was it indeed?" I commented rhetorically, surprised that so young a patient should know anything of herbal lore. "And pray madam what is your book?"

"It was my mother's," she told me. "It is the last of my possessions. We had to sell everything to buy food."

"And where is your mother now?" I asked her.

"Dead, sir," she drooped her head.

"You had best tell me all," I said. "What is your name?"

She whispered, "Phoebe Stanhope," and then asked, "could I have a drink of water?" Cursing myself for my lack of hospitality, I found her a cup of water and bread, cheese and apples and between bites and gulps and the occasional sob she told her sad tale.

She was the only child of a Derbyshire couple with some pretensions to gentility. I must admit I took this at first with a pinch of salt; how could an aristocratic daughter be brought to this sad pass? And yet her tale rang true. Her father was lord of the manor of a small village near the little town of Middleton and owned a mine in a great lead seam called the Dovegang Rake. However he fell foul of the High Sheriff, a devil incarnate it seems, by name John Gell of Hopton who had the lucrative calling of extracting Ship Money for the King. I had heard of landowners in Worcestershire brought to a sorry pass because of this same tax. Her father had tried to pay his miners something above the daily pittance, taking account of the dangerous nature of their work. Gell ruined him with his Ship Money demands and appropriated the Manor. Her father, depressed and it seems unable to interest his fellow landowners in his plight, died in her mother's arms in the lodge of his own estate after drinking himself into a stupor. Phoebe and her mother were taken in by a wealthy widowed cousin, also of the Stanhope family, but to their horror and consternation this same John Gell, now a knight, God rot him, came a-wooing their benefactress. Her mother could not support his company and they begged the widow to loan them a manservant and funds so that they could make their way to Monmouth where they had relatives.

They reached Tamworth without mishap but upon waking in their inn discovered that both servant and money had disappeared. Now they were dependant on the good will of farmers and carriers to continue their journey and began to sell their clothes and possessions. As they travelled with a carrier towards Dudley they were caught in a rainstorm that lasted the whole day. Her unfortunate mother caught a terrible chill, which soon became bronchitic. In the market at Dudley huddled under a fishmonger's awning, a poor woman found them and took them into her home. Her mother died soon after and Phoebe sold her few pieces of jewellery to pay for her burial. There was an epidemic of whooping cough amongst the children in that town and Phoebe began to cure them with an old receipt of her mother's, which used a tincture of boiled cabbage leaves to which honey, marjoram and thyme had been added. The children made good progress but then one died from an unknown cause and Phoebe discreetly decided to leave and make her way alone to Monmouth. She turned south and crossed the Severn at Holt Heath. Then she followed the Martley hills until she struck the much larger range of Malverns.

The account here became emotional in the extreme. It seems the old woman who tried to help her at the shameful scene I had just witnessed had taken her in but was terrified of being branded a witch. She too knew much of herbal medicine and scraped her living from the cures she could sell to her neighbours. However another old goodwife from a village near West Malvern had been burnt at the stake very recently and Martha had had many threats from Dodgeson and his foul bratchet of a son. Earlier in the day Martha had been with Phoebe in her garden, talking of the properties of parsley when the pedlar had appeared.

"Do you lack needles or thread, mistress?" he asked Martha pausing outside her garden gate She had gone into her house to find her purse." She was always loosing it." Phoebe explained but at that moment, the bull-headed evil Master Dodgeson and his vile companions had come swaggering onto the Green, first out of the Quarry. To Phoebe's amazement they began to tease and ill-treat the pedlar, beginning with nudging and supposed accidental tripping him. The rest of the Quarrymen followed but on seeing what was toward, hastened into the Inn, "as if they had seen the Devil himself." Phoebe told me, "which believe me, good sir, they had." Finally the cursed imps dragged the poor man over to the stocks, and placed him in that hideous throne, the better to stone him. At this point Phoebe could keep silent no longer. Lame and small though she was, it seems she was the only person there who could not stomach this appalling cruelty and disgraceful injustice. She screamed at them to forbear and with her fists sought to prevent them, the pedlar calling at her to desist, but then the devil's spawn turned their attack on her. She was crippled, undersized and a woman. Thank God their aim was poor. Even so, her back and brow were sorely injured. "And then you came, Sir. Like the Deus ex Machina in the old plays."

I was I confess acutely aware of the fact that her torn gown inadequately covered her full bosom. "Madam did these Jack Braggarts in any way violate your honour? If so, we must to the Sheriff......"

I stopped for Phoebe amazedly was laughing. "Well sir these wounds feel violation enough. As for my honour that is intact. Either those demons were too young or I was too unsightly."

I was at a loss to reply but was to learn that one of Phoebe's endearing qualities was ever to seek out the humour in a situation. I changed the subject and asked her if she had seen or heard of any troops of soldiers in the area.

"Talk, unending talk of the King and Parliament at odds, in Dudley while I stayed there. But here in the Malverns all is peaceful. The poor people seem mightily content to continue as their forefathers did: cutting stone and burning witches. Oh aye and stoning crippled virgins!"

I could not prevent a short of laughter and a half thought half possessed me, "How my father would love her wit!" But she had her destiny and I mine. "Come then, madam. I am bound for Ledbury. Let me at least set you on your way."

I was to stay some nights with a fellow physician who kept a lucrative apothecary's shop in Ledbury High Street. He had a very pretty daughter. Ben and I had been studying the work of John Parkinson, the apothecary of the old King James. Our friend Master Owen Lloyd of Ledbury had been dosing a cowman with tincture of Birch-sap for his painful kidney stones and wished to compare his receipt with that of the famous author. Our precious volume was entrusted to me so that Master Lloyd might copy those relevant pages.

And then before returning home I would visit friends of my father, a husband and wife and their sons who grew salad stuffs and other vegetables in gardens the western side of the Severn.

Today was Saturday 17th of September. There was much of melancholy and much of beauty in our landscape with Worcestershire already crepuscular and dim in the lea of the hills on our left, and Herefordshire golden with wheat and late sun on our right.

Hector clip-clopped up the High Street, the ass skipping and skittering beside him. I stopped outside Master Lloyd's shop as I wished him to approve my treatment of Phoebe as I feared her brow could be permanently scarred. "Why Thomas!" he cried as I stooped under the lintel. "You have been expected this many an hour. Haste you up to the house. Dame Pertelot and her chicken have fluffed out their best feathers for you." He was ever a jovial man but swiftly composed his features as I helped Phoebe from the cart. "Who's this?" he asked.

I told him how I had rescued her from a stoning and asked if my treatment needed alteration. He bustled about applying something I knew not called Tincture of Birthwort. Phoebe stood patiently allowing his ministrations, wincing slightly when the bandage on her brow was examined. I became aware of how strange and unusual she was. Abundant red-brown waving hair, features that were not "even" in the sense that she was not a Greek Goddess, for when she smiled and laughed, her brown eyes sparkled and her mouth, which was wide, red and generous, revealed an infectious love of life. But her unnaturally short left leg made her somehow grotesque, a misshapen Jack'o'Lent.....she did not so much walk, as bundle herself along.

"You have done very well, Tom there should be no scarring," he told me. "Now, Mistress, whither are you bound? Monmouth you say? And I say No, No and No. Firstly you must have rest for 24 hours and some days after if possible. Healthy scabs need to form on both back and brow. And let me tell you, the whole of Gloucestershire is alive with Parliament men. Go now with Tom here to the house and Tom, tell that most blessed of women whose price is above rubies, that Mistress Phoebe here is to sleep and rest in the truckle bed in the cookmaid's room until her wounds are all but healed. And tell my jewel among women that I am shortly to shut up shop and will want my dinner on the table sharp. And tell that idle Eleanour to stop prinking and preening herself and to be ready to serve her long suffering father. But Tom perhaps you have better things to tell her than me. Get you gone and God rest you, madam."

"I thank you, sir." said Phoebe and I could see that she relished his good humour.

The house was in the orchards to the west of Ledbury and the light was fast fading as we clattered into the stable yard. Eleanour, a vision of golden curls and sparkling white lace ran out into the stableyard and as I descended from the front of the cart began to chide me for my tardiness.

"Oh Tom you are late indeed. I have had to keep running from kitchen to parlour to pacify Cook and then to calm Mother who has decided that you had gone for a soldier."

Phoebe clambered awkwardly down from the cart and stood there crookedly, smiling at her.

"Why Tom," Eleanour shrieked, "God save us! Where did you get this hobgoblin?"

I gasped. I had known her for a lively chatterbox but this was sheer rudeness. "Why Eleanour!" I gasped, "Phoebe is a victim of churlish stone-throwing youths and your father ..."

Phoebe with a high colour interrupted me as I faltered, and spoke for herself. "Your father, madam who is a true gentleman as was *my* father, bade me come here to rest for a day or so in the cook's room, If that displeases you, I will be on my way to Monmouth."

By now I had found my tongue: "That was unmannerly and cruel, Mistress Eleanour. Poor Phoebe is the victim of a terrible attack. How could you?"

Eleanour had the grace to look ashamed. She bit her lip and hung her head. "Come Phoebe," I said offering her my arm, and led her towards the kitchen. But as we went, Eleanour behind us suddenly began to scream with hysterical laughter.

"That is what they mean when they talk of the long and short of it," she shrieked and indeed I suppose we must have been a pair of contrasts, I tall and lean and Phoebe a short round ungainly maiden. I felt her tremble under my arm but then was amazed to see that even in Eleanour's cruel jibe she could find a little humour. However we did not turn round but continued to the kitchen door, our dignity unblemished.

Later that evening at supper, Master Lloyd asked me how my father did.

I had seen him the previous evening at Ben's house in Newport Street where I now lived in partnership with Ben. He brought much good, fatherly advice and warned me to take extra care. I told the Lloyds of the King's raising his standard at Nottingham – to have it straight blow away into the mire in a monstrous high wind. And we knew that Robert Devereux, Earl of Essex was encouraging the Members of Parliament to pay and arm groups of followers.

"Aye, indeed!" said my host, "The devils are everywhere to the south …like a swarm of bees but not so useful. I hear there's a plague of them in Upton."

I told them of my father's warning, "that these same soldiers might feel moved to put their valour and training to the test. And woe betide the innocent bumpkin that finds himself in the midst of them," he told me, eying me sternly.

"Yes, father," says I, caution personified.

"Listen carefully," said my father, warming to his theme, "some of these Parliament men may lack their captains since I know not how a man may be a member of that great Council sitting daily and yet lead his men into the field. When men are far from home with the constraints of mayor or squire or parson far away, then villainy undreamt of, could prevail."

"Yes father!" says I, nodding sagely, like one of his old cronies in the Key Tavern. He caught my eye and made as if to cuff my head, but merely ruffled my hair in Farewell.

"So that is his thought on the matter," I told the Lloyds "Circumspection and caution."

"Good advice" said Master Lloyd, "save I cannot speak with such respect as he does of Parliament. Flatulence Fairground! And as for the King's taxes! Will there never be an end to them! Does he think when we sit on the jakes, golden crowns fall out?"

His wife and daughter were so outraged by his crude outspokenness that the table broke up in an uproar. "What will Master Thomas think of us?" cried Mistress Lloyd. But I was laughing so much I could not speak and vowed to remember this merriment to tell my father.

The next day was Sunday and I attended Matins with the Lloyds. The rest of the day was spent peacefully chatting on this and that. Owen Lloyd remembered my mother well and was able to share his memories of her with me. My father had tried to do this but had found such recollections, too sad and painful. When I went to bed on Sunday evening I felt closer to her than I had for some years. Meggie the cookmaid told us that Phoebe had rested well and intended to help her dry some herbs the next day.

During the next two days I helped Owen Lloyd as well as I could in his shop. The mercer's wife came in on Tuesday morning for a cure for whooping cough, two of her children were suffering and I remembered Pheobe's success with this particular ailment in Dudley. Owen suggested that I returned early to the house to ask if she would be willing to compare and share her knowledge with us. He also ordered that she was to attend the family meal later that evening. The two apprentices were also told to attend. I went back to the Manor House in the middle of the afternoon, that dead part of the day, when nobody usually arrives or departs. I dawdled pleasantly over the stable yard and went quietly into the kitchen in case Phoebe was sleeping and heard a loud voice issuing from her room. It was Eleanour.

"So please be assured, beggarwoman. For all your tricks, Thomas Fletcher is betrothed to me, or as good as! I have known him since my birth and our parents have often wished for our union. So have no loving notions of him. He is mine!"

I turned tail and quietly sped out the way I had come. A moment later the rustle of Eleanour's silk gown and the tap tap of her heels told me she had returned to the main house through the intervening door. Neither of them knew I was an eavesdropper.

I fled into the lane outside in order to collect myself. My face was burning with embarrassment. The notion of two young women having words over my future was a new departure for me. Then I realised that I had heard only one young woman expressing her wishes. Meggie came in sight with a basket of apples. I seized the opportunity to carry them into the kitchen for her and called to Phoebe to see if she was well enough to speak to me. She appeared a moment later wearing an old blue gown of Mistress Lloyd, cut down well enough to fit her. Her wounds were healing well and had ceased to give her pain. I noticed however that she was wiping her eyes, as Eleanour's cruelty clearly distressed her. I told her she was bidden to the meal that evening. She looked apprehensive but admitted that she owed the courtesy of acceptance to her kind host and hostess. She also agreed to come to the shop the next day and make a quantity of the whooping cough salve.

"What have you been doing today then?" I asked half expecting her to complain of Eleanour's cruelty. However she said nothing of that but made her reading a cause of merriment. It seems her precious book, sent to her mother some thirty years before by Lady Elinor Fetiplace, the author and a distant relative, contained receipts that Ben would instantly discard. She read to me,

"For the quinsy. Take rue and a white dog's turd ....now if you please Master Thomas, is that a white dog's turd or a dog's white turd?"

I laughed and told her I could not say. She read the rest of the receipt which concluded, "Lay it hot to the throat." She went on, "please Master Thomas, should I contract the quinsy, of your charity, spare me the white dog's turd."

"Indeed I will," I promised. She gathered mint and rosemary to make a sauce for the lamb that was even now cooking on the spit, filling kitchen and garden with delightful odours, and then disappeared to consult with Meggie about the apple pie.

The meal that evening was a merry occasion. Phoebe sat between the two apprentices, looking very handsome. Sitting down, she was not at all at a disadvantage and I noted she could make an excellent apple pie, flavoured with cinnamon and cloves with pastry light as a cloud. Master Lloyd laid down his spoon and wholeheartedly congratulated her.

"My heart," he said to his wife, "I beg you persuade Mistress Phoebe to remain with us a little longer. There are late gooseberries in the garden and you know I love a gooseberry tart above all other sweetmeats."

"My dear Owen," said she, "Mistress Phoebe must wish to return to her dear parents."

"Good Mistress Lloyd, would that I could, but to do that I would have to go to my grave," Phoebe told her.

"Who were your parents?" said Owen Lloyd gently.

"Sir Lewis and Lady Isabel Stanhope of the County of Derbyshire," said Phoebe, formally.

Eleanour froze, her spoon half way to her mouth. "And if you were an only child," Owen continued, "then you are in fact Lady Phoebe Stanhope." Eleanour nearly fell off her chair.

Phoebe smiled, "Sir, that may be. But I have found in my miserable travels that true nobility can be a quality known to the poorest of us and that the richest are not always the most compassionate. What use to be Lady Phoebe when you only have a ditch for a bedroom."

Mistress Lloyd turned on her husband and chided him bitterly for allowing Phoebe to occupy the cook's room. "My dear," he told her, "the fleas in the cookmaid's room are a specially selected breed, chosen for their ability to bite gentlewomen. You will find they bite as fiercely as those in the best bedchamber. And besides, Thomas here occupies that room. I do hope my dear, you did not mean country manners!"

It was decided that next day I should remain at home to, "dance attendance on the ladies," as Owen decreed. In truth I would have much preferred to accompany him to his shop. Eleanour had made me two handkerchiefs for my birthday, of finest lawn hemmed to perfection with my initials worked in Spanish silk - the finest materials and workmanship. I know 'twas so for her mother told me - more than once. I sat with Eleanour in the morning, her mother coming and going, seemingly speaking of a secret to her daughter for she mouthed something to her each time she returned and each time Eleanour shook her head.

Then half way through the afternoon the carrier came with a letter, which totally changed the atmosphere. It was from a cousin in Lichfield. The news it brought seemed to set mother and daughter in a flutter. Ralph Truscott, (I was told....more than once), was all that was excellent and was one of the chief merchants of that city. He was not needed in the shop for a few days and was coming to pay a friendly visit to his cousins.

Strangely, after the news that this phenomenon was shortly to visit, my standing seemed to decline with Eleanour. Her mother was ever courteous, talkative and responsive but Eleanour seemed luke-warm and lacking in interest when I embarked on an account of how I saved a young girl from drowning in the Severn last year.

"Yes, yes we heard all about that when your father was here last," she told me shortly. "Mother, do you remember what was Ralph's favourite colour?"

Finally I excused myself and went out into the garden, where I stamped about among the cabbages and tried to decide what I was feeling. I made myself be honest. Eleanour was devilish pretty, no question. I loved the way she looked but did I love *her*? The word "Hobgoblin," echoed again in my head and I realised that in fact I neither loved her nor did I *like* her, no matter how many handkerchiefs she made me. After a few moments I heard voices and laughter coming from the lane. Gilbert the elder apprentice had returned with Phoebe according to Owen's instructions as she had worked so hard and so usefully, he insisted that she must return to rest before dinner. It seems that the Mayor had come in for a cure for his gout and Phoebe had provided instant relief with a maceration of the humble herb comfrey. He had insisted that he paid her two crowns, which Owen was only too pleased for her to keep. She had administered her cabbage and honey potion to several little whooping cough sufferers and had made a quantity of this for Owen's future use, and finally she had copied out Parkinson's pages on kidney stones .....again! I had already done this but Owen had confided to her that my writing was like a regiment of crazed spiders and had noticed how clear her hand was. She looked suddenly stricken.

"Master Thomas, I do hope I have not given offence with Master Owen's criticism of your hand."

I pretended to be deeply hurt and acted like a silly miss but suddenly in spite of our mirth I knew what I must do, I knew that Ben and I were often overworked at both dispensing and consulting. Phoebe would be invaluable at both these necessary functions and would put children immediately at their ease, and also she could conduct examinations of female patients, without all the elaborate niceties of curtains and averted eyes that Ben and I adopted in the interests of decorum.

Gilbert went back to work and I asked her immediately.

"Phoebe, come back with me to Worcester and help us in our practice. You would have your own fine room in my father's house, and he would relish your company so much ....as would we all," I finished feebly.

She was laughing, "this is the best day, the very best day I have known for two years. Tom, what do you think? Master Owen asked me the same thing? Now I have the choice of the happiest of places, and am needed, you tell me."

"Indeed you are," I assured her and told her where we lacked a gentle woman's touch.

Then she asked, "is there a respectable woman servant in residence at your father's home, dear Tom? And are you sure that Master Ben would accept me?"

I answered heartily, "yes Phoebe" to both questions and she told me, "then I accept with all my heart. Master Owen is a great man in my view in every way, but I think his daughter finds me something of a fly in the ointment of her life."

"Then handfast and a bargain?" I asked her.

"Yes please" and we clasped hands on it just as Eleanour appeared I think to call us in for a cup of wine with her mother. She saw our handshake, sniffed and turned tail with a whisk of angry skirts. Phoebe was all for running after her and explaining but I was beginning to find such missish frets and sulks tiresome and tedious. I told Phoebe about the wonderful Ralph Truscott whose imminent arrival the young lady was using to put my nose out of joint.

And so it was that next day Thursday 22nd we thanked our kind host and hostess and set off with Hector faithfully pulling like a Trojan and Apple bobbing alongside him. Eleanour hardly seemed to notice our going. I thanked her again for the handkerchiefs but she seemed unable even to wish us Godspeed.

At Little Malvern we turned east and trotted downhill towards a hamlet known as Welland. The weather, which had stayed fine and warm for my holiday week, now began to look somewhat threatening and there were raindrops in the wind. And so it was we came to the Inn at Welland. And so it was I made the worst decision of my life. The innkeeper, Martin Beckford was a friend of my father, (but who in Worcestershire in those halcyon days was not a friend of my beloved father?), and had a very pretty daughter. As I write I believe, nay I know, if I and Phoebe and the horse and donkey had but trotted past that fateful inn and had not stopped for the night there, three innocent people who now rot in their graves would be alive and warm and happy for many years to come.

3

We reached the inn about two in the afternoon. We could take our rest and the beasts would be well served. To my great shame, as I remember this time, I had begun to feel something of an irritation that I had to be responsible for Phoebe. She rode on Apple alongside the cart, chatting pleasantly and commenting on the wonders of the Hills, but I fear I was somewhat less than courteous and answered without interest.

My mind was in something of a turmoil. I had abandoned my courtship of Eleanour. My conscience told me I was in the right of it but certain aspects of my physical self were angry that I would never possess her golden curls, white skin and feminine attractions, and that the perfect Ralph Truscott was the lucky heir to these seductive joys, devil take him. Was it so evil to respond to beauty? Did I have to be always Sir Galahad responding to the needs of ugly women? I brought myself up sharp. Phoebe was not ugly, not at all. If handsome is as handsome does, Eleanour was worth nothing and I had learned in less than a short week that Phoebe was worth a fortune. But my reason for arranging that we stopped at the Inn at Welland took no account of my abandonment of Eleanour, nor my appreciation of Phoebe's many excellent qualities. I confess I had a partiality for this particular hostelry and the guilt that I felt as we clattered down the hill should have alerted me. But alas, I was a slave to my own desires, which I did not yet understand, and to pretty women. The Landlord's daughter, Sarah, or Sally as her friends knew her, was perhaps even prettier than Eleanour, and to my untutored mind excessively good company. She had a ready laugh, white even teeth and an air of charming untidiness, which I was hard put to apportion to Art or Nature. So it was with aroused expectation that I, and my companions drew near to the Inn in the lea of the hills in mid-afternoon. There had been moments on the descending track where deep ruts from other carts and horses had made the road difficult. But with Phoebe holding the reins and I leading Hector's bridle all was well. However when we turned into the large open byre at the side of the inn, I was surprised to see two good riding horses, tethered inside the stables at the back of the hostelry. This inn was frequented by the countrymen who lived round about - the servants of the yeomen farmers, ploughboys, shepherds and occasionally a tinker. I attended to my beasts, leaving them eying their nobler relatives across the yard with some curiosity and munching the fodder the stable lad provided for them.

I left Phoebe with them, happily perched on the tailboard of the cart. Perhaps she sensed my change of heart, brought about I confess by the possible proximity of Sally. The shortness of my replies recently must have indicated that her presence was an embarrassment to me, ungrateful churl that I was. She had quills, ink and parchment and wished to record her mother's favourite remedies. "They were always effective," she told me, "and I assure you no dog turds."

Of pretty Sally there was no comforting sign, but two strangers sat at their ease beside the small fire, their leather buff coats opened. Two helmets lay on the floorboards beside them. There was an element of audacity about the elder that I liked not from the first, but when the landlord, Martin Beckford recognised me and bade me draw near, and take my ease, the younger of them, a fair haired youth about my age drew his chair to one side should I wish to warm myself for there was autumnal chill in the air and the sky presaged rain.

"Good day to you, sir," cried the older man, "and are you of these parts?"

"Indeed I am, good sir," says I, "but I think you are not."

They laughed somewhat sneeringly I thought. "You are in the right of it there, good sir," says the first. "We are from the great city of London. Have you never like your famous countryman, Dick Whittington - who came from hereabouts I think - have you never wished to see its wonders?"

"No," said I with my most courteous dog-fox smile, "and Dick

Whittington was Gloucestershire born and bred. Here we are well pleased with our country destinies," and our talk ceased.

I had never heard the high nasal voices of Londoners before - though I was destined to hear the tones of the capital many times in the next few years. I sat and drank my ale and listened to their talk. These men were of course soldiers. I began to think of my father's warnings. I cursed myself for my inattention and present lack of understanding. I had always told myself, "these matters are for the great statesmen to resolve and not for righteous men who ply their trades peacefully." It seemed though that those great statesmen had made no great shakes at settling the nation's troubles. The "hempen homespuns" drinking in the soldiers' boastful words as eagerly as they drank Martin Beckford's good ale seemed stupified with wonder and amazement at their glittering worldly-wisdom. The Quarter-Master had gold braid edging his buff coat which like the younger man's was new. The smell of the newly tanned leather of their coats competed with Martin Beckford's ale fumes - and with the tobacco the Corporal smoked in his little clay pipe. I too sat and listened - they spoke of their march from London to Worcestershire via, it transpired, the town of Northampton as if it were Thermopylae, Hastings and the Armada all in one, with them the triumphant victors when in truth so far they had not struck a blow. No, not quite true - for the younger and the more courteous to my mind, on hearing that I was by way of being a physician drew up his sleeve and revealed an angry wasp sting. He had it seems struck at the insect, seeing it settle on his arm.

"Have you a salve, good Master....? Would you honour me with your name?"

"Yes and No." says I, sweetness personified. "I have a salve and I will not honour you with my name. But if you have three pence I will treat your arm. I motioned to him to follow me and the older man, whom he called Master William came after us also, which I had not intended. It had begun to rain and the hills behind us to the West were already invisible in curtains of cloud. The dusk was drawing in. For some reason I did not comprehend I did not wish the Quartermaster to encounter Phoebe. So I lied. "I forgot," I told them, "I have left the tools of my trade in that cottage up the track.

'Tis a shepherd with a contagious fever. Pray return to the fire."

They needed no second bidding. All was well with Phoebe, the cart and the animals. I told her of my instinctive dislike for one of the soldiers but promised that I would ask the Landlord for better sleeping quarters for her.

"Of course I can pay now for my own room," said Phoebe, a touch airily. "A wasp sting you say? Mallow with oil should suffice. I saw some plants in the hedgerow as we turned from the track."

I had been going to rub the sting with thyme leaves but busied myself concocting her suggestion with pestle and mortar.

When I returned the soldiers exclaimed in admiration at the sight of my wooden box of tools and tinctures. From the corner of my eye I saw Will nudge his companion whose name I gathered was Philip Fosdyke. I busied myself, adding onion and a little vinegar to Phoebe's mallow poultice. The Quartermaster Will who wore a gorget of armour at his neck went to attend to their horses in the stables, I called Philip over to the back window of the taproom so that I could watch him as I worked. He looked once or twice towards the cart where Phoebe had prudently closed the leather curtains, but made no move towards it.

I applied the poultice to Philip's outstretched arm. "Shall you then ally yourself with the cause of Parliament?" he asked me, sighing in relief as the poultice took effect. "John Fiennes, our captain is as good a God-fearing soldier as you could ever meet with and a Viscount's son what is more. Old Subtlety they call his father. Should you not like to fight for your rights?"

"No," I replied shortly but added for good fellowship, "but the wasps in these parts are for the King."

He laughed far in excess of the jest's deserving, gave me three pence and asked if he could further reward me with another flagon of ale.

"No," said I, and then again relenting for he looked downcast at my refusal. "But a plate of Martin Beckford's jugged hare would be a handsome recompense."

I replaced the poultice. The swelling in his arm was declining and the angry colour fading. I gave him plantain leaves to rub over the sting, when the poultice came away, and then watched as Will Brigstock summoned the Landlord to speak about some detail of the horses' stabling.

When he returned he knew all about me. "You are Master Thomas Fletcher," he told me, "you see, you are known. A good man's name precedes him and I hear you are well skilled in the arts of medicine. I pledge you, sir."

Zachary Green, a ploughboy whose boots were always heavy but whose head was always light, opened his mouth to blaze forth my identity. "Ah yes, sir, Master Brigstock. 'Tis true indeed - Tom Fletcher's well known for his skills in the doctoring."

"Zach!" said I petulantly. "You have done your father a grave disservice by your free use of my name today. I fear his rheumaticks must now ever remain untreated."

"Oh come now Master Tom," says he, "I meant no harm - and nor do these gentlemen soldiers I am sure."

"Then you know more than I do, Zacharius." I said smoothly. "Are we to dine then gentlemen?"

I learnt during our meal that Will Brigstock was a tailor and Philip Fosdyke a goldsmith's apprentice. Both were from a place south of the great River Thames known as Southwark. They had known each other prior to their enlistment as they were it seems members of a Trained Band, a volunteer force who had over past years honed their military skills to perfection. Brigstock told us this several times lest perhaps we had not heeded his first announcement. I liked Philip well enough, though he seemed nervous of the country - and also of the night's dark pall. When we went out to relieve ourselves, he looked round constantly as if apprehensive of brigands or bogies. He was slight and pale, with a moustache, which he fingered about once every five minutes as if he feared the distempers of Worcestershire would cause it to moult and disappear perhaps. I conjectured that he was not quite so anxious to display his military skills as the Quartermaster.

Before we returned to the taproom, he placed his hand on my arm and asked me if he could speak of something that troubled him. I felt my heart sink for when young men catch a doctor on his own for advice, it usually has to do with matters carnal. "For whilst I take it you are about my years," he told me. "You seem a man of parts, travelling alone with the tools of your trade at hand and well trusted by your master." He then came to the root of the matter.

26

"Master Thomas," says he, "what think you of the theatre?"

"Of the theatre?" I repeated. This was a strange pastime for a fire-hot man-at-arms to concern himself with.

"Ay, the theatre. The drama - the plays of Shakespeare, Dekker, Jonson. Think you that they drive a man to sin?"

"Good Master Philip," says I warming to the man, "my father and I, and my master Ben Knowles love nothing so much as a good play. Whenever the Players visit the larger inns in our city they are well patronised, I do assure you. Why should plays lead a man to sin? 'Tis otherwise for sure. For when one sees folly mocked and evil punished, we must needs learn from these examples."

He laughed in relief. "So think I, Master Thomas. It is that there are chaplains now who preach that the theatre is the Abomination of Desolation where all Vices may be learned. But I think as you sir. List you. I am from Southwark where the theatre flourishes. There are many playhouses, built to the purpose where one may take one's ease and a bottle of good beer and view whatever piece is toward in comfort. Ask for me if you come there at the sign of the Golden Harp. Thank you for that assurance good Thomas. You have eased my mind somewhat and spoken good friendship. Would you like to have this?" he asked me drawing a pamphlet from his pocket. "Have it as a gift. 'Tis a very mirthful matter by Taylor, the waterman."

I had heard something of this water poet and accepted gladly. I placed the work, which at a glance seemed to be in the form of a mock-sermon, carefully into my box, placed it beside Parkinson and locked it.

"If I meet you again, I promise I will return your kindness," I told him.

Then he asked me again in his half laughing, half fearful manner. "Should you think it will come to aught?"

"What?" I asked him.

The ale and the good repast had mellowed me somewhat. I began to like this man. Above all I sensed that he was but a half-hearted soldier. He seemed alone in a huge unknown landscape, a stranger in a strange land.

"Will it come to blows I mean?"

"How could it?" I said as comfortingly as I knew how. "Save

the wasps, I know of no enemy in these parts, waiting to strike you."

"No," he said reassured. "Nor I," and we went back inside to the gathered company.

Will Brigstock I liked not at all. There was a calculation behind his every friendly word that was unnerving. He had a fine head of waving brown hair, a neatly trimmed beard and a flattering tongue. His eyes were never still but darted hither and yon. Certain sure for new soldiers and a new army, they were well accoutred, fine linen, new buff coats, basket handled swords and new pistols. These they handled with consummate ease, demonstrating their efficiency to the country lads who surrounded them. They stopped short of actually firing them off, much to good Martin Beckford's relief. But in his eagerness to demonstrate his aiming skills, Will Brigstock aimed his elbow by mistake into the wine pitcher. Red canaries splattered my working breeches and a great stain spread like a river in flood over Phil's buff-coat. Will catching the eye of the landlord discovered perhaps for the first time in his military history that discretion was ever the better part of valour.

"Mine host!" says he, all courtesy and craft. "I fear that we must trouble you betimes as tomorrow morn we must be up and away before the milkmaids. The muster is at Upton an hour before dawn."

I wondered much where Martin's daughter was, but had not asked in the presence of the soldiery. If I was honest I would confess that her absence engendered my surliness towards them. When they had removed themselves, Martin confided that news of the soldiers' arrival had preceded them, and, with perhaps unnecessary prudence and caution, (at so early a time in these civil disturbances), he had ordered pretty Sal to her chamber with a candle and her sewing. At the time this seemed a sad hardship for me, but Martin had his reasons.

"Master Tom," said he, "it sorts not well to trust to the soldiery. A man who is a good honest citizen, sober and upright can turn into a devil if you put a weapon in his hands. Terrible horrors have been told of the doings in High Germany. Murders and rapings and torturing. Why 'twas but yesterday that Petey and Moll from Master Bartlett's on the Common came in weeping and wailing and saying that these same Parliament men, come up from Gloucester, had stolen all the cooking pots. I had to lend Molly a cauldron so that she might at the very least make a supper for the good family. Best not to tempt fate, Sir. So Sal don't exist here the day, Thomas. She ain't here now nor she never was here, not while the militia rush hereabouts like raging lions, seeking what they can deflower. Would you want me to lend you blankets, and you can bed down for nought by the fire here, or you can have a bed upstairs if you can pay?"

"Neither sir," says I "I'll do well enough in my cart in the byre, if you have no objections. But I have a friend, a young lady in my cart whom for decency and her good virtue, I must ask you to accommodate safely indoors."

It seemed Phoebe was destined always to be bundled away into the cook's room. But this was warm enough, the cook Lizzie, attending her sister in Ledbury for her lying in. The landlord refused her offer of payment and in truth the room was comfortable enough, one wall containing the kitchen fire which smouldered merrily still.

I ran out to the byre through the rain, which was now pelting down in good earnest, grinning at the notion of Phil Fosdyke as a raging lion. A raging rabbit perhaps. There was a palliass stuffed with hay in our cart, which had proved useful in the past for transporting injured souls to Newport Street for treatment. I was afraid that Will Brigstock might have taken it into his head to steal my box of tinctures and instruments, or even the treatise of Master Parkinson. That loss Ben could not have countenanced.

So I made myself comfortable enough and guarded our treasures. Hector was tethered, but was taking his ease on the straw bales placed for his comfort alongside the cart. In the light of my candle begged from Martin, I could see the square bulk of Apple who rarely lay down, standing over Hector, seeming to keep guard but in reality dozing.

I lay with my head to the open end of the cart, which faced towards the rear door of the inn. The rain battered on to the thatch of the byre relentlessly. I blew out my candle and made myself snug. I thought back upon the three short years that had led to my qualification and cursed myself yet again for my foolhardiness that had caused me to think suicide, the solution to my dislike of the butchery trade. It was the easiest thing in the world to talk to my father on any topic that presented itself. How could I have contemplated souring his life, with my premature and predetermined death?

I remembered so clearly the next day at our Charnel School. I realised that my Primer must now engage my attention and that I must not waste my time in Sports. If I was to be a true doctor, I must not inflict bodily pain uselessly as so often happened in our bouts with quarterstaffs. I took the taunts of Matt Hailes and his followers in my stride when I announced that I could not enter after all for Victor Ludorum as I had no stomach now for wrestling.

"What?" cries Matt. "Someone has tried to strangle you! Have you quarrelled again with your father? It is not stomach that you lack but neck, Master Mackerel-Back."

"Do not speak, ill of my father, Master Hailes" says I, "or I must teach you civility!"

"Teach away, varlet!" he cries, clenching his fists and coming to pull me from my desk. So I slowly stood up to face him. Perhaps my brief dance with death had lengthened me, for we stood, not eye-to-eye but eye to bandage.

Because I merely stood and looked at him, he grew even more unmannerly, and turning slyly to his fellows, cried out: "The great baby is afeard. Even though he's grown apace of late, his courage still lies in the nursery."

I smiled courteously, locked his hands behind him with my left arm, picked him up, with his legs kicking away in front, and deposited him back in his desk. "There is your lesson, sir," said I. "Now do you still wish to try a bout with me?"

"Nay, I'll not meddle with you, Fletcher!" he muttered.

"Then now you know! 'Twould be no contest. Where is the sport in ill matched rivals?"

He nodded and sat in a sulk. But then he shouted half in jest, half in earnest, with something of his old friendship: "But what a sad old misery, you are become, Tom. Always in your dumps. Surely if I had a father who could give me so good a start in life, I would be merry from dawn to dusk."

"My dumps are over, now," I told him, "I look to you to teach me to be a gamester like yourself, Matt. In any case it is hard for us to be merry and at ease here in this cramped charnel house."

I spoke truth, for we had lost our College Hall, four years before when Archbishop Laud, King Charles' counselor, had instructed Dean and Chapter to house us boys in the Charnel Chapel. To the consternation of Master Moule, his usher, Master Taylor, us scholars, and our parents, we must lose College Hall, our wholesome airy schoolroom, and shift our scholarship to the old Charnel Barn. All of us knew that beneath the floor of this ill-fated building lay the mortal remains of the monks of St. Wulfstan's foundation from which our great cathedral grew. We knew, too, that they lay not peacefully in slumber as a mortal should surely lie in death, but higgledy-piggledy, an arm here, a skull there, thigh bones and rib cages all a-tangle. After this banishment certain of my fellows began to suffer from chest pains, colds and agues. My father consulted with Ben on this, thinking to take me betimes from this "place of pestilence" as he termed it. Ben agreed that the damp from the wall was more like to cause the younger boys congestion of their breath, but that the poor old tatterdemallion monks were too far gone down the road to eternity to influence or infect the living, being now but clean bone. But the knowledge of their presence there caused many of the smaller boys to fear and weep, particularly in the winter, when we began and concluded our studies in the dark

Many citizens believed that the visitation of the plague in our city, which followed on the heels of Laud, was begun in our cramped miserable schoolroom. But who could be certain? My mother died in torment from this scourge, and yet I, who trudged every day to and from the Charnel Chapel, books on shoulder, I remained ever sturdy, lusty and in perfect health, unbroken in body as was my father. I know that Ben looked at my increasing height and at my ruddy face often with a questioning air. Sir Nicholas, his adoptive father had died from the plague shortly after my mother. Lady Alice had followed him within the year from a wasting fever. But why had they died? We ate the same food, drank the same water, breathed the same air. Why were some marked for an early death and some spared? Why after two men have drunk two quarterns of ale from the same barrel, did one fall drunk in the gutter, his legs on loan to the devil, and his fellow go straight back to ploughing....and plough a straight furrow, ...almost? Why should the youngest daughter of Thomas Price, the wainwright perish from a fever of the lungs, when her two older sisters were the rosiest healthiest girls in the county?

These were the concerns that I had to ponder in my last months at school. I had, I think, become something of a sobersides, with the responsibility of my chosen profession, a pleasant weight on my mind. I began to deserve the reputation of a scholar (for the first time) but I also took care to laugh and jest if the occasion demanded. I knew I had now to learn in earnest. There was considerable leeway to make up. I had sullenly told myself through the last year that I had no need to construe Latin, when all my future care must be to learn how to dismember bullocks.

Master Moule had sensed my pain and had not chided me unduly. Now he welcomed back his prodigal if not with open arms then with open books. I told him of our new plans and he rejoiced with me, finding a herbal treatise for me to translate.

"It is width and breadth of vocabulary that will serve you best. Let us let Aeneas go hang and Achilles cool his heels. Your concern is with "genus" and "species". We will together prepare you for your trade with Master Ben, and God grant that you may never need your skills save in peaceful times."

So said my good master, and I, a reformed scholar set to, with a right good will and in the few months left before my birthday in September, the date set for my indentures, gained some knowledge of the rudiments put forward by Galen and Hippocrates.

Believe it or not, Ben seemed pleased with my progress. For three years I laboured hard beside him and learnt my trade. Our profession had its darker side. There were agues that we could not begin to understand or cure....the creeping cancer that invades a woman's innards and ceases not until it has choked the means of digestion so the poor wretch must needs starve, the sudden on-slaught of mortality from within a man's brain, that leaves him either dead to all good purpose or if he is more fortunate, dead indeed, those swift pangs of the heart that sometimes ring a warning bell and sometimes toll a death knell, aye, we could recognise them and to some degree alleviate the pain, but we were powerless to cure or to divert such maladies.

But many ailments we could cure with tried and careful use of herbs and tinctures. The simple nettle infused could relieve the more painful effects of rheumatics. Borage, its bright blue flowerets and its hairy leaves appropriately distilled could alleviate the fervent flush and pain of fever....particularly that one which can develop from a cold. A woman giving birth for the first time found her pains eased somewhat by a draught of infused raspberry leaves and ginger. The proportion of ingredients was vital and I grew practised at measuring and distilling and compounding. I tried always to prepare palatable medicines and experimented a little from time to time and began to realise that sick young children would be less likely to wail and moan at the sight of the surgeon if their tincture tasted of rose hip and blackberry syrup.... a pleasanter encounter for all parties. Ben had not explored this route and gave me great credit for my enterprise in that part of our practice.

Thinking of herbs I began to test my memory of the potion for whooping cough that Phoebe knew to such good effect. I tried to remember the ingredients and proportions and must have fallen asleep, still pondering.

I think I had been asleep for about an hour. I suddenly shot from slumber in an instant. A woman's voice was whispering my name.

"Thomas! Tom Fletcher! Awake! pray, sir, awake!"

4

Sally Beckford, a black cloak clutched around her with one hand, held high a candle with the other and was crouched beside me kneeling on the floor of the byre with her mouth delightfully close to my ear.

"Why, Sally." says I, thinking with delight for a moment that at last my luck had changed. "Sally? What's the matter?"

"Master Fletcher!" whispers she. "You must go now. The soldiers mean you ill. I could hear their talk through the gap at the bottom of the wall. They mean to steal you - to make you fight for them or, at the least, doctor their troop. I know not what - but you must go."

So my suspicions were not unfounded. "I knew they had an eye to my instruments," I mused, "but I did not guess that my person was so desirable," and lustful oaf that I was and still half asleep, I attempted to draw her down beside me.

"Master Thomas, in the name of God, go." Sally hissed. "The older man said he would wake at cockcrow and then they'll make away with you, Tom. They'll take you at sword point to this muster at Upton at the crack of dawn. Come on now. Saddle up and get off by the field path."

That was far easier spoken of than performed in secrecy, for Apple had an open personality that sorted ill with night and silence.

"The ass will bray Farewell at the horses. You know how he is. Should I leave him? But he'll create at our parting. What's to be done, Sal? How can I muzzle him?"

She thought for a moment. "Get Hector 'twixt the shafts quiet as maybe. I'll be back."

The rain was pounding down. She slipped away, a dark shadow

indiscernible in the gloom. As she opened the door for a moment I saw the square dim pool of light from the dying kitchen fire.

Hector was as always silently obedient to the bridle and the reins. I whispered to him softly adjusting the bit and promising him a good meal of mash when we got home to Worcester on the morrow. Apple was stirring now, snorting gently, somewhat bemused by the notion of night time activity. Then Sally, blessed girl was back, wet through, with a leather bag of windfalls.

"You lead Hector. I'll take this gentleman." She held out an apple to him and tugged him gently by the mane. As we left the shelter of the byre, the rain hit us like a barrage of shot. I was soaked in an instant. Mercifully the gate to Martin's field was open but our going was desperate slow. As Apple finished one windfall, Sally would stuff in another, but as he stopped to allow his jaws to gain an accurate purchase and as the earth was all churned up into mud our progress was snail-like. Perhaps the storm drowned the chink of bridle and hooves. As we gained the slight ridge at the far end of the field and tried to look back through the sheets of billowing rain, we could see no lights and no sounds of pursuit followed us.

"I must go back now," said Sally, whispering still although we were now well out of earshot. "Two fields away and you are on the road to Hanley Swan. The oaks at the crossroad will give you some sort of shelter. The leaves cling still,"

"Sally," I cried, water streaming down my face. "The younger soldier - was he for robbing and abducting me with his elder?"

"Nay, I know not," she told me. I could hear his voice but not his words. "'Tis best to trust neither of them."

I caught her hands and drew her to me. Till the day I die, I will remember the sweetness of the midnight rain upon her lips, and I cannot say how long we would have stood if Apple bereft of his midnight feast had not suddenly remembered his new acquaintances at the inn, and brayed across dark rain-swept acres a last trumpeted farewell. Sally scrambled to find him another apple and we froze again in fear, straining eyes and ears for the least movement or sound from the direction of the inn.

There was nothing. A pressure of hands as she gave me the bag of apples, last words of thanks from me and a tender farewell from her, and Sally was gone, a dark shape seen for a few seconds in the gloom flitting close and low to the hedgerow. The beasts settled to our midnight flight and I walked between them, holding Hector's reins and the bag with my right hand and my left resting on Apple's mane.

A sudden violent gust of wind from the North caused me to halt. My thoughts were disturbed not least by the notion of Philip Fosdyke's treachery. I had started to think of him in friendly fashion and it seems he was an Iscariot, intent on treachery. I thought much too of Sally's plight. Suppose the soldiers had waked at Apple''s summons and she ran back into their arms upon the stair or in the kitchen? Then I bethought me of stout Master Beckford, which calmed my fears. But as the storm ceased its shrieking for a moment, I thought I heard my name - or a part of it. "Tooo......!" The wind raged on and for a moment I wondered had I dreamt the sound. I pondered for a moment and decided I had to be certain that all was well with Sally even if to return to the inn was to embark on a fool's errand. Looping the reins over a hawthorn stump in the hedge, I snatched up my box of medicaments, left the beasts and crept back down the field, my eyes straining against the dark. There seemed to be a white blur on the ground near the open field gate. I crept closer. The white blur was a woman's petticoat. Throwing caution to the winds I ran into the inn yard. Muffled sounds of movement came from the ground near the stable. The Quartermaster Brigstock was astride her, with one hand over her mouth. With the other he was attempting to remove her clothing. He could not see my approach as his back was towards me.

She was fighting as if her life depended upon it, for although she could not scream, her hands were free to scratch. As her nails raked his face and he knelt upwards to avoid them, I brought my right boot into sudden intimate contact with his miserable arse. He shot forward and crashed brow, eyes and nose into the stable wall. He bellowed in pain, staggered to his feet and turned to face me, his hands grasping for my throat. But I stepped to the left and somehow my wooden chest of remedies made unfriendly contact with the side of his head. After that he seemed to lose interest in trying conclusions and lay down to rest.

Sally staggered to her feet. "Are you hurt?" I demanded. "Say the word and I'll kill him." To my relief she shook her head, stumbled to a slurry drain from the stable and voided up the contents of her stomach. I followed her, but 'twas plain she was shocked and distressed beyond measure by Brigstock's assault. Finally she gave me her hand. "Go, now Tom. God bless you for returning." She turned from me and went in at the kitchen door.

It took me some time to drag Brigstock into the shelter of the byre. (I knew from his steady pulse that my blow was not fatal but exposure to the night could prove so.) The howling of the storm covered the sound of my exertions. The rain meant nothing to me now. I was so wet I had forgotten entirely the notion of dryness. I left Brigstock lying on his back at the foot of the bales of hay. He had previously unbuttoned himself in the hope of accomplishing his foul intention. I pulled off his breeches and threw them in the drain. With any luck I reasoned a rat might gnaw away his genitals in the night.

I took one last look at the dark low building and started violently. Two figures stood framed in the doorway, the fire flickering behind them. One was Sally tall and slender, the other child-sized .....

Sweet Jesu, I had forgotten Phoebe!

My embarrassment knew no bounds. She had woken at Sally's return, hearing her distressed sobs and had instantly found her a cup of water. There was a confused conversation during which I promised Sally I would return, but what role she thought Phoebe played in my life, I do not know. In any event we had to leave at once. As we crept across the stable yard I was reassured to hear Brigstock snoring and snorting like the diseased goat he was.

I paused as a candle flickered alight in the room I took to be Sally's. Was it my imagination or did I see the faintest gleam of a face, for an instant at the window next to it?

We set off up the field path to where the cob and donkey waited. I wanted to be well away from the Welland Inn when Brigstock awoke. If he or Fosdyke wished to follow me, it would be hard to trace the prints and wheel ruts as the force of the downpour was enough to muddy and disperse our tracks.

Other farmers were not so careless as friend Martin, and it was necessary to open and close the field gates that enclosed their stock.

In one field we could not find the gate and had a sad time of it pounding the boundary until we came upon it in the most westerly corner. In another field a herd of heifers suddenly reared up from the wet darkness, causing my heart to lurch like a field-gun and Phoebe to scream. A snort from Hector and a few gentle words from me and the good ladies let us pass on our flight, moved as much by fear as curiosity. At last we gained the path to Hanley Swan and as Sal had predicted, ahead of us were the dark shapes of massive oaks. It could not be said that they gave us shelter as such, but the main thrust of the rain was kept at bay.

I sat upright in the cart dozing with my hands on the reins, whilst Phoebe slept on the paliass. I was I must confess something shocked and confounded by my own responses to Brigstock's atrocity. If Sally had nodded when I asked if he should live or die I knew I would have bludgeoned him to death. As it was I judged that he would wake with a monstrous headache, a broken nose, a black eye and a sore backside. But somehow my violent response had tainted me with his own foulness. In the years that followed during the moments following the pressing necessity of self-defence, I have always been assailed with self-doubt as to the justice of my actions and my cause. Would Ben have acted as I did? He had always been my pattern of excellence. My drowsy thoughts wandered to the past and Ben's strange appearance in the town when he was only about six years old, when I was not even borne.

The tale is like one of the fables the old gossips tell at their spinning or the old gaffers at their drinking....a Winter's Tale in every way. Firstly it was the story for a long night when the teller draws out the thread, or refuses to drain the glass. Secondly it was like the Winter's Tale of Shakespeare. Ben, the chief protagonist, was a lost child and thirdly that child was found in Winter.

One February night in 1622 after his servants were abed, Alderman Knowles, as he then was, heard a cat cry in the street outside. Being a kindly man and knowing that earlier there had been a dusting of snow, he unlocked and unbarred the great front door of the Newport Street house to give poor Puss shelter. There was no cat but a child was huddled in his doorway. A six year old or thereabouts....a boy who called himself Ben when he had been warmed and fed and washed. He was wearing only a filthy shirt and ragged coat and small clothes. Alice Knowles who was my father's cousin, had at one and thirty considered herself as childless. Little Ben coming cold, hungry and friendless into her home seemed like the answer to her prayers, ...a miracle almost.

There had been Egyptians or gypsies in the town earlier in the week and it was thought that Ben had perhaps been orphaned, and abandoned by them as a consequence. The Alderman sent after them, not because he wished Ben to be reclaimed but so that some knowledge of parentage might be established. But the gypsies like the dusting of snow had vanished. The Alderman traced their passing to the Hereford Road but at the foot of Fromes Hill, none could say if they went West, South or North.

Ben thrived exceedingly. His new parents were rich....let us not mince words. Sir Nicholas who bought a knighthood from King James, had inherited a prosperous clothier's business in Worcester, and had interests in the north of the county where metal goods were manufactured. Lady Alice's mother was the sister of my father's mother. The sisters were the only daughters of a wealthy Herefordshire farmer who had bequeathed them his land as jointures. My grandmother thrown friendless but not penniless had married my grandfather, a Master Butcher of Worcester, and her money, when her lands were sold, had served to enlarge and improve our premises in Fish Street. Her sister had retained her portions of land, which her daughter, Lady Alice, had inherited and which were now let out at good rents to several tenant farmers. In all Ben wanted for nothing except perhaps brothers and sisters and a pedigree.

Like myself he was a scholar at King's School, but as he was seven years my senior had been taught first by the illustrious Master Henry Bright and like his teacher Ben gained his degree at Brasenose College, Oxford. His parents were overjoyed at his proficiency for study but then Ben near broke my aunt's heart by pleading to be allowed to study medicine for two years at Bologna University in Italy. We had scarce heard of Italy in Worcestershire, and as for Bologna it could have been on the moon. The same old gossips and tale spinners predicted that Ben would not return to his doting parents but would disappear as mysteriously as he had arrived, thirteen years before. But return he did, as I well remember.

39

On Thursdays when I was a King's Scholar we had a half holiday, and for our sport on this day we ran races in the fields near the old Frog Mill. So complicated was the course which we were attempting....we had arranged several tree trunks as hurdles to be leapt....that I did not see my father's old journeyman, Jacky Grove, until suddenly there he was before me, panting and gasping, just as I, in mid-flight, was jumping a hurdle. If he had no breath before he had even less when I cannoned into him and for a moment we sat winded and equally outraged upon the grass to the laughter of all who witnessed the collision.

"Master Tommy," he finally managed when his speech if not his dignity had been restored, "you must come at once. Master and Mistress stay for you. Your kinsman Ben Knowles is returned and his parents are feasting the prodigal."

Ben was back! To me, he was the paradigm of all that was wonderful. Learned, travelled and a great horseman. I remembered with great affection and pleasure the rides he had given me on Jupiter, the horse on which he had ridden to and from his Oxford College. As we hastened past the Cathedral I bombarded Jacky with questions. "When did Ben arrive? How long was he staying? Had Jupiter been sent for from the farm? Was Ben different?" to none of which could the poor fellow make answer.

My parents awaited me with impatience. They had both changed into their Sunday finery. My preparations were simple. I stripped off to my small clothes, while Jacky held me under the pump, and then my dark hair was slicked back and I was crammed into my best doublet. We were ready. We made our stately progress along Bridport Street, my mother complaining bitterly of the mud, and down Merrivale and into Newport Street.

And there was Ben, taking his ease at his father's board, accepting the congratulations and good wishes of his parents' friends and neighbours, with a casual yet courteous grace, his mother beside him hanging on his arm and on his every word. At our approach, as honoured relatives, he did bestir himself so far as to rise, greeted my father lovingly as his good uncle (although in fact my father was his second cousin), asked after my mother's health and my studies, and was in every way the Ben we remembered. A little browner maybe but even I knew that in Mediterranean lands, the sun was hotter

He began to make changes in the Knowles household almost at once. I remember about a week later when I had gone thither with my mother to pay a courtesy call, he asked us to accompany his mother and himself to take the air beside the river. We passed out of the city's bounds by the Saint Clements gate and strolled through the fields with the river on our left. I approached as near as I dared to the swans' nests that lined the bank at that time, and when the old cobs threatened to give chase, darted back to the safety of our company. A low alehouse used by sailors and watermen lay perilously close to the river, a tumbledown jakes hanging out over the leaden stream. As we drew near two carters' lads raced out of the inn and ignoring the privy proceeded to relieve themselves, in robust competition into the waters of the Severn.

Our mothers turned in some embarrassment from this display but Ben was delighted. "There, madam. What more proof need you that Severn water is tainted?" Apparently I learned this had been a cause of contention since his return. Ben claimed that pestilence could travel even in running water, that even though it looked and tasted clean, it might in its higher reaches have been polluted. When Lady Alice thought that she had been boiling her mutton in the selfsame water into which low wretches had voided their urine, she needed no further persuading. Sir Nicholas was less eager to embark on the expensive enterprise of obtaining pure water for his household. He was, however, the grateful recipient of a tincture which his son had prepared for him the day after his homecoming. It had relieved him entirely of a troublesome cough that had been plaguing him. "Where would you look for an untainted supply?" he demanded, after we came to him in his counting-house after our walk, "how could you transport it and how could you ensure its continuing purity?"

Ben only asked to be allowed to try, and the next day set off on Jupiter westward with two small barrels on his saddle-bow. He returned in the evening in triumph. He had found, he told us, the purest spring water the further side the Malvern Hills which rising from the solid rock, naught could contaminate. Both households continued to use Severn water for washing, but for all consumption, Ben insisted that his water from Colwall must be drunk.

He began to doctor the Worcester citizens and achieved considerable success and renown. At length his father accepted that his son had skills ands gifts that were marketable, and part of the buildings at the rear of the Newport Street house became his dispensary and surgery. As I grew to eleven and twelve years, I was ever to be found there, pestering him with questions and accompanying him not merely for the Colwall water but also for herbs. By his discreet questioning he learnt which old wives and widows from the nearby villages had the knowledge and knew the whereabouts of certain herbs.

Then in 1637 the plague struck our city. One fifth of its citizens died, amongst them my mother, who had never ailed before and Sir Nicholas. Lady Alice "for a little tried to live without him, liked it not and died" - a noble epitaph extolling marital devotion. I know that there were many times since my mother's death when my father could have wished to have accompanied her to the graveyard and beyond.

A sad rift grew between my father and myself. He had it in his head that I must follow in his calling. For some reason I could not bring myself to explain that I was not a butcher, and could never be one. But after the day in May two years later that we called the Hanging Sunday, the three of us found a familiar harmony and were well at ease indespite of the losses we had sustained.

Suddenly my thoughts were dispersed and I shook myself alert. I had been sitting, dozing on my cart for what must have been some hours. Far to the south-east came the faint notes of a trumpet, the call bidding the soldiers lodged hereabout to muster in the town and with that clarion, all my anxieties and fears assailed me again. Perhaps an hour later, the first faint welcome glints of dawn appeared in the eastern sky. There was no cessation of the rain however and after feeding and watering Hector and Apple, I woke Phoebe and explained that we would set out on the road to Guarlford rather than turning right to the highway from Upton to Worcester.

I encouraged my two poor friends along the muddy track, and as I did so farm labourers began to stir abroad from the little cottages that lined the cross roads. I asked one if he had heard or seen ought of soldiers in the last few days.

"Oh yes, master. A-many of them are all around Upton, these two days past. 'Tis said they be a-going to move Worcester way. I keeps out o' their ways. If you be thinkin o'goin to joining 'em, sir, think again I begs 'ee. If you've run away, run you back, sir. There's no good to be gained from all of this."

I had, it seemed, questioned the village philosopher (or prattler.) I thanked him for his news and on we went ponderously slowly now, as the ways were churned up into quagmires. I turned off right to Priestfield and then made my way through Porlocks End intending to cross the highway there to Clevelode by the Severn where lived my father's old friends. But as we toiled our way easterly I heard ahead of us from the highroad, perhaps two hundred yards away, the sound of many horses trotting, harness jingling and the low sound of many men's voices - hundreds in truth, two hundred? - four? - I could not guess.

"For God's sake, keep the ass quiet!" I hissed to Phoebe, and for the second time in twelve hours, he had a feast of windfalls. I pushed Hector's nosebag round his neck and he buried his muzzle in its contents.

Brush and trees shielded us from their sight, and in truth I had no wish at all to see them. Brigstock unbuttoned and vulnerable was one thing but I had no wish to meet him accoutred for the march with some few hundreds of his fellows to support him. We paused there still and silent, my hand on Apple's muzzle for some more minutes till all sound had faded northwards, and then allowed my animals to graze for some while, with Hector still harnessed to the cart. Poor beast. I judged the time to be about ten in the morning. He had been between the shafts for nearly nine hours. There would be good stabling for them and a hot meal for us a scant mile off at the Severnside homestead of the Baileys.

As we came to the highroad I lodged the cart under a tree and went ahead to ensure the way was empty. The rain had declined to a steady drizzle, and there was that strange silence that seems to descend after much human activity and movement. Not surprisingly the way was churned up into pools and swamps. A lone horseshoe glistened beside a pile of mud. I returned for the cart and we swiftly crossed over and took the track to Clevelode that was half hidden from the south by a great thicket of hawthorn standing in a bend of the road.

The Baileys had land on the banks of the Severn, which they had farmed or gardened for three generations. Master Adam Bailey's grandfather had bought the land and dwelling from King Henry's commissioners about one hundred years ago. The name Bailey, it was thought derived from Bailiff and this first Master Adam was rumoured to have been a close man with money. Certainly he must have carefully secured and harvested his treasure for some years in order to have bought the freehold, which extended to several acres. Perhaps he supplied those same Commissioners with useful knowledge of other Church treasures hereabouts for which he was rewarded by this parcel of land which he kept in despite of the re-endowment of the Abbey property back to the Cathedral. Still, since that time the Baileys' secular hands had tended well these fertile river meadows. The dwelling had been a chantry chapel where the monks had lived. They had grown vegetables for their great Monastery in Worcester. The Baileys continued with this calling and as the years had passed had added thatched rooms to the original chantry, which was now in a state of some disrepair. They lived ever in fear of floods, which whilst they rendered the land fertile beyond belief, caused much inconvenience and distress to Master Adam and Dame Joan. It was hard to place the family. They were not gentry, although they owned much land. They were not peasants although they tilled the soil. They were not merchants although they sold their produce for money. Perhaps it was this strange lack of a status that made them friendly to all alike.

They had three sons, two of whom lived with them and helped to sow, tend, till and gather. The eldest had had a great disagreement with his mother and gone his ways to make his fortune so he said. Dame Joan was a woman much given to ordering any who came within her compass, and there was no doubt that her sons chafed at her government. But her husband, a man of sweet and noble disposition, was stone-blind. His wife no doubt had had to assume his role gradually whilst his affliction took its course. Ben had treated him when he returned from Italy. At that time the vague shapes and colours of his inheritance were still visible to him but now - in his fifty fifth year he could hardly tell night from day. Ben could ascertain that curtains had gradually spread over his vision, and that, had we the skill to cut them back, maybe some measure of sight would return, but, alas, we lacked that talent. Dame Joan cared for him lovingly, deferred to him discreetly, and did her utmost best to make his life endurable. They were always together, she leading him patiently by the hand, guarding his every footstep. It was with great surprise therefore that when we emerged from the trees that lined the ridge above the water meadows, there was Master Adam quite alone, standing beside the path, clutching a sapling, his blind face turned in the direction of my jingling cart with an expression of great fear.

5

I called out "Master Adam! Fear not! It's me. Thomas Fletcher, Amyas' son. Why are you alone?" At the sound of my voice his features broke into his gentle welcoming smile. "Thomas, true Thomas. I would be blessed indeed if you could help me home. 'Tis my own folly I'm at this pass, good Tom."

"Where's Dame Joan?" I asked him tucking his hand under my arm, at the same time steering Hector round the ruts and pools of the path. Phoebe slipped down from Apple and came to his other side and took his right arm.

"Why, who's this?" asked Adam, "This hand is small and wondrous loving. Who is your companion, Tom?"

I told him briefly of Phoebe and of our good fortune that she had agreed to help us in the apothecary's shop, as she was skilled indeed.

"But how is it that you are unattended, Sir?" I asked him

"Nell the cook-maid came running to tell us that a brave company of soldiers were passing up to the town, so Joan ups with her heels and runs with the boys to see them. I waited and waited and could hear no sound of their coming. After a while I thought to meet them."

"And met us instead," I said. "Truly Adam, I have seen none of your sightseers on this road. Would they not have run northwards to Pole Elm to see them pass higher up the road?"

Adam stopped still so suddenly that we were all hard put to keep our footing. "Thomas, to be sure. What a terrible blind old fool you have in hand - and there was I certain sure my Joan had been taken by the soldiery."

"It's a braver soldier than I'll ever meet," I thought, but said aloud - "We had best hasten then, Sir, for when she and Roger and

James find you gone, there'll be a rare outcry."

"Young Tom," said he after a few moments as we walked. "Or perhaps you, gentle Lady Phoebe. Would you oblige me kindly and tell me of the crops and fields? They lie to our left now. I am sure. Would you tell me what you see? I must now see through the eyes of others. 'Tis as good as a play to me to hear what grows in my gardens."

"Willingly, sir," said I, "and to begin I see some of the best beans as a man could ever see on a day's march. There are about fifteen rows stretching down to the Severnside. Here now we come to your orchard with Pearmain and Pippins a-plenty. And now cabbages, sir, already round, fat and green, like so many cannon balls" - and so we progressed, until a bend in the path brought us almost up to the bank of the river itself.

"And here, sir is your great irrigator, Sabrina fluens, stealing past silently, almost to your very door. Had you missed your footing here, sir, I fear we should have had a less merry..."

I stopped as a shriek rent the air. "Your wife, sir?" I asked. He chuckled and said "Yes, indeed," and the unmistakable voice of Dame Joan scolding someone floated towards us on the breeze. I could see the kitchen smoke above the trees some short distance along the bank and could hear the inevitable uproar that was breaking forth at the discovery that the master of the house was missing.

"Come on, Sir. Listen you are sought for." A good stone track rose proud and well drained above the last small field, already ploughed for winter. It served often as a causeway in times of flood. And here came Dame Joan, pell-mell, across it to greet us, screaming and crying at her husband's recent defection.

"Adam - merely the briefest of jaunts to see the soldiers - why could you not have waited? What, Master Thomas Fletcher? We have looked for you this many a day and only today Jacky floats down in the ferryman's boat to tell us to tell you if you come here you are not to linger. You are wanted at home it seems. Master Ben has need of you. Husband, you wicked runaway."

She took Adam from me with all tenderness and preceded me across the barton. Husband and wife were laughing together at their recent alarms and fears. "And did you see the brave soldiers

47

then, my heart?" he asked her. "Yes, faith did I and a more mud bespattered company you'd never see. But so many of them. Eight troops, so Roger says, have been straggling along the road since cockcrow, about eight hundred poor sad souls in all, bound for Worcester and then Shrewsbury, 'tis said to fight the King. Can you believe, fighting against the King? Such wickedness! Master Thomas Fletcher, come you in now and rest you and never mind Jacky and his prognostications. There's lamb stew in the pot and beans and apple pie so sit you down and James see to those poor horses - nay, not horses - though I have no doubt they can both neigh well enough, eh Thomas? You must forgive me running on. It is getting to be such a treat to see you - so like your mother in the face and your father about the shoulders. A very proper man he is, husband. But who is this?" she stopped abruptly, looking at Phoebe needing both breath and information.

I was for once spared my explanations. "My dearest heart," said Adam, raising his wife's workworn hand to his lips. "This is a damsel in distress like the old tales with Thomas her true knight. And such distress! Perhaps they will tell you all over an early dinner. I can smell a most savoury smell coming from your kitchen. Suffice it to tell you, my dear heart, that this is a most brave excellent and clever young lady."

"Dame Joan," said I, "Know you of what sort of need this is, that Ben sent Jacky for me?"

"Oh, now, Nell, can you remember, girl, why Master Tom must hurry hence? Did Jacky say ought to you when you drew him beer?"

Nell looked confused. She was not renowned for her intellect but after a moment's careful thought told us: "King's Men from Oxford who've fallen sick on their way hither."

King's Men - in Worcester - the soldiers at Welland and the troops on the road to Worcester we had all encountered that morning had been Parliamentarians. What could or would be the outcome? Might there be a battle? "So when did they come to Worcester, Nell?" I asked her. She looked even more perplexed but Roger replied, "Nearly a week past now Thomas. There was much talk in the alehouse at Powick of their coming. 'Twas a week indeed for 'tis Fridays on the even that I walk up there if the night be fine, and mayhap I'll go tonight for 'tis Friday again!" he concluded with a bold look in his mother's direction. But Dame Joan was placing a bowl of hot lamb stew before me and took no heed of the rebel in her ranks. The fragrant smell was irresistible but my mind was much troubled. On the very day - the sixteenth last Friday - that I had begun my country jaunt leaving Worcester by the bridge, Kings men must have entered the city from another direction.

"Dame Joan, I thank you heartily, indeed for your good cheer," I said rising, "but Ben has been striving for a week now alone, all unbeknownst to me, while I have been junketing and idling my way through the country."

"Poor Hector has not been idling," said James coming in from the stable. "He's quite done up. If you're for leaving, Tom, you'll have to let him rest here for a day or so. In dry weather well and good, he can manage the cart with ease but a fetlock seems swollen, Tom, and you'll do him no good if you force him on."

"You shall take Walter," said Joan "We'll not need him till Market day next week. Will the shafts serve? But no more words, Thomas. Sit. Eat. Your mother, God rest her, would never have forgiven me if I let you pass hence without good food in your belly."

There was no gainsaying her and in truth I was both hungry and weary. She and Master Adam sat and ate with me and talked of the old times when they and my parents were young. I confess that in my youthful weakness, I fell asleep over Dame Joan's reminiscences and pie, and I think they left me slumped in my chair for an hour or two. Meanwhile the boys had most kindly busied themselves preparing the cart, the shafts of which needed some alteration to accommodate Walter, a young cart-horse who would make short work of the muddiest road. We saddled him up and it was about three in the afternoon that I bade Farewell to Master Adam who thanked me again for rescuing him as he called it. "I knew where I was by the lie of the land, wife," he explained to her, "but had thought to meet you long before on your way back. I had somehow forgotten the other road."

For once she was silent, smiling at him sadly. "All's well that ends well, dearest," she said at last gently, then turning to me, "There is elderberry syrup and Valerian Root ready prepared for you, Tom. You can pay me when you bring Walter back."

The rain had stopped some hours before and now a warm harvest sun gilded the Severnside. The trees, limes and poplars for the most part were assuming their yellow and orange finery before winter reduced them to sad nakedness. It was piteous to see Apple torn between two loyalties. He trotted from Hector's side to follow me, then ran back to Hector and then finally coaxed with his namesake yet again, he threw in his lot with the travellers, and allowed Phoebe to mount him as before. Roger and James came with me to see me on my way. As soon as we were clear of the house, that is to say out of his mother's earshot, Roger who at seventeen was thrust clear in an age of revolt began to ask me about the chance of apprenticeships in Worcester. His mother plagued him mercilessly he told me. He claimed it was, "Roger, do this," and, "Roger, come here," the livelong day. At this point James rising fifteen and an excellent horseman chimes in: "But your life is as Paradise when set beside mine. I can never rest. She is a terrible scold, Thomas - we cannot play Sports with the other lads hereabouts - we are too well-born it seems but if we are well born who then...."

I touched his arm alarmed by a noise some thirty yards ahead of us. There was a crashing through the undergrowth, which lined the river bank at this point. The bend in the path prevented our seeing the source of the noise and at that moment James cried out "Look! Look there!"

He was pointing to the centre of the river. We had a clear view of the whole central reach at this point. Gliding slowly downstream, turning lazily in the current was an object I could not at first descry. A piece of fencing perhaps? An old cart abandoned? Thin protuberances seemed to wave from the main body of the object which then turned over and then over again - but in that moment of movement we had seen all. It was a drowned horse.

Lazy farmers upriver, thought nothing of heaving dead livestock into this useful oversized drain that flowed past their land - but this was a young chestnut - a riding horse, the delicate thin legs seemed almost to wave a crazed greeting in our direction. James, the centaur, half horseman but still half boy burst into noisy tears. "I always wanted a chestnut," he sobbed. "Look at her. She's only young. Why couldn't they have buried her?"

He turned and ran back - I suspect to glean comfort from the mother he had spoken of so slightingly.

Roger and I exchanged glances and started off again. The sun hid itself behind a cloud momentarily. The path now left the side of Severn and meandered up to Callow End and the main way to Worcester that the soldiery had taken and we were turning our backs on the river when the sun's renewed glitter made me pause. Some yellow leaves, brighter than usual, perhaps, were ambushed by a hawthorn trunk, which leaned into the surface of the river. I looked again. It was a buff-coat - a new one. Silently I gave the reins to Roger and eased my way down the bank. I crawled some little way upon the trunk. I grasped the coat at its upper edge and pushed it floating still, in spite of its weight of water into a hollow of the bank. I climbed round to the tiny cove and dragged the coat and its owner who still wore it to dry land. A redder wine than Canaries now stained his garment. A sword gash through the chest had killed him. The ragged edges of the wound were partly covered by his shirt but there could have been no doubt that this had been a final thrust upwards to his heart.

Even now the horror of his face haunts me. The one side, pale, amazed blue eye open still, gazing in surprise at the mortal outrage offered by his slaughterer, and that fair silky moustache of which he was recently so proud. The other side, a mass of bloody flesh where his slayer had sliced his face away, the blood still seeping into his hair, the bones of teeth and jaw and eye socket gleaming white through the shreds of his cheek. It was without question Philip Fosdyke.

6

In the silence, a blackbird sang. The golden babble came from the hawthorn thicket arching above our heads. Across the river towards Kempsey another answered from a beech copse. The afternoon sun was warm on my back and I became aware of that strange musty smell like old houses that hangs over running water. I remember thinking idly: The Baileys must live with this same smell, day in day out.

"Tom, what shall we do?"

Roger was leaning across the corpse, shaking my arm. "Tom, come on man. What shall we do?"

I looked at him, fairly coolly, I think and said: "I know this man."

Yes, I knew this man. Yesterday fleetingly I had glimpsed the hopes and aspirations that had moved him to ally himself to the Parliament cause, and in so doing had had to accept the leadership of a mad criminal like Brigstock, his officer and mentor. Like me, he had had no real awareness of why King and Parliament were at odds but now had died, still unaware of the reasons for their quarrel. I had told him I knew of no adversaries in the area, and truly at the time had known nothing of King's men in Worcester. I had sensed his dislike of his soldier's trade, had known he feared to kill or be killed. In his moment of death, he must have thought me a traitor.

Roger was gaping. "How could you know him? What's to be done?" His eyes swept the river as if he would find inspiration there. "Tom, there's another. Look!"

We scrambled down the bank, but this corpse was well out mid-stream destined to float heedlessly at the whim of the river for many miles. "Tom!" cried Roger again, pointing upstream. Another horse and two more bodies were drifting down in the current in hideous procession. One of them trailed rags of orange cloth. Beyond them I could see other specks, which on a happier day I would have dismissed as driftwood.

Roger said strangely, "I am happy that my father cannot see this."

I tried to shrug off the horror. Phoebe who had stayed with Apple on the path, now dismounted and gasped in horror at the ruin of Philip's face. "Go on, up to the road," I told her roughly. I had work to do in Worcester. I took an old blanket from the cart and helped by Roger together we wrapped Philip in this shabby winding sheet and placed him in the cart. There was nothing for it but to take him with me and bury him in Worcester. I owed him that at least, I who had unknowingly told him I thought there was nought to fear. I dreaded now as to what might have taken place there on this endless day.

We reached the high road, where Phoebe was waiting patiently. The mud was beginning to dry a little, but the going was still heavy and arduous. Roger was for continuing still with us but I sent him back, telling him he was needed more at his home at this time than any place else. I would bring Walter back, as soon as was possible next week. He left me angry at the knowledge that his fate was, "to kick his heels forever at his mother's apron strings," as he termed it, but aware of the logic of my advice, and anxious, I think, to protect his father.

Phoebe and Apple were hard put to it to keep pace with Walter and I again regretted not for the first time on that fateful jaunt that I had been soft hearted enough to allow the donkey to accompany us. He was not an animal for crises. I halted Walter yet again to allow the wretched creature to hurry himself to catch us up. As I tarried, the sound of galloping hooves from up the road grew ever louder. I drew Walter into the side, fearing that whoever was coming at such a gallop, might not take kindly to our presence in his path.

About six troopers, dressed something in the way of Brigstock, thundered towards us. Cursing and swearing for their way whilst not blacked by my cart was rendered something narrower, they reined in their horses to pass two abreast casting frenzied glances back the way they had come. I saw fear writ large on their faces. They had lost their weapons save for one who sought to load his musket as he rode, I think to no avail. One of the last ones shouted to me - a warning - as I later surmised. He and one of the others wore sashes or scarves over their buff coats like Philip and Brigstock wore, like to the orange tawny rags that trailed the drowned men in the river.

I could make nothing of the warning but the reason became all too clear a minute later. Three men came running down the track towards me, again clad like the fleeing Parliament men, although one had cast off his coat. A horseman followed them and for a moment I thought that perhaps it was another escaping trooper. But as I watched he leaned from his horse and sliced and thrust at the last man with his drawn sword. His victim fell with a shout and groan into the ditch and the mounted man turned his attention to the others. One at last followed his wit and ran off the road into bushes that lined one of the tracks to the hamlet of Bastonford but the other in dire panic could think of nothing but running forward. The horseman had paused to consider whether he should follow his quarry who had turned aside but then followed the runner towards me and the cart. I looped Walter's reins over a hazel branch, Phoebe slipped off Apple and we watched in amazement. The runner was wounded in the arm. As he approached me and the cart, he tripped and fell sideways onto a heap of stones on the left hand verge. Some farmer had placed them ready to improve and pave the road. The horseman rode at him, sword poised for the kill.

But I was already there, between his horse and the stones, facing upwards towards him as he raised his arm. Seeing my person blocking his killing purpose, he changed his intent, and drew back again to thrust at me. I ducked and as the force of his intention drove him forward grasped his thin right wrist. His left hand by instinct pulled on his reins, I think, but at the same moment, Apple becoming aware of the strange horse set up such a caterwauling by way of greeting, that the mount in curiosity must needs leave his rider, who having now loosed the reins to scrabble for his dagger, slid easily from his charger's back, over its tail, and down on his bum - with his sword arm still in my loving grasp. The handle fell from his fingers now, and I took it in my left hand. Only then did

I let the young popinjay loose, for he was so little in beard that I scorned to fight a child for in truth he was no more. His feathered hat was something askew now and his fine lace collar torn. I judged rightly as it transpired that his guardians would be seeking him.

He began to scream at me in a language that I took to be French. "Perfide traitre!" he shouted again and again, looking up the road towards Powick and Worcester as if he hoped that reinforcements should be there. Then as he saw the wounded man stagger to his feet catch the charger, (no hard task as it stood nose to nose in silent communion with Apple), and mount it by the simple expedient of using the heap of stones as a block, the young Frenchman's fury knew no bounds. He launched himself against me trying to scratch and beat me into submission with his left hand. I twisted his right arm up behind his back and waving his sword before his face reminded him who was in possession of the weapon. The fugitive on the stolen horse was by this time some yards away, shouting out to me: "Thanks friend." At this final proof of total discomfiture, the French youth could play the man no longer and lapsed into boyhood, weeping at his defeat at the hands of one who to him must have seemed no more than a peasant. I had a rope in my snapsack and for my own safety, after making certain that he had no other arms, tied his hands behind him, not too tightly, and as he was not of sturdy yeoman stock, but light of build thought fit to place him on Apple to return him to his guardians. Even I, untaught as I was in Politicks and the affairs of the realm knew that a young Frenchman, friendless and alone in an English country would have a poor time of it. The French Queen was not well liked.

It transpired that the three men I had seen him hunting down, were not his only prey. He craned to gaze at the poor fellow I had first seen him attack, who lay his head at a skewed angle to his body, and as we travelled I saw him eying other corpses by the road with every sign of pride and defiance. He would turn slyly to look at my reaction to his prowess. "What is your quarrel with us, then?" I asked him but he could not reply. "Pourquoi?" I asked him remembering suddenly a word of French I had heard in a play of Shakespeare's. He let forth such a flow of violent invective in which the words "perfide traitres" figured alarmingly. "But I am no traitor," I told him. "I could have killed you. Now I am returning you to your friends."

As we came to Powick Ham, the common meadow before the bridge over Teme he became more and more excited. There was much activity. Soldiers, Royalist troopers I realised, were clearing the path to the bridge of the fearful and tragic victims of the conflict that had ensued. I had seen dead men before Phil Fosdyke, but they had died in the course of nature. To see the unhappy remnants of these poor vanquished fellow mortals heaved about like so many sacks of turnips caused me much sadness, but my young captive much glee. His crowing laughter caused the Royalist troopers to glance at him at first with disapproval, but then they too began to laugh but at my prisoner, not with him. And indeed we must have seemed like the clownish interlude of a tragedy - the rough little cart, pulled doggedly by stout workaday Walter, the rakish ass with Mounsieur Puny Jackanapes in his tattered finery up atop, and myself leading the beasts, and looking I have no doubt a true Tom o' Bedlam, the veriest clodpole, with bloodstained shirt and mud stained kicks, hair like a black haystack, face and hands as filthy as the backstone of the hearth.

The low chuckles that had heralded our approach to the bridge travelled with us as we crossed it, as men turned from their tasks at our passing. My captured Jack with the Feather seemed to lack approbation - indeed the occasional groan escaped from those who had perhaps had cause to suffer from his unrebuked sauciness.

I learned later that most of the Parliamentarians who died in the battle perished at this bridge over the Teme, when a hasty retreat back to Upton had begun. I could later never find out how many drowned or how many being dead were flung into the river. Some of the dead who lined the lane beyond the bridge - Cut-Throat Lane it was known, (an uncanny rural prophecy), showed no signs of battle scars.

"How came they by their ends?" I asked one man who was busily stripping the good shoes off a corpse to replace his own which were both down at heel and out at toes.

"Crushed at the bridge there. How the traitors ran! They ran into their fellows as they were a-crossing back there and in the crimmage met their ends. We've cleared it so that dolts like you can enjoy swift free passage."

"Have a care to his fellow, there," I advised him pointing to the body beside the man he was pillaging. "He lives."

The musketeer stared at me. "How know you that?" he said standing up, one shoe off and one shoe on, like a grotesque Diddle Diddle Dumpling.

"By the slight movement of his chest," I told him. "By his colour which is not yet that of the pallor of the winding-sheet - and....," but at that instant the man of whom we spoke groaned and stirred a little.

"But our surgeon pronounced him dead not ten minutes since. Are you a witch?" he cried crossing himself.

"No, but it seems a better surgeon than yours. Cover him with your coat, I beg you for charity." I left Phoebe feeling his pulse and speaking to him softly, encouraging him to wake. I promised to return as soon as I had delivered up my young Mounsieur Hot-Head who was growing increasingly restive, to whomever should claim him.

We passed down the lane that led to Worcester and turned through the field gates of the great field that lay between Teme and Severn. Most folk call it Wickfield. I have in my life seen many battle fields - more than once I have been forced to abandon my Aesculapian calling and fight for my very life - but this first scene of death and slaughter stays ever clearly in my mind. And yet the Battle of Powick Bridge as it came to be known was a mere Harvest Junketing compared with the horrors I would later encounter. The Royalist soldiery - poor tattered Northern scarecrows for the most part - could not resist removing the clothing from the dead Parliament men who had been newly serviceably and warmly clad. There was no slaughtering of the wounded though and it seemed that injured Parliament men were assisted by Prince Rupert's surgeon. But all of this I learned later.

Now groups of men were making fires - and cooking! A few King's men of the nobler sort were in fact making shift to dine, attended by their servile lackeys. I observed this with some amazement. I had yet to learn that the murder of ones fellows was hungry and thirsty work and that our well-born betters must always refresh themselves after a hunt. And that was in effect their view of the day's work. They had had a rare day's hunting. But their quarry was their fellow men - not the poor gentle deer. A tall, dark man, his fine shirt sorely stained, perhaps four years my Senior reined up beside me, laughing heartily. His face was smudged with powder shot.

"Gerard, que faites-vous? Why sir, look I in a glass? We are like to two herrings perhaps?" He spoke English swiftly and well but laced with strange phrases.

"Who are you Sir, and know you this youth?" I asked, helping my prisoner from the donkey's back. He launched into a flood of French invective, as I untied his hands. I knew he was casting me in the role of cruel tyrant.

A servant approached, bowed low to my questioner. "Will you take a cup of wine, Highness? My Lord Digby drinks to your good health and continuing success." Was this then the King? I scratched my head wondering how much longer I could count on its proximity to the rest of my person. This though was no vengeful conqueror. He took the wine, pledged me, then pushed the glass into my grateful hands. "Drink, you are thirsty I think." The French child now at liberty began again to berate me with his fists, but this great lord spoke but once and instantly was obeyed. "Arretez, Gerard. Ce gentilhomme avait tu donner grand service. Connaisez-vous le pays d'Angleterre? Je ne pense pas."

"Oui, mon Prince," sulkily replied the discomforted youth. My dark haired friend turned again to me. "His uncle, my good comrade Mounsier de Lisle will be most pleased and grateful with you sir." At that moment, a fine gentleman rode up, crying aloud with joy at the sight of the Frog Prince. He dismounted and clasped the fiery brat to his bosom and they proceeded to converse in their own confounded tongue.

"Who are you, Sir?" I asked again as this man to whom all deferred as to a King turned to me.

"We want to give you gold - a present for his safe return," he said ignoring my question. "His uncle wondered at your choice of transport for his cherished nephew, but I reminded him that better men than young Gerard thought no shame to ride in triumph on an ass."

"Sir, I need no gold," and in truth I was heartily sick of Master Gerard and wanted nothing more than to be about my calling. I pointed to a hastily dug pit made to accommodate the Paliamentary dead. "Sir, I beg of you, be sure that these corpses are corpses in truth. Can you imagine a worse fate than to be buried alive? To wake only to suffocate? Sir, I have already seen one man left for dead, move and groan. May I examine them prior to their burial, good Sir?"

He laughed again, the victor on the crest of invincible elation. "As you wish. A name for a name. Yours is?"

"Thomas Fletcher, Apothecary and Physician of this city. I even now hoped to see my master here. He is Ben Knowles, a fine Physician."

"To my knowledge only the Israelite came hither to help us from the city. Could that be he?" He pointed towards a fire at the far end of the field where wounded men were sitting or lying. One man was tending them. He had stripped to his breeches, ever Ben's wont when great efforts were in hand.

I rushed to the cart and retrieved my box of instruments. For a moment I contemplated abandoning Philip to the burial preparations here, but then resolved to inter him as a friend and a brother in our own plot.

"Farewell, good sir." I cried out to the great Lord who still laughed as the Frog Prince told his angry story. "That is Ben. I must tell him I am here but then I pray you, let me examine the dead."

"Willingly Master Surgeon, and I thank you indeed for your pains," he called after my retreating back.

"And where in Hell have you been a-gallivanting, whilst I have been wearing my arse to a gnat's pizzle?" were Ben's first snarled words.

"List, Ben, whatever surgeon gave the order for the burial of the Parliamentary dead near the river knows not his trade. As I watched one so-thought corpse groaned in pain. The King's Commander is content that I should examine those set aside for burial. Shall I try if they are dead indeed?" He straightened up and stared at me, his brown chest stained with another man's blood, his mouth a thin hard line.

"Tell me then how do we distinguish the merely comatose from the worms' meat?"

"The faintest film on mirror or glass held near the mouth?

Their colour? If they still retain the body's heat?"

"Well, well," said Ben "Off with you. I've made shift so long, t'will be no hardship without you now. But for the Lord's sake, Tom, where is the clean water? God knows what impurities I am washing into these wounds. And where in Hell is Parkinson?"

"Safe, quite safe," I shouted as I ran back to the cart. "Here in our chariot!"

I took a barrel and bowl and clean cloths from the cart. Phoebe was bathing the swordcuts of a man whose arms were crossed all about with red wounds. I ran back with Ben's requirements and flung them down beside him. Then I ran back for my box of instruments and hastened to the lane side where I had left the shoe-stealer and the man near death whom I had asked him to guard. The plunderer had decided to let no grass grow under his newly shod feet and had disappeared but my "dead" patient had been spat back by the Devil and was sitting up on the grass very carefully nibbling a piece of cheese.

"How do you?" I asked him. "I saw before you were not for the Day of Judgement. You can eat without pain?"

"Aye, marry, can I," he told me, "But I've a monstrous great ache here in my side."

I examined him. He had cracked or broken a rib which was causing him some pain, but not so much that it could not be endured, I thought.

"You were trapped or crushed, sir, at the bridge. But you will mend over months. But you must live quiet and godly. Can you go back to your home?"

"If they are taking no prisoners, I have money for my journey as I think." Very carefully he felt in his pocket. "Aye, the king's menials have left me that at least. And have no fear, good Master Doctor, I hail from Northampton where we all live quiet and godly."

I bade him Farewell and hastened to the burial pits. Their future inhabitants were being lifted in with rather more courtesy than when they were simply obstructions at the bridge. A Royalist Sergeant in charge of proceedings approached me

"His Highness warned us you would wish to examine t' corpses," he told me. "But hurry thyself up lad. Bastards are swarming up from Evesham. If thou cannot haste thysen I cannot bury. We are for Shrewsbury post haste."

A quick glance northwards confirmed his words. Troops of King's Horsemen were even now gathering at the Worcester end of the field, ready it seemed to ride off in rough military formation.

Men who have been crushed for any length of time may have sustained grievous internal injuries. Broken ribs can pierce the heart chamber and no immediate sign of hurt may be visible for some time. Of the twenty men laid out, the first twelve were dead indeed. A few had sustained fatal sword cuts and Rigor Mortis had begun. One whose arm hung by a few poor scraps of flesh had perished a few moments before I came, the Sergeant told me. He had lain amongst the ranks of the wounded crying and moaning most piteously. "And when it finally pleased t'Almighty to receive him into his bosom, it were a blessed moment for all on us I can tell thee, sir." I judged that his death occurred as much from the knowledge of his horrific plight as from loss of blood, though that was extreme.

Another man although he lay inert and still, I could not for my life, (or rather his), pronounce him dead. No film on my glass, when I held it near his lips, no pulse but no stiffness and his flesh though it was cold to the touch, had not the heavy unwieldiness of a joint of beef. When I raised his arm, I could not truthfully perceive or sense the stiffness of death. I passed on but asked the diggers who were already filling in the pit, to place him gently on the side and wait. Three more were grave matters but the seventeenth quite clearly breathed still. One of the burial party after I had invited him to place his hand upon the barely moving chest, told me: "This was or rather is a Captain, sir. He was rallying them round him like a demon, but as I remember we dragged a dead horse from him at the bridge."

I bade them fill in as far as maybe and busied myself with my two patients, trying to make them warm. Phoebe brought over the cart, so that I could find coverings for them. Suddenly the first of the two, he who breathed not but who had no stiffness came to himself. I was chafing his hands trying to raise warmth in him, when he opened his eyes, murmured: "Elspeth," turned his head to one side and plainly died. My standing rose amongst the burial party. The Sergeant praised me saying: "And we thought as how he was so much mutton when all the time life of a sort still clung to him."

As my other patient began to breathe more deeply I straightened up and took my ease for a moment. "Who is that young commander?" I asked him. "He is a Prince I think, but the King's sons are children still."

The sergeant laughed. "That's young Rupert - Rupert of the Rhine as he's called. King's nephew. He's nobbut a youngster and yet he's spent three year behind bars somewhere o'erseas. King loves him well and he's not one o' your dainty Jacks, afeard to dirty his hands."

I watched Rupert in his stained shirt riding down towards the Teme, rallying his troopers. A horse thrashed still in agony, its dazed owner helpless in horror beside it. I watched Rupert dismount, and hold his flintlock to the horse's head. He fired, and fragments of its brain and skull flew everywhere. He ran then to a stray charger whose rider - perhaps a Parliamentarian was dead or fled - and exhorted his follower to mount and ride. As they passed us, he called out to me, "Farewell Master Surgeon."

I proposed to the Sergeant if they would now place Elspeth's lover in his last resting place, I would make shift to care for the unconscious captain. They completed their task. I watched them as I tried to force a little clean water from the flask I carried at my waist between the lips of my last patient. Through all this activity I seemed to be as it were observing myself from above and admiring my own coolness. How could I view this carnage, these scenes of mortality with a level head? In truth, when all was known, the action this day of Friday the twenty third of September took place when Englishmen cherished still some sort of care, one for the other, and when to kill a countryman because he held a differing notion of how the realm should be governed, was a most unnatural act for most men. But this was by no means the philosophy of all. For an evil minority our terrible Wars, which began in earnest on this day, were simply an opportunity to obtain an ill-deserved prosperity. Some wicked protagonists in this bloody drama cared nothing for the high ideals of either King or Parliament, but were concerned only how swiftly and how best to line their pockets.

Others whose perverse desires and fantasies had been kept in check by the mundane habits of their past daily life were given an unbridled opportunity to indulge their hideous hidden lusts. Such a one was William Brigstock. I was swiftly to learn these truths in a tragic and terrible manner, which was to alter the course of my life for ever.

7

My father, hearing that there had been a battle in Brickfield and in Cut-Throat Lane, hardby Powick, had crossed the bridge with some fellow merchants to the village of St. John's to learn more of events. They were in time to see the King's men ride away to Shrewsbury. As he and his friends watched Sir Richard Crane's Lifeguards cantering northwards in the rear of Rupert's army along the muddy track, I think they hoped that this was the last they would see of soldiers on active service. In this they were sadly mistaken.

I saw him scanning the field as I toiled towards the bridge, Walter pulling the cart, which held one dead man and one living. Ben had in his charge two King's Men from Staffordshire who were far too sick to ride off with Rupert. One clung to life by a hairsbreadth. My hand was under the elbow of another, steering and steadying him as he lurched along. Ben had bandaged his head but the sword cut he had sustained across his scalp was bleeding again and the poor fellow knew not what he did.

I see my poor father now in the theatre of my mind, looking everywhere for me, as he knew Ben had sent for me, recognising his Prodigal, waving joyfully in greeting and hurrying towards me, faithful Jacky at his heels. "Dear son, I have been so afeared for you." He clasped me to him briefly, "God in heaven, you stink like week-old fish!" then looking at the wounded men and at the bodies in the cart and asking briskly: "So, what's to do here?"

"Could you aid this poor man and his fellow in the cart there? Could they lie in Fish Street for a day or two? Ben and I will doctor them, round the clock if need be but they are poor men, far from home."

"Bring them, bring them!" shouted my father, "Jacky, run ahead of us and tell Gill to get the press beds prepared for them in Master Tommy's bedchamber - and tell her to put on pans of water for the young master. He smells like the town sewer, save not so sweet!"

"They are King's men, Father, but so terrible hurt they could not ride off with Rupert. He's a fearsome cool blade. What sights I've....!"

I gulped and lapsed into comfortable silence. My father ever aware and alive to my feelings was silent also as we trudged homewards to Fish Street. On arrival I saw my invalids who were Lord Digby's men - a ploughboy and a farmer's son I think - as well disposed as their wounds allowed. In truth I had little hope for the second. When he came to himself which he did in great pain and distress, all he could think of was that his parents would be at charge for the horse he had borrowed and which had been killed under him when he had taken the massive cut across his chest.

After Gill Cook and Jacky had helped me lay Philip on the great trestle table in the parlour and old Tabitha had been summoned to prepare him for burial, I led poor patient Walter back again to the field to bring back Ben, Phoebe and the Captain. She was dipping cloths in cold water and holding them to the Captain's brow as Ben instructed. The patient was conscious now and after a while with our help could walk or stagger rather to the cart. Ben asked her to protect him from the motion of the cart. I gave him some notion of her history and he said shortly, "She has more than proved her worth this day. Would you could both have been here earlier."

As I went to take the leading reins, I tripped and fell - from fatigue perhaps? I know not. Straightway she was there, assisting me to my feet. Then unasked, she took the reins and led the way, thanked courteously by Ben.

A number of Parliament men fell in behind us. I looked at them questioningly and one came forward and told us they were the Captain's men from Herefordshire. "Thanks to his good judgement, not a man of us is harmed," he told us. "When he saw the press at the bridge he made us make for a ditch and lie low. Rupert's men never bothered us, and in minutes it was over. But the Captain here rode from us into the skirmish when he saw a Scots major, a noble friend, beset by the Cranes. We saw his horse roll on him and thought all was over for him and for us."

The Captain's name was Robert Burghill and at last he was made comfortable in one of the guest bedchambers of the Newport Street house. We had done all that we could for him and the two men from Staffordshire. The man with the chest wound, which Ben claimed had missed his heart by inches, was near mad with sorrow at the loss of his horse. The other, one George Preston, was more philosophic and tried to comfort him.

Ben came to dine at Fish Street bringing Phoebe with him. As there was presently so much work there at the moment it was decided that she should stay in one of Ben's guest rooms for the time being, although my father, having heard her sad story had already begun to plan how best she could be accommodated with us. Jill had roast mutton and caper sauce for us, a dish I loved well. I learnt of the happenings here in the last week - the arrival in Worcester of the Royalist Sir John Byron and his dragoons by road from Oxford on the same day that I had left for Ledbury. Sir John had a precious cargo - the silver plate from the Oxford colleges to be minted into coin of the realm to pay the King's army. ("Soldiers are good eaters but not always good payers," said my father wisely.) Then on Wednesday last, (whilst I was determining in Ledbury to cease dancing attendance on Eleanour), there had been an attempt made by Captain Nathaniel Fiennes, (brother of the John Fiennes of whom Brigstock spoke), to enter the city arms by Sidbury Gate. His intention was to steal Byron's plate. It came to nought. My father saw the whole incident.

The Parliament men made a small hole with a pick axe through the gate and then fired one shot through it. This was enough for Sir William Russell who had volunteered himself to take command of the defence of the city. Some few of Byron's troopers who stood ready, rode forth through Sidbury Gate which they had newly fortified and taught Fiennes not to covet his neighbour's goods. They did this, to such good effect, riding forwards with valour, and then riding backwards with discretion, that they came off light with a few scratches, but four or five of the King's enemies were heavily brought to God's justice something earlier than they had hoped.

"So then Captain Nat not liking his lesson overmuch makes legs down river, east side Severn and encounters other companies by Upton Bridge, I take it meeting with the Captain, Ben is tending now. And there am I beside myself with fear for you Tom, you clown, knowing you are dallying around the Southern end of the Malverns. And then up rides Captain Nat today, west side Severn, helter-skelter into Rupert's loving arms, closely followed by my wandering rascal here. And in truth, son, you say Rupert spoke to you?"

"Certainly he did." I told them, "But how come he was there at all?"

It seems Rupert rode from the King now in Shrewsbury down the West side of Severn to ensure Sir John's peaceful passage to his sovereign, as there were so many reports of Parliament men in these parts. I remembered the Yorkshire sergeant's words. "'Twould be good to lock up doors," I warned, "Essex' army is on its way here from Evesham."

They looked at me. "I heard talk of that from the wounded," said Ben. "All who could heave themselves on horse, no matter how cut about they were, made shift to do so when word came Essex was moving hither. Ah well! I must return to tend the Captain. Tom, I'll need you in good earnest tomorrow. Time enough then to prepare for Essex' occupation."

But the morrow was too late. I woke to my father's bellows of rage. The rain had returned and with it, Essex' horse and foot. Parliament men were everywhere, cold, wet, bewildered and angry at the lack of bespoke billets for their comfort after days of unaccustomed travel. They were it seems emptying my father's store of the carcasses hung ready for sale. I peered out of my window through the drizzle - and swiftly withdrew myself. The man ordering this wholesale theft was none other than Quartermaster William Brigstock. As I squinted round the leather hanging to my shameful delight, I saw that he sported a rich black eye and that the edge of a bandage was visible below his hat. When he bowed to make obeisance to a passing Captain, it became clear that that part of his cranium between crown and brow would bear the scars of Martin Beckford's stable wall for some weeks to come. A ragged attempt had been made to cut and shave his hair around the wound. I decided discreetly to postpone our reunion.

My father's store was now obviously empty. Brigstock ordered the Parliament thieves to carry their loot to some pre-arranged point of collection and turned away with a last vicious glance at Jacky who had been knocked into the gutter as a side of beef was clumsily borne away. I began to fear that he had connected our name Fletcher hung over the sign of the Hereford bull, with his recent close contact with my medicine chest. I watched him as he swaggered up Fish Street after his plunderers. He had an air of owning whatever place he shamed with his presence - Martin Beckford's parlour - the city of Worcester - it was all grist to the mill of his vile ambition. As I watched his retreating back, a man on horseback clattered down and drew up beside him. The rider muffled up in his cloak leant downwards to try to hear what Brigstock had to say - obviously a matter of some secrecy. Brigstock strained himself upwards but the horse was so high, that its rider must needs dismount in order to preserve the clandestine nature of Brigstock's news. But now another difficulty arose. The muffled rider was so small a man, Brigstock had to stoop to mutter in the fellow's ear. Both looked back to my father's shop sign and then Brigstock cupped his hands so that the Jack o' Lent warrior could remount and ride swiftly back towards the High Street. Brigstock paused, annoyed that his hands had been muddied by the rider's little boots. He spied a poor girl passing with full buckets from the well near St Albans. He called her over and washed his hands in her clean water, despite her protests. Then with one last sneering glance over his shoulder at my father and the group of neighbours who had gathered to share his outrage, Brigstock passed out of my view.

I hastened down to warn my father of Brigstock's nature. He was not in a mood for reason however and swore a great oath: "Let him be the Devil's Quartermaster - he shall go his ways to the Gaol House by eventide."

"Father," I pleaded with him, "Have a care! This is no country bullfinch! I have not told you all I know of his exploits. He would have ruined Sally Beckford if I had not prevented him. He has an army behind him now. For aught we know his commanders hold him dear,"

"All the more reason to tell them of his villainy. Assaulting that innocent girl you say? John Fiennes his commander? I'll to the Mayor first to report these outrages!"

I could not persuade him to stay indoors but he must be off and away to redress wrongs. At the door he paused, "And Tom. Give that poor good girl the contents of my purse and tell her where the mercer's is. She deserves to be better clad, poor sweet maid. What times! What trials!"

I let him go his ways and tended my invalids. George would make a good recovery, but the other poor fellow was in the delirium of death. His eyes started from his face. "Set Giles to bird-scaring!" he ordered me. I agreed and he seemed to sleep but 'twas not the wholesome sleep of health. I dressed his terrible wound yet again with Pare's lotion of egg yolk, turpentine and oil of roses and prayed for him. There were no other remedies.

George sat and rested holding his head in his hands. He had contrived to leave his bed to relieve himself and now told me of an occasional blankness before his eyes and a headache, which throbbed and flared like a foundry. Still the wound on his scalp was clean. A scab was beginning to form.

"You need rest and food," I told him. "Gill will bring you the second and I, as your physician, must help you back to your bed to gain the first."

I wondered how Ben was faring. I decided to go to work, in despite of my dread of meeting Brigstock. I had bested him once I told myself and could do so again. But two days ago he did not have eleven regiments of horse and foot at his beck and call, so it was with caution and circumspection that I ventured forth. As I turned the corner and went through the arch towards Bridport Street I carefully surveyed the passers-by lest I should come upon the evil bastard. Quartermasters there were aplenty knocking on doors and informing the good residents of Worcester that now their joyously anticipated occasion to assist the cause of Parliament was come at last, and that quiet godly guests in the persons of reputable military ambassadors of the great Earl of Essex now sought their hospitality. I noticed Mistress Harrison, the wealthy widow of a rich cloth merchant, standing in her doorway looking askance over the shoulder of one such officer, as an "ambassador of Essex" vomited cider into the gutter. There were such soldiers everywhere, following in the wake of their Quartermasters, looking about them in the rain, buying penny loaves from the baker's shops, making fires at street corners. They had even made one such cooking fire in the square before All Saints, around which a whole company seemed to have gathered. They did not molest me being intent on eating and drinking, and one kindly fellow even invited me to a slice of roast mutton - no doubt from the same carcass which had been hanging in my father's store that very morn.

There were twenty or thirty of them waiting for treatment in the courtyard at Newport Street. I could see that Ben was already at work in his Dispensary so I pushed through to the kitchen and thence to one of the guest chambers to see how the Captain progressed. He was sitting up and eating a piece of bread with some Cheshire cheese with infinite care and was much rejoiced to see me. He had been told by Ben and Phoebe that I had saved him from a premature grave. He gave me grateful thanks for his deliverance at the hands of Royalist ignorance. He had a great soreness about his ribs and if he moved quickly the pain was impossible to bear. Ben had diagnosed three cracked ribs and thought also that the shock of more than one violent impact had caused his death-like state.

"Yes, indeed." I remembered the Sergeant's words. "You were grievously crushed. But they told me that you fought like a demon...."

"What of my men?" he asked suddenly.

"They have been somehow accommodated in our stables," I told him. "The horses have been put to grass - what little there is - in my father's paddock."

"My horse..." he said dreamily, then asked me sharply, "dead, I take it?"

"I fear so, sir." I told him, "or else captured by Rupert's men."

After a moment he said thoughtfully: "I hope that was the case, indeed. Did they take many prisoners?"

"As far as I know they took only one man, one Edward Wingate, a Member of Parliament," for so the rumour went.

"I know him well. I doubt much his treatment will be over courteous...." but at that moment Ben stormed in.

"Tom, are you blind? Am I to doctor these rapscallions all day alone unaided? Forgive me Master Robert. I trust you are recovering. I must wrest your companion from you to help me treat your comrades in arms. Now list well," as he hurried me over the courtyard. "Most have the sores and blisters of unseasoned travellers. If they cannot pay or if they are drunk they must wait whilst sober payers are dealt with. Do you hear?"

I heard well enough and forgave him his irritation, for as he said, as we toiled all day with blisters and saddle sores, Byron's men whom Ben had tended alone had suffered from similar complaints, and these Parliament heel kibes or arse abcesses were in fact lacking in poetic appeal or medical interest. A sore bum is a sore bum, whether its owner is for King or Parliament. At length we were done, the last thigh anointed, the last foot bandaged and a fair quantity of silver collected for our pains - or rather our patients'!

I made my way back to Fish Street, the drizzle continuing and unhoused soldiers who had thought it best to invest in cider rather then lodgings stood or sat in the mud and grime. I wondered if I should remonstrate with them for their health's sake but thought better of it for they might not relish my help, rather might view it as officious interference. When I reached home, Jacky told me my father was still abroad, going from Alderman to Alderman to seek support for his grievances. At length he returned, his individual cause diminished by other outrages committed in the name of Parliament and so-called good government. It seemed that the Mayor, Edward Soley, had been taken up by Essex' men, imprisoned and there was now talk that he would go to London to stand trial for allowing the King's Men to enter eight days before.

"And if my Lord Essex can suggest a means whereby a peaceful city of unarmed burghers can gainsay an hundred men a-horseback with swords and muskets with walls and gates for the most part in ruin, then I would wish his Lordship to enlighten us, for I know not how we could have diverted Byron. My case is as nothing compared with the fate that awaits the poor Mayor. If men need meat I will always give them food for charity. It is the theft I resent, not the loss. How do the invalids?"

"George Preston is stronger still." I told him, "but as he thrives his fellow wastes. I doubt that he will see tomorrow even. I will fetch Ben for him in the morn to see if there is aught he can prescribe that I have neglected."

The next day, the Sabbath, the 25th of September dawned clear but again I was awoken by my father's bellow of rage and again I ran to the window wondering what further thefts from our premises the Parliament had sanctioned under the name of law and order. Citizens of Worcester up betimes stood and gaped at the obscene show. The soldiery had it seems visited the Cathedral, soiled and looted the precious robes of office of Bishop, Dean and Prebendaries and were even now capering about the streets flaunting their disrespect in the eyes of the early church goers. Although they had not forced themselves again into my father's store, another butcher further up Fish Street, hardby St Helen's was shouting curses and imprecations on seven or eight of the villains who had availed themselves of his stock. A newly slain calves' head had been placed atop a richly decorated green cope. One of the felons, the worse for drink for sure, had torn crude gaps for eyeholes in the gold embroidery and had pulled it over himself, and was dancing blindly past our windows, cheered on by his fellows.

I dressed myself speedily and ran down to try to prevent my father from remonstrating with the criminals. He was wearing his Sunday robe, a deep blue threepile velvet doublet, his high hat with two proud plumes, lying ready on the table.

"Don't go out, father!" I begged him. "Don't speak to them."

"Nay son," he said calmly. "We are gone too far for that. I will not speak to these braggart Jacks. It is their master I must confront. He must know they have desecrated what we regard as God's house. See to your poor fellows above and bid Ben and that clever young lady to dinner. In spite of their robberies, Gill still has beef for the spit."

He picked up his cane and his hat and left his house without another word. I went back upstairs. George spoke to me pleasantly with gratitude saying that he and his fellow had no pence to pay me, but when he reached his Staffordshire village, he would send money to us by the carrier. "There is not need of that," I told him.

"Think no more of it." I looked at his fellow who had lapsed into unconsciousness. "I fear that today...."

He looked at me. "I fear that too," he said slowly, "but his poor parents will be comforted to know that he died in a good house, not cast aside to perish in some ditch."

I decided to fetch Ben there and then to get his opinion. In truth the poor man had lost too much blood and with it I believed his strength, for all some doctors believe that bloodletting purges the body. As I passed along Merrivale I saw one profane knave pouring beer from a tavern into a gold chalice, holding it aloft and declaring: "Here is the King's blood soon to be spilt for all." Whilst those with him laughed, they looked round as if ashamed and apprehensive of his lewdness, half expecting reproof, like children who expect and need guidance. I hurried past, went through the great arch of the Knowles house and found yet more groups of soldiers, already standing around waiting for medical attention whether is was the Sabbath or not. I noticed the man who had told me of the Captain's bravery and care of his men, painstakingly skinning a hare.

In the kitchen Ben was gazing in some concern at Phoebe who had brought news. Robert Burghill had left his bed for the first time and sat in his shirt at the table.

"Tom, has my uncle gone to Matins at the Cathedral?" Ben asked, "If he has, it is likely he will not like what he sees. Phoebe here went earlier. It seems that Essex has ordered that the Parliament horses may be stabled there."

I sat down, not knowing what to do. "He has already gone to Essex to complain of desecration." I told them. "Chasubles, copes, chalices, all are pilfered and paraded round the streets in scorn." "Think you, Captain," I asked him, "that Essex will listen to my father's complaints?"

"He might," he answered guardedly.

"In any event Ben I am come to ask that you return with me to examine the Staffordshire fellow with the chest wound. I think I have done all I could - in fact I know it - but if you...."

I stopped suddenly. My name was shouted. A small figure hurried through the arch, shouting for me. He brushed aside the groups of soldiery and hurled himself through the kitchen door.

73

"Master Tommy! You must come at once! The soldiers have broke into the store again."

And my father was from home! Although I had no doubt that it was provisions they sought, I realised that the two King's Men could be in great danger if the villains wandered upstairs. I ran through the streets unheeding of the abuse that my haste occasioned in the loiterers standing and sitting at every street's end. I knew not if Jacky or Ben followed. As I ran the words, "My father's house. My father's house," echoed through my mind like to the hoof beats of a galloping horse. I ran through the arch of Cooken Street, almost tripped over a drunken fool lying near the horse trough and round the grey stone corner of St Alban's. The door of the shop stood open. There seemed no-one about until I saw Gill lying at the foot of the stairs where she had been roughly pushed aside. I took her in my arms, lifted her easily into the kitchen, set her in my father's chair and brought her water. She opened her eyes and seeing me, knew not whether to cry for sorrow or groan for pain. She could not speak but with her head motioned to the stairwell. I left her and raced up the stairs to my room.

George lay over the bed of the other. A sword cut had severed most of his head from his body. The other man, whose name to my shame I never asked, had died from a swift stabbing to the throat. A red sash that George had treasured as his insignia from Lord Digby had been torn to shreds and lay puddled in his blood, which still dripped from the bed. He had put up a fight. My old ill-fated joint stool lay broken at last by the wall, and above it a gory smudge, which I judged to have been caused by one of his assailants.

I began to fear I knew not what. My father was somehow at the root of my terror. If they could kill wounded men as they lay sick and in pain, what atrocities might they not commit? It might be that my father would be seen as disloyal for agreeing to house the two King's Men..... Gill had recovered somewhat. "Do not go upstairs!" I instructed her, "and if your master returns tell him for God's sake to lock all fast and stay indoors till I return."

Jacky came in. I asked him briefly for news of my father but he had none. "I heard tell a great body of people have gone over to the Corn Market," he told me, gasping for breath still. "It may be Master's gone too to see what's to do."

The streets were emptier and strangely silent. At least it was easier to make my way without running the gauntlet of the groups of jeering soldiery but the quietness was unwholesome. As I ran down the High Street looking everywhere for the two proud plumes in the high black hat, I heard a great moan or sigh as from the throats of a crowd of hundreds. I turned the corner of Goose Lane and saw Ben and Phoebe coming up from the Meal Cheapen. Ben customarily a man brown of hue was grey faced. Phoebe was supporting him and hurrying him along. They both saw me of an instant and Phoebe leaving him leaning by a shop wall came to me calling, "No Tom, you must not go there!" I looked at her uncomprehending, then brushed her aside. Her balance ever precarious due to her disability was lost. She fell near to Ben, but I would not wait to aid them. As I passed the corner by the Trinity Almshouses I looked aside and saw not my father, but his tall hat. A Parliament man was aping good manners to some young girls some yards down from Goose Lane. He was bowing and scraping to them like a painted popinjay, removing and replacing the plumed hat with each obeisance. I was less courteous and grasped him by the throat.

"That is my father's hat," I told him through clenched teeth. "Where is he?"

He gazed at me wide-eyed, clearly scared witless by my sudden onslaught. As I flung him from me and turned and ran again, he called after me some warning, some imprecation, I know not what.

And then, as the road widened near St Martin's, I clearly saw my father. He was high above all, still as stone, hanging from the town gallows, with Essex' rope around his neck. I stood for an everlasting moment numb with disbelief.

Then as I slowly entered the Cornmarket there was a murmur from the people at the sight of me and I saw Alderman John Elmbury stand up to the soldiers who were there - Essex Lifeguards I was to learn - and demand that the body be cut down and be delivered to his son who had come now to claim him.

I think that the Captain of Guard answered something to the effect that he had orders for my father to remain on the gallows as a warning to all other spies. At this reply the murmur grew to an angry shout, and other merchants came up behind John Elmbury. A few lads with cudgels were pushed forward and the dozen or so

Guards were surrounded. With them was the muffled horseman I had seen with Brigstock but of Brigstock himself there was no sign.

This same small officer had obviously great powers for at a word from him, one of the soldiers climbed the ladder and with his sword, cut through the rope. My father fell with a crunch of bone upon the wooden platform.

They let me through then so I could climb up and take him in my arms. In my heart there was the silly hope that just as he had interrupted my feeble attempt at self-slaughter three years ago upon that other Sunday, that now I was in time to bring him back to life. I performed the same offices he had tried to do for me. I loosed the rope, kissed his poor face suffused red with his own blood, pleaded with him to wake, stroked gently at the terrible burns and bruises round his neck. The townsfolk stood around in silence and as the realisation that all I held dear in the world lay inert and lifeless in my arms, and as my grief broke bound, I tried to move him and my sorrow from their prying eyes.

I could not do it. He was a big man, too heavy for me to lift, unaided. As I struggled the stench of his bowel voided after the moment of his death was perhaps too noisome for others to come near. Then, suddenly my old schoolfellow and rival Matt Hailes was beside me. In kindness he took my father below his arms while I took his soiled legs and slowly we passed him down to a group of fellow merchants who stood ready to receive him. Slowly then for we had to stop to stem my grief and rage at intervals, Matt and I carried him to nearby St Martin's and laid him down before the quiet and deserted altar.

"Stay a short vigil for me, Matt," I asked him. He nodded and I lurched out of the church by the side door running again until I caught sight of the murdering Lifeguards joking and laughing as they marched down the High Street towards the Cathedral. I guessed they would be returning to report to their master. I remember little of my journey save I kept them ever in my sight until they knocked for admittance on the door of an absent Prebend's house behind the Cathedral.

I drew back behind the College Gate and waited until they had been admitted. Then like a mad creature I raced over and hammered on the door with my fists. Of a sudden it opened and I threw myself inside pushing by the serving girl and roaring for Essex. She was too frightened by my wild look either to call for help or to tell me where he was. As well for him, for I dearly longed to kill him. But Ben and Robert Burghill rushed suddenly through the great door I had left open.

Ben tried to hold me. "Tom, Tom, dear cousin, softly, gently now. I have lost my beloved uncle. Let me not lose my cousin - all I have left."

He knew that this appeal to family loyalty was the only curb that would stay my hand. I leant against the oak wainscoting and stared at him and Robert. The blood lust went from me and I could think only of the horror.

A voice from the staircase said: "What is the matter?"

Robert Burghill who should never have walked abroad staggered slightly. He had been hastily dressed and hurried here by Ben. His orange scarf with the silver edging that proclaimed the officer had been flung about his shoulders.

"My Lord General," he said haltingly, "I am come..."

"Who are you?" asked Robert Devereux, Third Earl of Essex, the pompous little whey-faced swine.

"Captain Robert Burghill, Sergeant Major of Lord Fielding's regiment. I led my own troop of horse at the recent engagement and but for this young surgeon, Tom Fletcher here, would have been buried alive by the enemy who thought me dead as a shotten herring. I am still ill, my Lord General, but have come hither from my bed...."

"Then I pray you return thither," said Essex cold as charity. "What do you all here in this house?"

"You killed my father!" I lashed out in fury. Ben and Robert made to drag me from the house. In the dimness at the stair's head, his Life Guards moved forward slightly but Essex by a gesture stayed them.

"Who was your father?" he asked me coolly.

"Amyas Fletcher - Master Butcher of Worcester...."

He interrupted: "Yes, indeed. The spy."

"He was no spy," I shouted. "He respects our great cathedral. Our forefathers built it and men who defile it as a stable should be accursed."

He laughed shortly. "Men who shelter the renegade Stuart's men in their homes, it is they you will find who are accursed. A man who deceives the great commanders of our Parliament into thinking all is safe for them to advance - such a man will be cut down in his prime and his devilish works ended for ever."

I had no notion of what he spoke but gazed at him in utter bewilderment. Again it was the good Captain who came to my aid. "They were wounded men my Lord General, in Amyas Fletcher's house." Robert's voice gained in volume as he realised he had a hearing. "Master Amyas took them in out of charity from the field two days ago to give them lodging and care, just as his nephew here has assisted me. This family have not as yet given allegiance to either side. But these men were poor men, sir, one very sorely wounded, both from Staffordshire and far from home. And also..."

"Luke!" suddenly shouted Essex . "Were they wounded, the Royalist fugitives your men found?" There followed a discussion we could not hear. He suddenly bawled out: "Yea or Nay, Luke?" Again there was more mumbling and muttering. I realised that the sight of Captain Robert Burghill standing there and speaking for us had unnerved his murdering creatures. As I watched I saw again the little man at the Gallows, looking down at us. He turned to Essex and whispered something, then fell back out of my sight.

Essex turned to us again. "It may be that unnecessary zeal has turned God's servants momentarily from the paths of righteousness. But that still does not absolve this youth's father from the charge of treason. He was seen by a scouting officer of Sir Samuel Luke's near Powick on Friday morning before the battle. How came it that the Captains of the troops deemed all was safe to advance?"

"My Lord, I was one such Captain and that is a damned calumny. I never saw Amyas Fletcher at Powick. A number of villagers there told us there were no King's men to be seen in the fields near the bridge over Severn. And truly then on Friday morning that was so. And indeed, my Lord," and his voice grew even louder. "How comes it that Rupert was not in arms and ready for us when we chanced on him? He and his men were stripped off in their shirts as if they had stolen some moments of repose to take their ease. If there had been spies abroad, why had they not informed him of our coming? In good faith my Lord, he was as surprised to see us, as we to see him. Ask any of your Captains."

There was another terrible pause. "Luke!" bellowed Essex. The little man appeared again at his side. "How answer you that?" Essex asked him. Luke began to whisper again. "No, sir." Essex bawled at him, "aloud I pray you that all these may hear!"

"I had cause to believe that Amyas Fletcher was not friendly to our endeavours," he announced in a thin precise voice.

"What cause was that?" I asked. Ben spoke now. "My Lord, I can produce many witnesses that will tell you that Amyas Fletcher was in his slaughter-house on Friday. It is the day that farmers roundabout are used to bring their beasts for slaughter and sale."

"Yes, indeed," said I, "for how else could your thieving Quartermaster have availed himself of the contents of my father's full store, to feed your soldiers?"

"Enough of this," said Essex. "You may be certain it will be carefully considered. As I said, zeal for the Lord's work can occasionally drift awry. I will see what can be done. Go now all of you. Master Burghill, I am glad indeed of your recovery."

Robert tried to hustle us away. I was for going. The fight had left me again. But Ben, diplomatic careful Ben, he would not be silenced.

"You will see what can be done, sir? Why, what can you do, sir? Can you not feel for this youth? Have you forgotten your own father's fate at the hands of Elizabeth? Could you raise him from the dead after his shameful public execution any more than you can resurrect my uncle?"

There was a terrible silence. Then Essex said: "Your uncle, Israelite? Then a new heaven and a new earth must indeed be near at hand for I see my actions this day have assured the conversion of the Jews. Leave. Now. Before I order more shameful public executions."

As we got to the door he called to me. "You! Young Fletcher!" I turned to face him.

"You may bury your dead," he told me.

8

Memory, which had ever been my faithful slave, flees from my service in the days following my father's murder. For it was murder. Brigstock had fed Samuel Luke damned lies. I now had no doubt he wished to punish me for impeding his foul purpose with Sally. I knew I would have to return to reality to clear my father's name, even - and the thought was alien to me then, either through weakness or cowardice - to wreak revenge. But I could not think of that. I had to dispose my father fittingly. That for the present was all my care.

Only one event clearly emerges. The rest is blessed obscurity. I suppose I must have eaten, drunk, spoken, slept but can remember nothing of the details of my existence except that Ben and the servants kept me ever in their eyes, fussing over me like an orphaned lamb. On the Monday after - after his death I suddenly left my father's coffin set alongside Philip's, broke away from Ben's anxious questioning and care, and hastened to Sidbury Gate. The soldiers challenged me but I hastened past unheeding. I knew of plenty of breaches near the Frog Mill should they refuse to let me return. I walked past the Wylde house and up the road to Evesham for some little way, then turned aside into woods - Perriwoods they are called - where my parents had often walked with me, a troublesome brat of six or seven, questioning everything, running everywhere. I remembered so clearly one such happy afternoon. I had scrambled down a bank in pursuit of a vixen, thinking to capture a cub for a pet, should she have a litter. The vixen swiftly evaded me and I thought to return in secret to my parents to startle them for a jest. I accomplished part of my plan but stopped in my tracks behind a hawthorn bush beside the path for there they stood locked together in passionate embrace with seemingly little thought of me. I remember my father cradling my mother's face with his large hands, looking at her almost in wonder before he kissed her again. I felt alone and friendless for a moment, but then my mother ended the kiss and looked around for me, calling, "Tom, where are you?" I appeared and stood before them at a loss, not knowing what to make of their display of affection for they still had hold of each other like young lovers.

"Come Tom," cried my mother ever sensitive to my moods, breaking away from my father and holding out her arms. "Come and let your parents kiss you." They knelt, both of them and held me for a moment, the three of us clasped together on the woodland path, the sun peering through the tender leaves of Spring.

I realised with the hindsight of adulthood and loss that her words and actions were in some way a pledge of continued love and devotion, and that I was the living proof of their joy in each other. I needed to find that grove and to remember the sensation of their arms around me. I blundered through the copses and along the rides until I came to a clearing that seemed to me to approximate to the place I sought. I threw myself onto moss and leaves at the foot of an oak and wept for my loss. I was so alone. Apart from Ben whose ties were adoptive merely, as far as I knew, I had no-one in the world.

And then as I lay there, my mother sang to me. I sat up and heard the words clearly echo through the trees. It was a song she used to sing when she dressed me, or when she prepared my bread and milk in the kitchen, or when she tended my hurts.

"You and I and Amyas
Amyas and you and I
To the green wood must we go, alas,
You and I and Amyas."

You who read my tale will say 'twas a village girl wandering home alone to Warrenton or some such hamlet who happened to sing to please herself, and for you that will suffice. I know my mother sang to me. I had not heard or thought of that silly song since my mother's death. Only my mother could have known its significance for me. Or so I think. In some strange measure, it comforted me, brought me back to my present responsibilities. I felt a little, a very little better as I wandered back to the city. The

81

guards at the gate had gone off duty. As I trudged up by Edgar's Tower, I saw Phoebe hastening towards me with her disfiguring lurch. I wondered idly about her. It almost seemed as if she had been with us all my life, instead of only a few short terrible days. She was clearly agitated and as she approached me, wiped away clumsy tears.

"Ben sent me to look for you," she told me and tentatively tucked her arm under my elbow. "There was no need," I said heavily. I let her lead me back to Fish Street, and I confess I was glad of her sturdy support for all the top of her head was a good nine inches below mine, for I was suddenly more tired than I could remember.

I had come somewhat to myself on the day we buried my father. On Wednesday the 28th we laid him to rest beside my mother in the graveyard of St Helen's, where his parents also lay. For Philip I purchased a plot in the same churchyard. I had not kept vigil after my walk in the woods but on that morning I managed to persuade Doctor Potter, the Dean who had respected my father even if they had been at odds over the Dean's support of Laud in Oxford, to say a Requiescat over the two dead men in private in the house. It was too dangerous in Worcester at that time to resort to the well loved old words in public. Robert Burghill had asked to be present and sat reverently with my father's friends and servants. There were a few raised eyebrows at his presence but I cared not and I knew Ben had come to trust him. After the short service - we dared not for our lives take any form of communion - Robert stayed looking on my father's face as it lay serene and pale now, his body packed about with sweet smelling herbs.

He then asked a strange thing. "Tom, I hope you will not take offence but I would wish to look upon your friend Philip Fosdyke before such examination is no longer possible."

I felt slightly ill. Even poor old Tabitha who laid out the dead had found the task distasteful and she had innards of leather. Philip lay with his head decently covered with the cere cloth, rather than distress my father's many mourners.

My silence must have unnerved him for he asked again. "Tom I have thought long and hard about the manner of his death and I do not think he was killed in the battle. May I look upon him?"

I nodded. To my shame I could not come near. Robert gazed on his shattered face for some moments then drew back the cloth to examine his chest. After a while he stated, firmly, "I do not believe that this man died in the battle at Powick Bridge."

"But I took him dead from the river. Many of the Parliament troopers fell or were pushed into Teme," I told him. "It was at full spate after the rains. And from there they drifted down the Severn."

"Would it distress you unduly to tell me how you found him?" Robert persisted.

I told him what I could remember, of how I drew him from the river by his coat "Think well Tom," he exhorted me. "Was he facing into the water or floating on his back?"

I remembered very clearly. "He was facing downwards. I pushed him round a tree trunk to get a better purchase on his buff coat. I drew him out by the collar whilst Roger grasped his legs."

"So you took hold of his coat at the back. Now tell me, was the back of his coat as you drew him out, wet or dry?"

I looked at him dumbfounded. I could almost feel it again under my fingers. The light of Robert's thought began to dawn on me. "It was dry!"

"Well," conceded Robert. "If he had floated on his face all the way from Powick Bridge there is the chance I suppose that the sun might have dried it."

"No, no," I said warming to the theme. "Not so! Philip was the only corpse that was at the river side. The current is too strong mid-river - and also as we watched the dead horses and men in its power, they constantly turned in it, over and over."

"As I suspected. So when you looked at him full in the face, (and I know what a nightmare that was for one unused to the horror of violent death), and saw half of his face had been sliced away, did aught else suggest itself?"

"Oh dear God!" I sighed, "Of course. He was still bleeding from that wound."

"Are you sure?"

"In fact his blood stained the blanket in which I wrapped him. From his face - not from his chest. Think you he had been killed before his face was mangled?"

"Indeed I do. And saw you, Thomas, in your examination of the dead at Powick Bridge, amongst whose number I was placed, saw you any wounds like to this," he looked again at Philip - "this slicing away of features?"

"No, none. Sword wounds to the body, blows and cuts to the head, broken ribs a-plenty but nothing of this nature. Oh God!" I cried again, "Now I remember! We heard something - the two Baileys and myself heard a strange sound ahead of us in the bushes near where I found him, but just as we heard it, James saw a drowned horse midstream, became greatly upset, cried aloud and ran back for his mother."

"As well he did or it might be that all three of you now could be worms' meat or fishes' food. Do you remember what he cried aloud?"

I racked my feeble brains. "It was something like "Look there!" So Philip's murderer thought he was perceived. He only had time to destroy one half of his face."

"Exactly! I believe that you heard Philip's assassin dragging his body to the river. I believe that on the river bank he mangled one side of his face and was preparing to slice away the other side to prevent his identification, should his body ever be found. I think that he then heard the boy's cry of horror at the dead horse, and fearing discovery tipped Philip into the shallows, face down and escaped to the muddy road. There I believe he rode in the direction of Upton. I do not believe he was ever at the battlefield."

"It is Brigstock you mean," I said slowly, "but he professed friendship to Philip. Why would he kill him?"

"Because Fosdyke knew of the attempted rape. Did you not tell me you thought you saw a face at the window? My guess is that he intended to inform their Captain, John Fiennes. I know John Fiennes would not countenance such a criminal in his ranks. He would have had him thrown into gaol...."

"So what should I do?" I asked helplessly. At that moment Gill came in wiping her hands on her apron. "Please you, Master Tommy, Sexton asks if they can carry the departed now while the light lasts."

"Come then, Tom," said Burghill and of a sudden it was as if my father spoke for me. "Indeed, yes." I cried out almost laughing. "It smells like the town sewer in here, though not so sweet." We left through the great front door and walked the short distance to St.Helen's, the same way my father had hastened when I last saw him alive on Sunday morning only three days before, seeking out the desecrators of the Cathedral. What had seemed like laughter became terrible dry sobs. I wept into Ben's shoulder in a terrible silence as we followed my father for the last time up Fish Street. I was aware that Burghill fiercely exacted respect and decorum from the troopers gathered under the house eaves. Some of them, Burghill's men, even followed our small silent procession but whether it was to honour a man unjustly murdered or to pay their last respects to their comrade, Corporal Philip Fosdyke, I knew not.

When at last it was time to bury them I could scarce lift the spade. The thud of the clods echoed dully on the elm. Potter spoke again. He spoke only of my father, nothing of poor innocent Philip who to him was a rebel Parliament man. The pious Dean believed that my generosity in buying a plot of sacred ground for Fosdyke to be gravely mistaken. I snorted into my kerchief. My father would have loved such a grisly pun.

Throughout strangely it was the memory of my father's humour and tolerant delight in the vagaries and nonsenses of his fellow men that gave me a kind of wanton courage. When all was done I said aloud albeit with streaming eyes and blocked nose: "I pray you, if you will return to the house, my father would wish you to drink to his memory. There is little to be gained in drinking his health!"

This evoked a few grim smiles from his fellow merchants who pressed my shoulder as they hastened to do my bidding. The day was cold and dismal for September. I wished to stay a little longer with my father and promised I would follow. Ben led the way to play the host and Robert was engaged in earnest conversation with another Parliament Officer I had not seen before.

I sat myself upon an old grave whose owner must perforce forgive my incivility and looked at the heap of freshly turned earth that was my parent. I remembered how we had both stood near this same spot to bid farewell to my mother in the plague year, seven years before. "She had thought herself immune," my father had told me, "As a Welshwoman she told me she would be unaffected by an English pestilence. She had laughed as she carried a basket of food to a maid's house in Baxter Street. But within days she was gone." I had been sent from the house to a Herefordshire farm managed by my father's cousins and had been brought back to stand at her burial between my father and Ben, still numb and uncomprehending the nature of my loss. It was in the years that followed that I realised how much her love and merriment had meant to us both, and how in one part of his being my father had mourned her still....

A man stood before me. It was Martin Beckford. The large bluff landlord - the epitome of "mine host" was gone. Now he was shrunken, diminished. Great hollows were below his eyes and his hands shook. He stepped over my father's new grave as if he knew not what he did. I stood up as he came over to me. He took me roughly by the shoulders.

"It was an evil day for me when you first came drinking at my inn, Tom Fletcher. You have brought me the worst misfortune that a father can endure."

He said the words haltingly glaring into my face, so that I could smell the aqua vita on his breath. Usually he was a man abstemious in the extreme.

I suppose my lack of understanding must have shown itself in my face. He began to weep, long dry sobs without tears and then shouted, "You have robbed me of my child!" and pushed me from him with surprising strength. I staggered and would have fallen but Robert was there to support me.

The unknown Captain caught hold of Beckford's arm. "Have a care, good man," he ordered in the voice of one used to command. "This young man has even now buried his father."

Martin pointed to the grave, "That is Amyas Fletcher?" he whispered hoarsely - I nodded. "Then we are alike in grief. Yesterday my girl was laid to rest in Upton."

I could not understand his words.

"Martin when I left Sally she was well enough. Shocked but able to take herself - Brigstock was...."

"I know all about that. I shook it out of the poor zany, when he battered to be let out of the chamber where Brigstock had locked him while he slept. He told me he remembered Brigstock moving at the sound of an ass's bray. He heard him say something about

86

"Thieves being abroad." He then heard my girl scream, saw your return and struggle with the bastard but could see you had the best of it, so goes back to bed if you please without raising the house. They must hold women's virtue very cheap in that hell-hole of a London. Sal creeps in, poor lovely lass and lets me sleep throughout. In the morn Fosdyke hammers on the door, Sal in tears tells me of the Brigstock rogue's villainy, and out I go to the stable where you left him, to poke my pitchfork through his guts. But the devil has gone with both horses. The poor fool Fosdyke told all, then set off at a trot to try to catch up with his troop."

"Martin, there is Philip Fosdyke." I showed him the grave next my father's. "I found him in the river, murdered as we now think by Brigstock."

Beckford stood in a trance, "So this Brigstock! This is two deaths we know him to have caused...."

"It is three, Martin." A small cold rain had begun, pattering upon the freshly dug earth that blanketed my father. I could no longer bear to contemplate it. "Please, let us go back to the house. Robert, I beg you."

But it was not Robert who helped me along but Phoebe on whose shoulder I again leaned - as if I were the cripple and not she. Robert guided Martin Beckford and the unknown officer followed, leading the innkeeper's horse, which he had tethered at church-end.

The guests were speaking softly of my father's life and eating cold capon pie. Martin snatched at a beaker of wine Gill had left on the table and downed it at a gulp. But Sally, pretty Sally? I forced him to his tale. "So what then Martin?"

"List and mark Tom. After the noon drinkers had slaked their thirst, on that Friday - last Friday 'twas, though a lifetime has passed since then, I went to Upton to fetch my sister's girls to stay while the soldiery were ranging loose. I left Sal with little Joseph, the stable boy. He sets to his task to shovel hay from out the byre for my few cows. Now you know 'tis out of sight of the road. Of a sudden in the quiet, when he pauses in his work, he hears a horse shift feet and bridle jingle somewhere near. He looks out. There's no horse in the stable yard but he hears it move again. He peeps round the house and sees one of the mounts he stabled the night before come back. 'Tis Brigstock's horse, a chestnut. Joe runs back to peer through the kitchen window but is too late. He sees Brigstock run from the kitchen into the inn parlour and out through the door into the road to his horse. And he sees my girl. She is gone...dead, ravished and strangled by that that..." He broke off. "Her poor head all wrenched to one side - and her clothes...."

He sat down heavily upon a bench, the beaker falling from his fingers as he brushed away tears. Whilst he had spoken Robert and the unknown officer had listened to his tale.

Robert asked haltingly: "This Joseph...is he a true servant ?"

Martin stared at him for a moment, then understanding dawned. "Oh, I am with you there, master. Even were he not as true as steel, he is only twelve years old and undergrown at that. My Sal was like an elder sister to him."

I said wondering, "Then he must have killed Philip on the road to Worcester as the poor weak fellow hurried to rejoin his troop. He was on foot and far behind the main force. In fact as Brigstock stabbed him, the Powick Bridge action was over and bodies were floating down the river.

Robert now turned to me. "Tom, this is John Fiennes, Brigstock's Captain."

"I am sorry and shamed that it is the discovery of such an evil varlet that should have led to our acquaintance, Master Fletcher. He shall be brought to Justice if he can be found." John Fiennes bowed. What strange paths our thoughts take when we can least control them! In my mind I was resolving to tell my father that no less a personage than a viscount's son had graced his best parlour when in a trice Reality reminded me, "Your father is dead."

I nodded and thanked Captain Fiennes who had the air of one whose words are always heeded. I briefly told Martin Beckford of Brigstock's treacherous accusations of my father to Sir Samuel Luke and Essex.

"But," said John Fiennes, and the one syllable was like an aristocratic cannon shot. "There is a difficulty."

"What is that?" I asked. If we had convinced him as to Brigstock's guilt, what need of delay ere the devil was brought to justice?

"Early on the day of the action at Powick Bridge, he asked to be transferred to the Company of Sir Samuel Luke. He informed me that this person... a Bedfordshire Member I am told...., was actively seeking those who would and could find it in their consciences...," he coughed gently..., "to travel the countryside some twenty miles or so distant from the main body of the Parliament army to report useful information back to Sir Samuel. I understand that the Lord General has not yet recognised this system of gaining intelligence officially, but that unofficially he...... At all events, this Brigstock for whom I confess I had little liking, asked to be relieved of his commission in my Company shortly before we began our somewhat ill-fated attempt to enter Worcester from across the Severn. He produced letters from Luke enlisting his assistance. "In fact," he sighed heavily, "I do not now know where he is, save that he now reports and draws his pay.... rather more than the four shillings a day I am accustomed to provide for a QuarterMaster.... from Sir Samuel Luke. I will tell my brother of this affair and ask him to seek the Lord General's decision. In the meantime, may I present my most sincere condolences to you, Master Fletcher and to you too sir, on your most grievous losses so recently sustained, and may I thank you, Master Fletcher, in the name of the Parliament for your charity towards my corporal Fosdyke. His family shall be informed of his... whereabouts."

He bowed, gallantly declined further refreshments, and took himself and his lordly eloquence elsewhere. My father said inside my head, "Yon burbler breaks wind with Master Mumblematins." I laughed suddenly as if he had spoken the words to me aloud at my elbow. Ben was beside me, ever-watchful of my welfare at this time. I was suddenly desperately weary.

"Ben, I must go."

"Where?" he said suddenly alarmed.

"Only to bed. I pray you, tell Gill to make ready a bed for Master Beckford. He can have mine." I was by this climbing the stairs. I went into the great chamber where my father had brought my mother as a young bride and where he had lain alone for seven years, fell onto the intricately carved bed she had brought with her so proudly as part of her dowry, and slept.

9

October 1642

What more could I lose? I had buried my father, the best parent ever mourned by an unworthy son. In the next few days I ranted and cried like an unschooled babe, refusing to see even Ben, demanding answers from the silent walls, throwing myself onto my parents' bed in an agony of grief. Why was my father so untimely taken from me? An innocent man in the prime of his life! Into what Hell were we careering, when an evil bastard such as Brigstock could ride free unchallenged, and my good father be ripped from his life at a liar's word, at a tyrant's whim. Why? I screamed at the wall.

And poor lovely Sally. There had been a world of promise in that stolen midnight kiss in the rain swept meadow. And Philip whom I knew now to have been my friend. Then too my mind dwelt on the terrible murder of the two from Staffordshire, cut down like vermin in the room above me. Somehow all these deaths lay at my door, my actions over the last ten days had caused them to be snatched from their appointed lives. But over all my grief hung the image of my father's fearful ending. Much as I had liked Philip and George and perhaps even loved Sally a little, and could have loved her a lot, it was the loss of my father that caused me to weep and cry, immune to any comfort others who mourned him also, might have for me.

After one such bout of uncontrollable self-pitying grief, I saw poor Gill standing in the door, tears streaming down her cheeks. She held out the beaker containing the posset of honey and Aqua vita and elderberry which she had prepared for me over my days of mourning believing it would strengthen and cheer me. Alas, it merely made me drunk as a fish, but I could not chose but humour her and down it, good loyal old woman that she was.

I drained it and thrust the beaker again into her hands and she turned to leave me. As she got to the door she looked to their bed and said: "His great desire was to be with her Master Tom, though you were all the world to them both. He has his wish now, dear lad."

She went her ways downstairs, but she had left me with a touch of blessing. I could always know, could always rejoice in the knowledge and memory of my parents' love for each other, as well as their devotion to me. Should I not celebrate that love in my own life? I lay quiet for a while, then roused myself, dressed and went to the Knowles House to seek Ben.

When I saw him, sitting silent at the end of the long table in the kitchen, with the observation records he kept carefully for each patient unheeded before him, I realised suddenly that I had paid no heed to his loss and everything to mine. My father, his adoptive mother's cousin, whom he called uncle, was the last of the generation who had reared him. Worse than that he had seen his beloved uncle die a hideous death. I had kept my grief a private thing when Ben perhaps needed to remember with me, the times happy or sorrowful of our shared past. I pressed his shoulder as I sat beside him and as he turned to look at me, he smiled.

We were silent for a while. Phoebe was making some sort of sweetmeat, which was fragrant with cinnamon and aniseed. Captain Burghill sat near the fireplace reading, what I had thought might be the Bible, until Phoebe asked him for directions. "And so drive it thin, and print it in your moldes," he read out sonorously. It then transpired that he was obligingly reading aloud the instructions for her receipt from Ladie Elynor Fettiplace. As she saw my bemused face she explained: "The dough sticks so to my fingers, and my receipt book is all I have that was my mother's. The Captain kindly undertook to help me."

"You see, Master Thomas, I have abandoned the Principles of the Art Militaire for Culinaire," Robert told me.

"If only they would use Phoebe's gingerbread cakes instead of the accursed lead balls, this conflict would soon be at an end," said Ben with a laugh.

"I know not what to make of that, Master Knowles, and so I would ask that you are first to taste my wares," said Phoebe. In another woman I reflected such a riposte would be saucy but with Phoebe there was.......

I could not believe myself. I had not thought of my father and of the way he died for a full two minutes. I clasped my forehead ashamed that I could so easily be drawn into pleasant idle chat.

Ben was watching me. "No, Tom," he said softly, "there is no harm even now in laughter. No man in Worcester loved to laugh more than your father. So let it be. In remembering him for his jovial kindly nature, we honour him." He paused. "Though I would give all I had to hear him jest in truth."

I laid my hand upon his arm in silent agreement. Ben had aged. His face had still the grey tinge that I had seen appear when he saw his uncle die. His nose, high and hooked like a bird of prey seemed now to stand out of his face which had suddenly become thin and lined.

"I am sorry, Ben." I said after a moment. "All of these sad troubles are my fault."

He looked at me in wonder, "How so?"

"If I had not gone to Ledbury when I did, I would never have met Brigstock. If it were not for Sally's desire to help me, and if the ass had not brayed in the night, he would never have woken and stolen down to attempt her virtue and then if...."

"Tom, in the name of God enough of that," he said sternly and then, "If Ifs and Ans were pots and pans then tinkers would go hungry. If the King had not forced the prayer-book on the Scots, if Laud had not been so strong after dissenters, we would not now be hurtling headlong towards civil war. Is that your doing? If the Earl of Essex had not accepted the position of Lord General of the army of Parliament - well, well, we can "if" our lives away! But "ifs" can lead to good fortune as well as bad. If Phoebe had not taken it into her comely head to make us gingerbread we should not now be breathing these delectable aromas."

Phoebe giggled. I glanced at her fleetingly.... and made a joke that only she would understand, "I trust you are not suffering from the quinsy, Mistress Phoebe."

"Indeed not, Master Tom, I thank you," she told me. "No white dogs I assure you."

I had picked up my father's great purse as I had come out. I drew out several sovereigns. "Phoebe, these are for you. My father wanted you to have fine new gowns......"

I put them on the table in front of her. She was about to protest but I went on "Don't gainsay me - or him. It was in a way his last wish." I turned abruptly to the Captain I had a question for him that had been scratching at the back of my mind.

"Captain Robert?"

"A moment, Thomas. Then, Mistress Phoebe, you must dust your moldes with Cinnamon, Ginger and Liquorice, being mixed in fine powder. And then if you please you must bake your moldes in your bread oven. There I have done." He closed the book and turned to me. "Now Tom." (The Captain was of that cast of mankind that cannot easily think of more than one matter at a time.)

"Why was Essex willing to give so much heed to the little whisperer - Luke - he called him?"

"Samuel Luke like me leads his own troop. But he has never ceased to agitate and demand that Essex consider the possibility of gleaning advance intelligence of local loyalty. He would claim that such knowledge could save the lives of Parliament's followers. Who better for such a task than the Quartermasters of each troop? They are already a law unto themselves."

We lapsed into silence. I stayed and ate a little with them. The dish was excellent - partridge with a red currant sauce.

"Partridges?" I asked. With one voice they answered "Ralph!" But then Robert explained more fully: "He is a good helpful fellow whom I am training in the duties of cornet. 'Twas possibly a heaven sent escape for him to follow the drum with me as his commander. He has a strange talent for finding dead animals. A landowner whose estate marches close to mine, was all for forcing him into an intimate acquaintance with the pillory."

"A useful man for an army on the march." I could not but agree. But then overcome with a strange tiredness I rose to go. Walking out through the courtyard, I observed that Robert's men had three of these same partridges roasting on a neatly contrived spit. Ben walked silently back with me to Fish Street.

"Tom," he told me as we parted. "We must strive to help and protect each other as brothers. I know that would be your father's wish."

He could not know that that resolution was very soon to prove impossible for him to keep. John Fiennes had used the post runner set up between Essex' army and the Capital and had written to the Widow Fosdyke to tell her that her son had died nobly for the Parliament in the first blood of the conflict. When she heard the news and knew that I had disposed him honourably in St. Helen's churchyard, she wished so much to see his grave that Philip's old master in Southwark, a rich and much respected Portuguese goldsmith agreed to accompany her.

So it was that on the second day of October that the sexton brought news to me in Fish Street of the arrival of two travellers who had asked him to show them, the whereabouts of Philip's last resting-place.

I dispatched Jacky to fetch Ben from Newport Street as he was far more gifted than myself at the arts of courteous conversation. I hastened to the churchyard to ask them to return with me for bed and board after their journey. It was raining with relentless intensity, and a few great horse chestnut leaves were flapping down onto the graves. I see the two of them now beside Philip's mound. The Widow Fosdyke was weeping, kneeling on the ground trying I think to be as close as was seemly and possible to her son's mortal remains. The goldsmith stood apart from her, saying the occasional word of comfort but glancing cautiously everywhere about himself from dark sharp eyes above a hooked Roman nose. I told him who I was and bade him Welcome and he politely thanked me for my pains on the part of his well-loved apprentice.

Then Ben came, stepping among the graves. He bowed to the strangers, and began to echo my speech of welcome to Worcester but then he stopped short in wonder staring at the old man who in his turn was gazing at him as if he were a ghost.

Ben said strange words in a tongue I had never heard him utter previously. It was "Meu Pia" and the old man caught his hands and cried out something like Benjamino Perdido. They could neither of them speak further but looked long and hard at each other's faces. All this while the Widow Fosdyke sobbed on the ground, unaware of the drama that was unfolding above her.

I had often asked Ben if he could remember his early home. He knew that his parents must have been people of substance but could remember little else save that from birth he had been schooled to be secret and to say little about his home. It now transpired a careless nursemaid had let him wander from her side in a London street. He could remember a strange journey with men and woman who ate in the open round a great fire. They had chided him a great deal for crying and told him if he did not stop, he would be burned on the fire. Finally they had abandoned him in the streets of Worcester, and here my father's cousins had taken him in and treated him as their own son in everything.

But how could Ben be sure that this was indeed his father? But as I looked from one to the other, I too could see a distinct resemblance. They were of a height, both a little shorter than myself, both were lean and spare of build but it was in the caste of feature and the play of expression that their near kinship blazed forth. The sight of his father had kindled in Ben the long forgotten memories of his first six years. Haltingly he tried to speak again in the unknown language, which later I learned was Portuguese.

Isaac Nunez could not now for his life, after embracing and weeping and exclaiming over his long lost son, allow him out of his sight. It was indeed like the end of their Winter's Tale. They were Marranos, Jewish people from Portugal who lived very secretly and quietly in small but wealthy communities in London and Bristol. Indeed Ben without knowing had followed a family tradition. A relative had been the former Doctour Hectour, well known to Queen Elizabeth not merely for his medical skills but who had also given that sovereign lady and her government, important information from Spain and Portugal. A strange irony! My father had been hung for supposed spying and Ben's relation had been honoured for it.

I said with some asperity, "And all this while we have called our cob after your great great-uncle."

In all of this confusion the poor widow's grief was forgotten. At length it was decided that she should stay in the guest chamber at Fish Street and that Ben should entertain his newfound parent at Newport Street. Indeed I think it would be true to say that Master Nunez was pleased to be granted sanctuary from the conversation of his travelling companion. I had liked Philip well enough but perhaps had not known him long enough to justify the constant rehearsal of his virtues. I suppose I should have been more sympathetic. After all we both mourned our dearest relatives but her conversation wore down my spirits and two days later I escaped to the bridge and watched the Severn gliding serenely past. There Ben found me.

"What will you do now, Tom?"

"Do?" I replied unpleasantly. "Why what should I do? What would you have me do? I have lost my father and it seems you have found yours." I could not hide my bitterness. Ben looked carefully at his shoes and then at some swans that sailed below us, hoping for stale bread. I was unjust. I knew it. His emotions were now if anything even more in turmoil than were mine. He had lost a loved uncle but found a lost father all in a week. It was truly the stuff of fairy legends.

"Tom, I am ever thy loving cousin, brother if you will."

"Indeed," I said scornfully, riding high on my bitter steed, "You ask me what will I do. Then tell me, Benjamen Ben Isaac Nunez what will you now do? Will we have the good widow and your father round our necks for ever?"

While I spoke such discourtesy I knew well I was out of all governance. Yet Ben merely sighed and seemed to forgive in an instant. "Well the poor widow tries me sorely with your poor friend's many virtues. There, forgive me again, Tom. I know you liked him well. Here, this is for you." He held out a parchment. I took it and read. He and his father had visited a notary and drawn up a deed of gift. In brief Ben gave me everything that was his - the house, the doctor's practice, the rents from Dame Alice's land in Herefordshire, from Sir Nicholas' interests in the iron trade near Stourbridge.

I spoke what I dreaded. "You are going back with him to London then?"

He did not answer for a moment. Then he told me. "Tom, I must. He is my father. He is old and a widower. My mother died ten years ago. I must go back with him to help and protect him. You heard Essex call me Israelite. I have long begun to suspect my parentage was from that source. In Bologna they called me 'il Ebreo' no matter how much I protested and professed myself an English Christian. Do you know why I have never married? Be-

cause I knew that there were differences - not important perhaps -
but once I began to understand the organs of regeneration I knew
that as a babe I had undergone some small surgery, which Chris-
tians do not practice. And I was waiting Tom for this reunion. My
father" - he smiled - "my father...."

"Your father what?" I asked as unmannerly as a mad dog.

"My father makes me laugh. Like Amyas he sees the world as a
constant source of humour. I am sorry Tom, but I cannot again lose
my delight in his company. He thinks as I do but with more
wisdom. I mustn't lose him again."

"Am I then so tedious and humourless?" I asked him waspishly.
Then swiftly for fear I might not care overmuch for his answer, in
curiosity I asked him: "What are you then - Christian or Jew?"

Again he laughed: "Nay I know not and I wish with all my heart
I did not need to answer. This I will say Tom. The ground grows
bread, the sun shines warm, mankind, ay, and womankind repli-
cates him or herself the same way, come day, go day. I agree with
St Thomas More of blessed memory. God did not give us windows
into our souls. If I am a Jew, so be it. If the words and wisdom of
Christ seem to me a worthy pattern, so be it." He pointed to the
Cathedral, towering upon the river bank to our left. "You remember the old tale of the Jew in that Cathedral and how Jesus, Mary
and St Wulfstan persuaded him to part with 10,000 crowns for
repairs and upkeep?"

"Persuaded?" I cried for I knew the story well, "No! No! As the
legend goes he was tricked into parting with his money. It is a
shameful story. It was much more like to have been a greedy
bishop, that tricked the poor man, rather than that sacred trio!"

"Tom, Tom," Ben was laughing again. "Have a care that the
world does not identify you as the Jew. Persuaded or tricked, no
matter. All I would say is that Cathedral is my investment as well
as yours. So - will you come to London with us to keep holiday at
my father's house."

Hating him and hating myself more, I told him evenly "I'll see
you in Hell first," and left him.

But Ben would not allow me to proceed in so unmannerly a
fashion. He followed me and pointed to the Deed. "Do you not
see, dear Tom, that I have left you my horses - and that includes

Jupiter?" He looked at me with a hint of slyness in his smile. Jupiter, the best riding horse in Worcester, a few years younger than myself, given to Ben by his doting parents when he returned from his studies. I looked at him and felt my mouth unwillingly twisting into an answering smile.

"It is a handsome gift," I said slowly.

"So have a care to that," he said, pointing to the document.

And when I got home, I still had the Deed of Gift held tightly in my hand. And I did not throw it away like a jealous girl. I locked it in the closet in my bedroom.

I tried my best to hate his father. I tried to foster in my heart all the myths and stories of the Jews in England - mean grasping Shylocks who ate Christian children, but began to laugh aloud at the prospect of Isaac and Ben sitting down to such a ghastly meal. Indeed Isaac confounded my evil imaginings at every turn. Apart from his generosity to me, which I could churlishly argue with logic was to sweeten the prospect of Ben's imminent departure, he was courtesy itself to Phoebe. The second day of his stay he instructed her to show him the best cobblers shop on High Street, wishing he explained to purchase a pair of slippers for a young woman in his employ. Phoebe's feet he believed were of a size. Three days later a special pair of shoes were delivered in Phoebe's size, the one with a much higher built up sole. Her joy and delight at this gift was such that I felt deeply angry with myself for not having thought of such a simple strategy.

I at last found my manners and stood with Phoebe in the courtyard of Newport Street and bid them Farewell and Godspeed. Prior to that I had even brought myself to thank Isaac for the generous Deed of Gift. It was good and gracious of him so to reward me. He and Ben could so easily have placed an agent in Newport Street. Oaf and lout that I was I finally managed to mumble something of my gratitude. I had lost all my family but had gained considerable wealth, in but a few days. As I remember that time I blush for my unmannerly behaviour. I tried to thank him for his generosity.

"Thomas," he said, "your family gave my son all that he is. It is right and fitting that your aunt and uncle's wealth should be restored to you. Now I have my son again, he will want for nothing. All that is lacking is his bride."

Then he went on to say that he knew how sad my life was, but that out of my sorrow, perhaps one day I could be magnanimous and not begrudge them their joy, that I was as another son to him, that I would ever be welcome to their home in Southwark.

"As a Christian Prodigal perhaps? " I said waspishly, but Isaac, good old man that he was turned my ill humour into merriment.

"And on the day you come dear Thomas, no likelihood of the husks of the swine, but the fattest calf in London."

So Ben was gone. As I watched the rumps of their horses turning from Newport Street to Merrivale, I was left with my terrible inheritance of land, money, grief and bitter thoughts. So much to happen in so short a time. My ill-fated journey had begun on Friday 16th of September, the battle one week later, and my father wrested from me on Sunday the 25th, killed by Essex and his murdering minions. The second day of October brought Isaac and the Widow to Worcester and the 7th saw their departure with Ben, my only relative even though 'twas merely by adoption. Ben was also (I thought, indulging my pathetic melancholy) my only friend, and now he was gone.

I wandered about Worcester, leaving Phoebe to deal with Parliamentarian blisters and saddle sores, although the flood of travel scars was at last diminishing. The Captain, his ribs mending fast, was much improved and assisted her to control the soldiery that still visited Newport Street. Jacky seemed to be coping with the butchery although I confess I had not concerned myself with that aspect of my inheritance.

And then two days later, Joan came jogging into the courtyard on Walter. She dismounted and without a word took me in her arms. I wept into her bony shoulder. After a moment she began to tell me of my parents' deep love for me, their clever handsome only child, and how I was a good brave boy, who would remember all my life how much I was cherished as a child. Between my noisy sobs she spoke of the need now to live *for* the dead as, "Alas they cannot live now for themselves, so it behoves us to live as well and as happy as we may in their honour."

I confess this was a new notion. I sniffed, wiped my nose and led her in and Phoebe, who not only dispensed well but who had also undertaken many of the housewifely tasks, brought in some wine and two goblets. Joan immediately told her "Another goblet if you please my dear girl - for yourself." Phoebe smiled and did as she was bid. I was suddenly aware how totally pleasing her expression was.

In brief Joan had come to me with a proposition. She had come to ask for lodging - nay for a home for her dear Adam and for herself and for Roger their second son, (and my favourite).

"Are there floods?" I asked at once.

"No, dear Tom" she told me "At least not of water. Simon our firstborn has come from London to claim his "birthright," as he calls it. And I can tell him that is toil, toil and yet more toil. That is the stupid lout's inheritance if the truth be known. And if we are to speak of truth, he has suddenly found that able bodied young men in London are required to ally themselves with a Train Band Captain for Parliament and to take up arms against the King. This has moved him to revive his love for the land." She paused, "Believe me it is not loyalty to his sovereign that moves that quakebreech but love of a whole skin. Still we could swallow the hammerheaded dolt's brand of loyal moonshine, if he had not brought his trollop back with him. He calls her his wife but I call her the Whore of Babylon. I will not share my home with his drab, no matter to how many Welsh Countesses she claims to be related."

Both Phoebe and myself were hard put to it not to laugh aloud and there was a sneaking trace of sympathy for the Babylonian lady. "What of young James?" I asked to divert the conversation.

"Oh that one will stay with the heir apparent, and indeed air is all they *will* eat if they do not work harder than I have known them do. James stays because his addle-headed eldest brother thinks he might breed horses. 'Tis well I have taught him how to trap and cook rabbits else they would starve, all. And speaking of breeding, I see she is with child herself. Let them manage without us, say I. Roger will always stay with his father and the poor simple knave feels something for his mother also. He does not like it that I am set aside by this pole-cat." She brushed away a tear.

"I am most happy to welcome you here, dear Joan and Master Adam and Roger of course," I told her. "It will be much better for Phoebe to have the help, companionship and guidance of a lady like yourself."

"Indeed it will, dear madam." Phoebe chimed in "I sorely miss my mother."

This was so very much what poor Joan wanted to hear. She clasped Phoebe's hand across the table with one hand and wept a little more. I put my arm roughly about her shoulders, wondering somewhat how the scheme would prosper. And yet there could be no doubt that there was work enough, here and at Fish Street for anyone who could help us. After a moment she recovered herself.

"And you are not to think we would come empty-handed. Believe me, Roger and I will earn our bread and we will have a princely income from Simple Simon. He is to give us half his takings and half his allotted harvests for inheriting his birthright before his allotted time. If my poor Adam were not so smitten..."

"Dear Joan," I told her "I see your coming as a blessing to us. Master Adam has always given excellent wise counsel and your skills will be highly valued. Phoebe has not known this but I have seen how hard she has had to work since she came here."

Phoebe made as if to disagree but I silenced her, "no Phoebe. You have had to shoulder terrible responsibility. I am aware of it, believe me."

Joan left promising to return with Adam and Roger the following week. In the meantime I told Phoebe I must concern myself with the butchery. I did not like the workshops at the back of the shop but there was Jacky, instructing a young man no older than myself in the art of chopping up a pig. My father had tried always to keep the slaughterhouse as clean as possible as he believed that the live animals waiting for their end, were affected by the smell of the blood of those who had gone before them. I could see from the clean floor and chopping block that Jacky remembered this.

The young man straightened himself and I saw it was Matthew Hailes, my old school fellow.

"Why Matt," I exclaimed, "I had thought you were your father's apprentice."

"I could not stomach it, Tom," said he "I have no head for heights. I always envied you your prospects here. But Jacky here has only hired me as a day labourer whilst you decided what should be done."

"Master Tommy," said Jacky, and he almost wept as he spoke. "I have not your good father's breadth of shoulder. I cannot heave the carcasses about as once I could. Young Matt here is a God-send."

I suggested that we went into the kitchen for a pint of small beer and Jacky praised Matt's strengths. "We can get to the cows again, Tommy, if Matt could be here to help me. He's powerful good at hefting them about and he's a wonder in the shop with the ladies, with something after your father's way of putting it into their heads what they want."

Matt had always been one for the girls. "Well Tom, you know me - (Must I say Master Tom?" I shook my head vigorously) "You know me, none better as a schoolfellow. But you also know that I cannot figure out like Amyas, Tom. The numbers run mad as May butter for me, always have and always will. But Jacky thinks I will make a slaughterman, a straight true final blow, so no suffering. It's not pleasant, Tom, but I can do it. And I think I know how to talk to the goodwives without causing offence."

"Does 12 pence a day suit?" I asked him. He seemed delighted, and so it was settled. I took the accounts back with me. I could see that there was some attention needed in this, but all else seemed to be prospering.

On Thursday 13th of October the courtyard at Newport Street seemed to be full of Baileys. I had helped Phoebe prepare for their coming. Beds were aired, blankets found, fires laid and lit and the house smelt delectable as Phoebe made small cakes and sweet-meats, as well as a hearty venison stew for their first evening. Simon and his wife had come with them, ("To make sure we have left the farm in good earnest!" said Joan bitterly), and were to return before nightfall but the smells of Phoebe's cooking were so enticing that it was difficult to persuade them to ride back. Finally I achieved this by the simple expedient of telling them it was what they wanted to do.

We had - not a merry meal – but a comfortable one. Adam was a most entertaining guest and Joan could not refrain from abusing the whore of Babylon, whom Phoebe and I thought well-meaning if disadvantaged beside Joan. I confess I did not know there were so many words in our tongue that meant Woman of Easy Virtue.

The list seemed endless. Then Adam set the table aroar by observing mildly: "My dearest heart, to hear you speak of her one would think you had no liking for our daughter-in-law." And Joan had the good grace to look abashed.

And so all would have been - if not well - at least peaceful in our household. Roger professed to enjoy working with numbers and was straightway burdened with the accounts for both Fish Street and for the Dispensing and Surgery. I enlarged my experience still further by delivering twins and successfully treating an infected ulcer on a soldier's calf. Phoebe gained considerable respect by insisting quite forcibly that children infected with measles must stay in a darkened room. The woman who disregarded her warning was heartbroken at the plight of her son whose sight was severely impaired.

And then I, great claybrained hammerheaded oaf that I was, behaved so stupidly that all seemed lost. We had an excellent harvest of apples in the Newport Street garden. Phoebe had done everything she could think of to preserve them, and hundreds were stored in the loft. As we had a surplus she was carrying a heavy basket of apples from the Newport Street house to give to a market woman who had no wares. I realised too late she had gone out with too heavy a burden for her strength and hurried after her. When I was still some distance from her I saw some apples fall and Phoebe stop to pick them up. But as I was hastening to help her, a great hog in armour seeing Phoebe bent over in the street offers her the crudest of assaults. He and his companions were clearly far gone in cider. The sight of her upended backside roused his craven lust and he aimed a great kick at her, roaring out "Hoddie Doddie! All arse and no body!"

These were the last words he said for some time, for I had knocked him sideways with a blow that made his teeth crack. Even now my knuckles tingle at the memory. His own body weight caused him to fall heavily and awkwardly, and to my shame I followed up my blow with a kick to those soft parts of his anatomy to which he must needs have recourse, should he e'er wish to duplicate his vile person.

His friends stood gob awry and one made as if to fight his cause but the other stayed him. "I know you, sir," he said. I knew him too. It was the man whom I had helped acquire the French child's horse on the road from Upton. "You saved me. Get you gone from Worcester now. Sir Edward Saunders, our Lieutenant has Essex' ears and thinks this Tom Billiard a rare good blade. I will hold off the reporting but leave this town now. There, I have paid my debt to you."

He and his fellow hauled Billiard to his feet and half dragged him away. I turned to poor Phoebe who stood terrified but completely unharmed at the side of the road. It almost seemed as if my father with what we had interpreted as his last wish had saved her. Her new gown had a bum-roll, that foolish fashion of dress which had completely cushioned her against injury. I helped her back into the house and gave her up to Joan's good offices, but, thanks to her weakness for fashion, she had not even sustained a bruise.

We held a swift council. Adam, on being told of this latest escapade by the admiring Roger, said gently "Dear Tom, your chivalry can never be questioned but perhaps an element of discretion might serve you better in the future." Robert Burghill was distressed in the extreme by the unmannerly behaviour of Billiard but agreed that my absence would at this delicate time be politick. Joan began packing up food and Phoebe rolled up my small clothes so that they could be crammed into my saddle packs. We decided that when Essex' men came to arrest me, Joan would tell them I had gone to visit a sick cousin in Hereford whose name she knew not. "They cannot inflict themselves upon us for much longer. Joan proclaimed. "Most of the poorer sort have neither food nor money now. They will have to go elsewhere to eat."

Meanwhile I would ride over the bridge at the end of Newport Street (that would bear out her Hereford tale) but once I was in St John's, I would turn off to the right into the thick woodland and join the way north, following in the wake of the Kings' Men who had taken that same road, three weeks before. It was only a month ago that I had left my home to travel to Ledbury. When I contemplated how much I, and others had lost in those short weeks, I could not believe that I could continue as the same Tom Fletcher, my world had changed so completely. Believe it or not, I had to forsake my home, or I had no doubt I would be gallows fruit, like my poor father. Essex' way was clearly "Hang First, Judge Later."

I prudently decided not to wait for his justice.

10

I left before sunrise as I judged that Essex would send his Life-guards for me as soon as the first light was in the sky. I had asked Robert Burghill who still lodged with us to protect my little household. He promised he would have his troopers in the court-yard that morning drilling and exercising. Essex' men would surely be deflected from their purpose at the sight of such Parliamentary zeal - and expertise. Robert cherished a rare respect for Phoebe and was outraged at the news of the scurvy bastard's rude insult.

I had kept my leave - taking swift and simple. Roger would help Matt and Jacky if necessary at the Butchery, and keep a day-to-day account of the buying in of stock, the slaughter and resale. Joan would take general charge of both households. I knew all would be well under her government. I was concerned for my patients but Phoebe had demonstrated that she had excellent skills in diagnos-ing and dispensing. Well so be it! I had to leave for my life!

The morning dawned fresh and clear as I cantered through the village of Hallow. It was tempting to put Jupiter to the gallop, but he was all I had twixt me and the gallows so I knew I must treat him with great care. If he should stumble - but he seemed confident enough. The ways were hard and dry and I thought he relished his freedom.

When we came to the inn by the bridge at Halt Fleet in the midst of good sheep pasturage, I dismounted and gave a stable boy tuppence to rub him down. It was mid morning. I had put about six miles between myself and the Earl of Essex. Was it enough? But I felt in need of refreshment. "Any soldiers?" I asked two shep-herds who had elected to combine the care of their sheep with a welcome quart of ale outside, with good views of both the meadows and the river. They shook their heads. The landlord who had seen the quality of Jupiter from his window welcomed me most courteously. A savoury aroma hung about the inn and as I entered the taproom I was immediately recognised.

"Little Tommy Fletcher, as I live and breathe!" It was Lofty, as tall as he was broad, a Severn waterman, and yes, yet another of my father's many friends.

"Sit you down, Tom, and name your pleasure. Poor lad. We heard about Amyas. I don't have the words, son." And he pushed a tankard of small beer into my hand, and turned to the company who were I saw to my relief, five of his fellow watermen. "Amyas Fletcher's boy."

They came to me and took my hands telling me of their sorrow for me. My father had been something of a hero to the Watermen. Whenever the City Council had wanted to collect tolls from them for their free passage up river, my father would come up with some harebrained scheme, which immediately demonstrated the Council's parsimony. For instance he suggested that the market men and women who brought in their wares to sell from the outlying villages, should be charged for the Worcester air they breathed on market days. When they brought up the question yet again he suggested that the King should man the tollgate since only he, if anyone, could claim the ownership of the Severn. In his way my father had worked for the freedom of the river and for the free trade and passage of the Watermen, who transported cargoes of fuel, metal goods and timber, thus ensuring the prosperity of the region. In Gloucester they had no such champion and so these same Watermen brought much of their drinking custom to Worcester where of course my father had known and cherished them all.

I could even now play the woman when my father's memory was invoked. I passed my shirt sleeve across my eyes and noticed that the company was silent in tribute. I toasted him again "His memory ! And all of you. His best of friends!"

"No truer word!" said Lofty, "But Tom are you for Worcester or upriver?"

"Upriver that's for certain! Putting as much ground between me and the Earl of Essex, God rot him!" I told Lofty briefly about my brush with Billiard. "So I thought I would be safest with Rupert."

"Safe! With that mad fearsome blade! I tell you Tom, we've just free floated down from Bridgenorth on a good fresh. And I tell you, with those King's men in Bridgenorth, a man might die of thirst for the alehouses are crammed with them. I'll wager there's not a quart of small beer in the whole of that town, and they were spilling out the quayside taverns as well. We're bound for Worcester to get a drink!"

I laughed, "Essex is still there, Lofty. You'll see merely the backs of Parliament men in the alehouses and precious little cider. Go to Newport Street and tell Joan Bailey to give you all good cheer. You say the King is in Bridgenorth?"

"Not now. As we welcomed this fresh, he was for Wolverhampton. Rupert dances about him like a flea round an old dog."

"Last we heard Rupert was in Kidderminster," another Waterman put in.

"No, 'twas Bewdley," cried another. And still another "Stourport, as I live."

At that moment a low whistling came from the trows, clearly heard through the open door. One of the shepherds burst in "Soldiers, on the bridge now!"

Sweet Jesu! I was more frightened than I had ever been, craven serf that I was! Essex had had me followed. They had ridden up east side Severn through Claines. All the horrors of hanging and the gallows possessed me! "What shall I do, Lofty?" I clung to him in terror!

In a moment he had snatched up a bowl of pease pudding and hurled it down my shirt. Then he pushed me down with my head under a rough hewn table. "Stay there, good and quiet, or snore and retch. Play the drunk. You hear me."

I could hear the jangling and hooves of many horses and the low voices of men. No shouting or roistering! They had come in earnest to hang me! Billiard had died perhaps.

Several pairs of leather boots entered the tap room. Then a thin reedy voice from above a most handsome chased pair that encased the longest legs I had ever seen, proclaimed politely, "God save all here!" The Watermen responded courteously and returned his blessing. "Landlord, God bless you Sir!" went on the high voice "We've come post haste from the bloody fray. In the great cause of Parliament. Could you make shift to feed my poor troopers? I am Lord Philip Wharton to let you know you have not riff-raff in hand."

Lofty's bulging calves came squarely into my line of vision.

"Alas, sir, we have even now finished this goodman's duck stew and uncommon toothsome it was, but dear sir if you but ride a scant two miles west to Witley you will find excellent good victuals. They have not had the honour of entertaining any armies on the Tenbury Road. Rupert stopped here at this inn on his way to Shrewsbury last month." (The handsome stork-like legs took a step back towards the door), "and poor Abraham is vexed out of his mind lest the pestilent knave takes it into his head to return here as he threatened. The Prince and his Lifeguards ride up and down this river like Saturn seeking what he may devour, and doing terrible damage to man and beast."

"Oh heavens!" exclaimed the Bird Man. "We even now escaped his attentions under Kinver Edge. What think you, Charles?" Two worn, mud bespattered boots stood to attention. I began to breathe more freely. If they had come from upriver there was no chance they would have heard of my attack on Billiard.

"My Lord, 'tis a good notion. We vex the peasantry less I think."

The Bird Man turned again towards Lofty, whose calves like cudgels were inches from my nose. "Witley is as I think under the Martley Hills, is it not, good sir? A straight road from Martley to Worcester I recall?" he asked Lofty. Truly for Parliamentarians they were polite as princesses! But just then the Bird Man noticed my legs." Why what's to do here?" I had the wit to give a great snore. I was I confess already ashamed of my earlier panic. Better though for my identity to remain unknown if they were bound for Worcester.

"Oh sir. My nephew! We know not what to do. Has your Lordship any notion as to how to cure an accursed sot? He has taken to Canaries and we cannot keep him from the drink and there are some here who think it good sport to encourage....."

He was interrupted by a trooper. "My Lord, there's a monstrous fine riding horse in the stable here. Do we acquire it?"

My legs must have stiffened with horror. Lofty gave me a gentle kick. "Oh my lord, breeding will out. That horse is none other's than my Lord Essex."

"How so, good fellow?"

"Oh, my good lord! A word to the wise! Mark you, you did not hear it from me. A childhood sweetheart, lodged even now, in Ombersley, a mile across the river. Even now you and your troop rode close to where the great commander takes his pleasure! I cannot say more, sir. Discretion, sir, is the word."

"Heavens! Yes indeed. Discretion! And Rupert may well be coming this way. It may be that the King is even now riding with his army from Stourbridge to Worcester."

Charles, who seemed far bolder and wiser than his master spoke. "Forgive me sir but indeed we don't know that. If t'were true, it would take a day for that army to move, not hours.... plenty of time for my Lord Essex to pleasure his doxy and return to Worcester. And in truth sir we saw precious few of the enemy on Kinver Edge."

"Say you so, Charles? Well your counsel is always wise I think. But we made a soldier - like retreat did we not? We'll haste to Worcester by the Martley Road, and I'll buy viands for the poor men on the way. And thank you for your good counsel Master Waterman for so I perceive you to be. Peter, Charles we'll make for Witley. And".....he was clearly ferreting about for a coin, "Three shillings for your pains." (He gave the money to Lofty who most graciously accepted it. Never was moonshine so well paid I think). "To horse then, good lads all. Peter and Charles take your ease for a moment. I'll assemble the men." He left the inn leaving the troopers to follow him.

"To horse, good lad," cried one and taking little mincing steps, imitating the extraordinary voice of his noble commander, he led his fellows laughing heartily out of the inn. "Enough!" barked one of the two lieutenants, following him to the door "If you can find a more generous commander than his Lordship, you dog, then I pray you take your leave."

The lieutenants who gave the impression of being serious professional soldiery, remained long enough to down a pot of ale which Abraham willingly gave them, delighted to see their departure. "But what grief, Charles, to leave the ordnances!" said one to the other. "In truth there were but few of the rogues," Charles replied. "But thank the Lord, (the one above not our gallant commander!), you had the wit to disguise the guns in the hawthorns when I signalled Rupert's approach."

"Alas" said the other laughing heartily. "I knew my playgoing would one day prove fruitful. Burnham Wood and Dunsinane. Can we retrieve them do you think?" and they crowded through the door. I did not hear the answer.

I was never more ashamed. I emerged from my makeshift hiding place to the congratulations of the watermen but my cheeks burned with embarrassment. Wanting to escape what I felt must be scorn, I ran out to see that Jupiter was safe. I was less at risk from Lord Philip Wharton and his men than from a gaggle of girls. I went back in, asking Abraham to fill the Watermen's tankards at my expense. "I cannot stomach the prospect of hanging!" I tried to explain weakly to Lofty and his friends, attempting to brush the pease pudding off my shirt.

"Well now! Here's a strange fellow, does not look forward to kicking the clouds!! You are not alone in that, Tom! There's no shame there!" he said with a grin. "What's to be done now, lad?"

An idea was slowly forming in what passed for my brain. "I had best try to find these ordnances they spoke of, and tell Rupert of their whereabouts. If he needs a doctor perhaps he will keep me with him until Worcester is free again."

"Sit first, lad and eat Abraham's duck stew. The ducks in these parts *will* fly into our nets. We try to stop them but they will not listen."

It was an excellent meal but I could not join in their good fellowship. Finally Lofty turned to me. "Listen Tom. I will speak plain. As I heard it, you saw your father hanging. That is true?"

I nodded dumbly. He went on "And no one can bear that horror for you. Of course you are desperate afraid of such a fate for yourself. You would not be human if you were not. And yet you tell me you gave a swingeing account of yourself with this abuser of ladies, this Billiard. You had no fear of him. You are not a coward. Only a fool would boast he does not fear death. Everyone has his reckoning. You will not be hanged, son. Come, let's get you on your way to find this mad knave Rupert. Look for your needles in a haystack or your guns in hedges."

And later at twilight I was in the field under Kinver Edge where the apparition of Rupert and his Life Guards had so distressed Lord Philip Wharton. I had left the Severn at Stourport and followed the river path by the Stour and skirted Kidderminster. Jupiter was enjoying a good meal of oats at Blakeshall where I was told by the landlord's buxom wife if I was for Kinver I would be in Staffordshire, but Blakeshall itself I was reassured was still in Worcestershire.

There was no sign whatsoever of any "bloody fray." All was peace and calm, with great chestnut trees surrounding the fields, sporting their autumn gold. There were hawthorn bushes a-plenty round which the sheep nibbled the soft turf, but in which were the guns concealed? I pulled out a long sharp stave from a hedge and began to poke it into the brakes to see where there might be metallic resistance. I realised this might be a tedious affair and then remembering my encounter with so many boots that morning, thought that footprints or beaten down grass might give the guns away.

And so it proved. A little more scrutiny of the grass, a prod here and a poke there and the three makeshift "bushes" gave up their secrets, the ground around them trampled and dirtied. But now it became clear that the leaves on the boughs that covered them were fading and falling faster than the mild Autumn weather dictated. I judged that each gun was perhaps six feet in length. I must find Rupert and report my cannons.

I slept soundly that night in the inn at Blakeshall. As there had been ground frost during the night, I delayed riding back to Kinver until noon for Jupiter's sake. My guns were as yet undetected, but I was puzzled by a roaring sound that came and went from above in the old village. It was like no sound I had ever heard before and emanated from a large brick building. As I approached a man, somewhat stooped and grizzled, wearing a leather apron came from the main door and leant for a moment against the wall. I dismounted and hitched the reins around a tree branch.

"What is this place?" I asked him shouting above the tumult.

"This? This is a mill, son."

I could not quite believe him. Mills I knew in plenty, windmills on hills where they could catch the wind, and watermills by lively brooks and rivers.

I tried again. "Do you know where Prince Rupert is?"

He grinned. "Indeed I do. By this time he will be at table with my daughter. Why, who wants him?"

Without waiting for an answer he turned back into the building and shouted some sort of command. Slowly the noise declined, whirrings and hammerings slowly fell silent, until only the sound of a hidden millrace could be heard. A number of men came out to eat and drink and take their ease, calling a greeting to the old man as they passed him. Some went their ways to their cottages nearby. The old man who was clearly the master of the enterprise, whatever it was, had come back with a leather bag. He took from it bread and a large lump of fat bacon, what my father called ruff-peck. He kindly made as if to share it with me but the sight of it gave me a distinctly wambly sensation in the stomach.

"I say again, who wants him?" he asked as he chewed his bacon. I told him my name and my calling, although by this time I had some doubts as to his sanity.

"Well, Tom Fletcher, I can tell you exactly where Rupert is. He is in Stourport with my daughter and my son-in-law and I can tell you too where he will be later today." He poked about in his mouth with a dirty finger and spat out some gristle.

"I wish to help him," I told him. "The Earl of Essex ...."

"What of him?" he insisted.

"He hanged my father."

He was silent. Then he said, "so you want revenge? But against who? Rupert will be here later at the Hyde with my son in law, Richard Foley. He wants me to make pikeheads and shot in my slitting mill here for the King's Men, instead of nails for ships and wheel-barrows. To be frank with you, I do not know that I want my brave new methods to be turned into weapons against my own people. Some men have been drained dry by the King's taxes. How do I know, how do you know that the cause for Parliament is wrong? Eh?"

He chewed some more. "How do you want to help him?" I decided to trust him and told him about the ordnances in the meadow below the cliff.

"Oh aye," said he. "These guns you have found, cannon if you will. They are fawcons, son. When this struggle ends and we are again as we were, will you be proud to know that these same fawcons have shot your countrymen to pieces? Eh? ....Master Doctor? Eh? Men who have done no wrong except object to being made paupers for the King? How does more killing help your innocent father?"

I sat down on a stone wall. He had somehow taken the glory from my enterprise. When I looked up again he was gazing at me sadly.

"I tell you this, Master Doctor. Rupert knows about your cannon. Oh aye! One of his men lay at cliff's edge unseen and watched their disguisings. That is another reason why they ride back here today. Now, with that news I have salved your conscience, Master Doctor. But what of mine?"

"Who are you sir?" I asked him.

"I am William Brindley, the Ironmaster," he told me. "And I was once as proud as Lucifer of my forge here. What a puzzle though young Tom! I make the pikeheads for money, Rupert uses them to shatter flesh and bone of our countrymen and you try to mend the damage. You are fortunate, you do not make the havoc. What would you have me do?"

I was silenced. I thought of Robert Burghill, a most comfortable wise support, a very present fatherly help in trouble, a man who had saved my life with Essex, to think of him killed through my actions horrified me - to think even, God help me, of the Birdman and his lieutenants - I wanted them to live and to live long.

I looked at his sad blue eyes and shook my head. "It *will* come to a battle," he told me "Oh! Aye! Perhaps more than one battle. A clear conscience - a luxury indeed. Come back at four and get guidance from Rupert. Though I doubt that his henchmen are ailing!"

I rode slowly about in the beautiful meadows and woods by the Stour, thinking of his words. I remembered Ben talking of him when I was a child. My uncle, Alderman Knowles had been impressed and excited by Will Brindley's exploits in High Germany. Apparently he had gone there to learn their new methods of smelting and slitting, been courteously denied this knowledge and so pretended to be the dullest of country bumpkins, playing the fool in their manufactories until he had the processes by heart. The Alderman had been so delighted with the tale that he had bought some share into this Brindley's enterprise. I clapped my hands to my head. Of course! What a fool I was! I had seen his name and that of Richard Foley on my Deed Of Gift. Ben had told me that he had written to all concerned to tell of a change of ownership. I judged by the sun that it was nearly four. I rode back to the Hyde and was tying up Jupiter when William came outside again to greet me.

"Thomas Fletcher of Worcester, nephew to Alderman Knowles. Did you come here a-spying to be sure your interests are well served?"

I slid down and made a polite obeisance. "Indeed I did not, sir. I have only just now remembered that I have inherited some interest and came back in haste lest you should think ill of me. I beg you be assured. The Deed took place only weeks ago. I do not know what I own, but as I rode I remembered my uncle telling Ben of your sojourn in Germany."

"Well what a lucky case you are in to be sure, Tom Fletcher of Worcester, not to know what you own. Oh Aye!" The men were filing past at the end of the working day "These poor men know well what they own, son."

We were interrupted by the barking and antics of a small dog. "Here, Boy," cried William, "Rupert is here. This is his pest of a dog." Horsemen clattered up to us and there was that same dark Prince, looking at me with great interest as he dismounted.

"I know you, do I not? Master Surgeon of Worcester. Are you come to fight for me and your King? How are your potions and your motions?"

His companions laughed immoderately as men will at a great man's feeble jests. "My motions and my potions are without equal,

Highness, and await your inspection whenever your Lordship pleases." I quipped back at him, my father's son as ever. Now he laughed as well. He and all his company gave the impression of having eaten well and drunk even better.

"Have you need of a sawbones, Sir?" I shouted above the tumult of his followers.

"I have not, but my uncle writes to me of agues and cibes, of sore bums and raw heels a-plenty. Will you take your ways to Wolverhampton and treat the army?"

"Every man jack of them." I cried entering into the spirit of his playfulness. "I will ride now. Where is the King and may I say you sent me?"

"As far as I know they may even now be saddling up to leave there. He had thought to stay at Thomas Holte's great wonder of a house in Aston. But with a destrier like this fine fellow, you should make good time and find them straggling off."

"In truth sir, yesterday this horse was nearly confiscated by Sir Philip Wharton at Holt Fleet." I told him of my adventure, to my shame making light of my terror and enjoying the audience. They roared at the prospect of the Earl of Essex creeping away to his light-o-love, and Rupert convulsed us all by proclaiming, "The Earl doesn't know his prick from his pipe!"

Through all this banter William Brindley stood and smiled. Then the Prince and his companions rode down to help members of his troop rescue the fawcons and left Richard Foley to speak to his father-in-law. I made as if to go my ways but William insisted that I stay, telling him "Dick I would have you meet Alderman Knowles' nephew of whom we heard but lately." Richard who like the Prince was well fed and watered, invited me to his house in Stourport, but I declined. I had the impression that he wished me to increase my share of my holding.

In fact I determined that I must now make for Wolverhampton in order that Jupiter might have good stabling that I could inspect whilst it was still light. I was told that the road thence from Kinver was fair and firm. I bade father and son in law Farewell whilst they still wrangled over the moral niceties of the manufacture of weapons. I sensed that Richard cared not for morality if there was a way to put money in his pocket.

My journey went as merry as a marriage bell. I put Jupiter to the gallop, which he seemed to love. We went along through meadows and thickets on the west side of the Stour and had just cantered through a village called Wombourne when disaster struck. I suddenly became aware that on the track before me a thin rope was stretched across. Jupiter could have leapt it but like me I sensed he had seen it only at the last moment and was somewhat laden with my person and possessions. I cried out a great "Whoa," pulled his head somewhat to the left and gritting my teeth, released my boots from the stirrups.

My horse, my magnificent horse, stopped dead. I, alas, did not.

11

From far away I could hear the sound of my mother's soft voice, speaking Welsh as she often used to do when she was alone. When I asked her why she spoke what I could not much understand, she would reply: "I get a good conversation that way, cariad. No arguments and everyone in agreement!" I smiled at the memory but then reality began to seep into my aching head: my mother was dead - and my father also! I forced my eyes open. The Welsh sounds continued. A young man was sitting beside me stroking my hand, speaking to me as gently as if he was encouraging a young child. When he saw my open eyes, he called to a companion, "Aled, Aled Bring his water."

Aled appeared magically from behind me, from a beech copse carrying my water flask which I realised had been removed from my saddle pack.

I sat up. I had been lying on a heap of dead leaves at the side of the track with a tree root for a pillow. When my head was still, it felt light as the King's groat, but when I moved, a headache like a hatchet split my brain. To my intense relief, Jupiter seemed to be unharmed. He was grazing at the side of the track. He looked at me questioningly and perhaps with a certain superiority as much as to say, "is this the kind of incident that I am to expect with you?" I called him over and he ambled across to me and nuzzled my neck. I heaved myself up and turned to the two Welshmen.

But there were not two. There were three. The third was lying on his back, beside a shallow ditch parallel with the track and was clearly suffering extreme pain. The other two had removed my chest of medicine from beside my saddle. Its contents were spread around them on the filthy ground.

"What are you doing with that?" I cried in a voice of thunder. They stared at me, terrified.

"We could tell you were a doctor, look, from this so we thought while you was having a sleep we'd see what we could do for Bryn here."

"You put that rope across the road!" I shouted. Never had I felt such righteous indignation.

"We needed to get him to a doctor, master. It's his leg. We had to stop someone, you see."

"I am a doctor!" I shouted "And you near killed me!"

"Yes but you stopped, master, didn't you?"

There was no refuting their logic. I passed a hand over my hair. There was a lump the size of a pullet's egg on my skull but the headache was a little easier. I had been lucky indeed. I groaned in frustration and began to replace my phials and instrument. When all was to my satisfaction, I said with the devil's irritation - "I suppose you will want me to look at him."

"If you please, master," said the one whose voice had woken me. I learned his name was Hugh.

Bryn lay on his back facing west due to a bend in the path, sore vexed by rays of the setting sun which shone fully into his eyes. He was wearing baggy fustian breeches, which prevented me from seeing the injury. I ripped them from his person to the outraged gasps of his countrymen. He had clearly dislocated his knee. It was swollen to an unnatural extent. The great thigh bone, the femur that ended in a ball of bone had left the socket of the tibia and was protruding somewhat into the surrounding flesh. As I felt the area, the poor fellow gasped in agony.

"How did this happen?"

"He had a bit of a fall, see," said Hugh.

"It's more than a bit of a fall to dislocate these bones." I told them "How far down did he fall?"

"Er, from a window to the ground. It was in Wolverhampton, see where we'd gone to join the King, but the girl's father came home unexpected and he had to jump for it."

"How did you get this far from Wolverhampton?"

"A farmer carried him to a place called Penn for us. After that we had to let him hop."

Untold damage had been done to the joint. If I did not get the ball back into the socket swiftly, I knew he would not walk again. As it was, the socket bone, the tibia might have been cracked irreparably and muscles and tendons might be torn apart. I looked at his sweating face and knew that this was an almost hopeless task. I felt the area again. I would have to push the femur up somewhat and then pull it down into its ordained place. There was one chance and only one, because after a botched attempt he would be so disturbed and hysterical with pain it would be impossible for him to allow any further interference. I asked them if they had any liquor of any kind. It seemed that all they had managed to carry from Wolverhampton was the rope that Aled had in his snapsack.

I placed myself beside the dislocated thigh, told Aled to hold down on the shoulders and set Hugh to the feet, thereby shielding Bryn's eyes from the insistent sun. I tried to tell myself, "If I cannot do it, I shall just ride away and leave them to their fate." As I prepared myself, feeling the leg lightly under my fingers, Bryn groaned and obligingly fainted. "Now whatever I do," I told his friends, "Do not let him go!" I steeled myself.

"Look there!" I shouted to divert their gazes. As they looked away, I jerked up the femur and locked it into the tibia. All Hell broke loose with Bryn. He came to with a vengeance, screamed fit to wake the dead and threshed about, called me every bad name in Welsh and English and then at length subsided again into unconsciousness. I grinned at his horrified friends. "He *may* recover now," I told them. "He may walk again. Not well, but he may be able to put his weight on the leg in a few weeks."

They glared at me. "Well, what would you?" I asked them, "The leg was useless without the joint in place." The only bandaging I could think of was my pease pudding shirt. I tore it into large strips and bound the knee as tightly as I could without constricting the flow of blood. The unnatural swelling was already receding. I set his friends to finding short clean straight boughs to use as splints. Now to get him to shelter. They had no food and no money. I gave them what food I had, forced water between poor Bryn's parched lips and found Jupiter's blanket. We had the rope of course and I had my dagger.

"Two more long staves, over two yards in length." I ordered them like a sergeant. After considerable crashing and thrashing (and swearing), they found the staves, we lashed the edges of the blanket round them and with meticulous care, edged Bryn onto the blanket, inch by inch.

His eyes were open now, following my every move lest I approach him again to hurt him. "How does your knee, Bryn?" I asked. "Better, by our Lady!" he whispered, "It aches like the Devil but it feels like mine again."

"We are going to carry you slow and steady back to Wolver-hampton, where I will find a good inn." I told him. Hugh had recovered from his horror at my makeshift surgery, though Aled still looked green and like to vomit.

I gave him Jupiter's reins and told him to lead the horse gently and firmly. I made Hugh carry the staves at the front where they protruded into handles and I took them at the back. We had to lift together, walk together and rest together all in time, and never was I more pleased to see the outskirts of Wolverhampton, for Bryn was tall and well made.

I would not stop at the ramshackle old taverns at the end of the town where they were all for staying but went to a fine building near the Church of St. Peter. It was the Hand Inn in Tunwall Street. The place was at sixes and sevens for the King's Command-ers, I learned who had stayed there, had within the hour ridden to Aston. Even so the landlady at the sight of my purse made shift to house and feed us all and Bryn was soon comfortable in a clean high bed. Aled and Hugh decided to sleep in his room on press beds and I was pleased enough to sleep in the best chamber that Sir Lewis Dyve had just vacated. The landlady who told me with a proud glare that her name was, "Betsy Smart, and proud of it" had been hard at the preparation of a magnificent meal for the King's Men, when word came that they were to go. The wonderful smell of roast pork and sage and apple stuffing influenced my decision to some degree. I supposed I could have ridden after the King but in truth I knew I should not leave Bryn. I felt guilty for the unspoken but uncaring thoughts I had had prior to my interven-tion. I had to care for the poor fellows as my Welsh mother had cared for me with so much love and devotion. They came from the town of Rhayader and spoke English and Welsh with equal skill. If Bryn lived through the night, then I would leave money for Bryn's doctoring and their board with the landlady. And the fragrance of the roast pork was a powerful argument for remaining in Wolver-hampton.

Bryn asked to sit up to greet me when I went in to my three Welsh "soldiers" next morning. I greeted them with "Bore da.Iawn?" and he replied with the others "Good day Thomas." I was delighted with their skill in caring for him. They had carefully retained all his urine lest I wished to examine it, and seemed disappointed when I explained that a joint and the urinary system could act independently one from the other. But they had kept him clean and fresh, preserving the sweetness of his spotless sheets.

I was even more delighted to see that Bryn could twitch his big toe and the one next to it. I told them I would find a doctor to tend him for a week or two. I went down to ask for food and small beer to be sent to him. Aled came down with me and asked if he could attend to Jupiter for me. The landlady looked somewhat grim when I asked if Bryn could remain here while his knee mended. I produced my purse and told her of my plan to find a doctor and explained that Aled and Hugh had cared for him in a most neat and cleanly manner.

I put on my dog-fox smile, and asked her to sit down and break her fast with me, as I could sense that she would prove a useful ally. She had prepared an excellent dish of eggs and sausages, truly some of the best I had tasted.

"Are you for the King or Parliament, madam?" I asked. "Neither, sir," said she. "I too," I told her. "I find that I am fiercely neutral in this matter."

"You are in the right of it, there Sir," she told me, "although it is rare that any man thinks to ask a poor female for her view. The father of this King, James had my father brutally murdered."

"How so?" I asked her gently, "Madam, it may be that we share a terrible grief. Tell me your story."

"My father Thomas Smart was hung, drawn and quartered for being loyal to a friend. He played no part in the conspiracy to explode the Parliament. I was born the same year as this King and at the age of five was made to watch my father's tragic end."

"Where was this, Mistress Betsy?" She gestured with her head. "Out there in High Green. He and John Holyhead were alike viewed as traitors when in fact all that they knew was that Catesby was a runaway from justice."

I told her of my father, my tale still raw in my eyes and throat. She patted my hand and told me "Yes, Master Thomas, we are alike in grief, but yours, alas, a recent horror." I told her something of Ben's remonstrance with Essex reminding him of his father's shameful death at the hands of Elizabeth. She laughed bitterly. "You say true, indeed. And she, also, (the so-called Virgin Queen, my arse!) had no compunction about condemning her cousin Mary at Fotheringay. And that was James' mother. I tell you, sir when you have great ones in hand, look to your future safety. They will use you and destroy you!"

She insisted then that I drink a cup of canaries with her and told me of a good doctor in Cock Street. She was clearly a woman of much respect in the town, for the doctor in question when sent for came at once to examine Bryn. We undid my bandage carefully and Mr Cook of Cock Street could see from the terrible bruising where the great ball of the femur had near pierced Bryn's skin. "Bend his knee gently with the greatest of care tomorrow when you are here with him." I told him, "But I beg you no weight or stress for at least a week."

We bound up the knee in clean linen provided by our Hostess and pinned it securely. In truth I think Mr Cook of Cock Street was somewhat surprised to have instructions from so young a physician but Ben's teaching, I had discovered, had been excellent and I spoke always with authority. I paid him for his future care, knowing that Betsy would ensure his attendance.

Then I turned to Aled and Hugh. They had been delighted with the notion of a doctor called Mr Cook of Cock Street and kept repeating his name with great relish and amusement. "You'll soon be well Bryn, bach!" said Hugh, "With Mr Cook of Cock Street to tend you."

"And Thomas (brother) we have determined who you are," he went on. "You are the Good Samaritan."

"Not so!" I told them with a grin, "I am the poor John-a-Dreams who fell among thieves. Aled, suppose Jupiter's legs had been broken on your rope?" His only answer was a shudder and a guilty look.

We went down so that I could pay for their food and lodging. But Betsy would not take anything for the two able bodied men from me. "You are a good man with a horse?" she asked Aled, "You can earn your keep as my ostler for a week or two. The man who was my groom has gone for a soldier! And as for you," she turned to Hugh who grinned and scratched his head "I know a fellow victualler who needs a potboy. I take it you know something about ale? This Goodman doctor has done way and beyond what was needed."

So, about noon I bade them all Farewell and pleased again to be responsible just for myself alone, set out for the village of Aston where the King was staying. My road was not so peaceful as one could expect in Worcestershire. There were a quantity of little workshops along the way from which came monstrous bangings and roarings. There was polished steel jewellery for sale and sword hilts and buckles, beautifully burnished, were displayed. As I rode through Bilston and Coseley, forges such as the one like Brindley's in Kinver abounded, though these were poorer enterprises, worked by one or two rough fellows. They were not so rough that they did not know a good thing when they tasted it. As I rode through Coseley I asked one such poor man where I might get something to eat. He told me that the pie shop in a back street sold the best rabbit pies in the world for three half pence. He was right! The village of Aston was a surprisingly humble place to house a king, although the forges and iron working had given way to vistas of fields, woods, churches and country houses, a landscape quiet and pastoral. I dismounted and asked in a baker's shop where the King was. The journeyman looked me over and told me slowly, "well, master, he *was* staying with Sir Thomas in his new hall. That was last night. Oh aye."

"Sir Thomas?"

"Sir Thomas Holte. He owns everything round here. Everything. Look to your horse!"

I followed his directions, riding a quarter mile or so from the village. Pleasant trees shaded the tracks in their autumn glory. I rode across a meadow with the sun gilding a herd of fine cows and gasped! This was the largest dwelling house I had ever seen. It must be a palace. I rode slowly round the walls, and in through an arch, larger than most city gates. I was in a large grassy space before a marvel. Where the sun touched the brick, the building glowed, a delicate pink. This was surely not simply the largest house I had ever seen, it was also the most beautiful. I reined in Jupiter and gazed in wonder for some moments. The towers, the great shining windows, the tall chimneys, all was strange yet perfect, marvelously designed, basking in the afternoon sun.

A voice interrupted my reverie. There were still heaps of bricks lying around, men were carrying them to supply others, building outhouses. A man whom at first I had taken to be the overseer of one such gang had left his work to admire Jupiter. He wore a leather apron and leggings and had black hair like myself, although his was streaked with grey. He was handsome but there was a meanness about his eyes which narrowed as he appraised my appearance. He repeated what he had first said that ended my dreaming, "A fine horse!"

I found my wits. "Nay! A fine house!" I suddenly knew without anyone telling me that this was its owner.

"God save you, sir," I said politely and dismounted, keeping the reins looped around my arm.

"He might, at that." said Sir Thomas and then more directly, "What do you want?"

"The King!" I told him.

"He's gone, thank God! But better to keep him and his creatures a day rather than a week - and then he reads me more lectures than I ever needed about my duty to my idiot eldest son. This morning he went north to spur on recruits. Why do you want him?"

I resisted the temptation to tell him that that was for me to know and for him to speculate upon, and bit back such a saucy answer. "To tend the sick, should it come to blows." "Oh, it will, it will, young man, make no doubt of that. He's taken our money. Now he wants our blood."

"Are you then for the Parliament?"

"Now when did I say that?"

"I thought" - I began.

"Aye, that's the mischief of it all! Too much poxy thinking! God rot all thinkers and philosophers. You're a doctor then? Is this your chest of simples? Have you anything for head-lice?"

"For yourself?" I asked him.

He snorted with contempt. "No, not for me. I have one pour cold water from the well over my head daily winter and summer. It stimulates my brain."

"Do you grow lavender?" I asked. He nodded. "Aye, great clumps in the garden: they made a great to-do pulling off the flower heads to keep their linen sweet in July."

"Crushed and infused in oil and rubbed gently into the sufferer's scalp, you will find it an effective remedy." I told him, making to remount.

"Wait, wait! Don't you want to see the house? If you'll treat them all, there's a good meal and a good bed for you tonight. Sleep in the King's bed if you wish."

I now had a notion as to what I had in hand. I guessed what motivated this grasping knight. "How many to treat?" I asked. "Ah, now," he thought for a moment. "My dear good lady wife, her maids, if you please. Then the children!" He began to count on his fingers. "Five of mine. Then there's the Roper brood, the poxy imps. Their father can no longer feed them, curse him. There's eight or nine. They can empty a table of victuals faster than a weasel through a warren. Say twenty or so. Something of a plague we have here Master Doctor, though whether of lice or children, 'tis hard to say."

"One shilling and six pence each," I told him.

"What?" he screeched.

"Say a job-lot for thirty shillings! If not ...." I mounted Jupiter and clicked him on towards the gate.

"Wait, wait!" he cried again to my retreating back. I reined in, and looked back at him. "For one so young, you drive a terrible hard bargain. Twenty five shillings the lot and a good meal and a clean bed."

"And my horse?"

"Oh fear not for him, he'll be well looked after!"

There was something in the way he said that, that I liked not. I resolved to be on my guard. I noticed carefully where he proposed to stable Jupiter.

I allowed him to lead me to the kitchen where a harassed cook attempted to organise a cackle of slatternly kitchen maids. One aggressive hussy approached us, eyed me over and seemed to be about to ask Sir Thomas for something. "No, not now Bet!" he snapped. "Who knows what is in the still room? Lavender essence you say young man?"

It seemed unlikely to me that any of them knew where the still room was, liveliness being more to their taste than stillness in any form! Finally one girl flounced out of the room, casting a black-eyed come hither glance at us to follow. She went up the nearby staircase, hitching up her skirts to afford her ease of passage, Sir Thomas and I in her wake.

The still room was something of a revelation. Spiders had made a city in there but Sir Thomas assured me that "Lady Grace, God rest her," his first wife, had spent many hours working on her herbs and essences and after her death, her old nurse had continued to replenish the store with enthusiasm. There was lavender essence in plenty. I took four phials and asked if there was oil in the kitchen. "Aye to be sure," said Sir Thomas, "Not now Nan." The young maiden who had accompanied us upstairs seemed to have had some accident with her bodice facings and required Sir Thomas to assist her.

"Come down this way," he told me, opening a door near the still room. I gasped. I was in a long gallery. It was a wonder. The late sun streamed in through magnificent windows that overlooked the park I had crossed earlier. We moved slowly down the room, revelling in the light and warmth that gave a sensation of lightness of heart and pure joy." You have made a marvel here, Sir Thomas," I said.

"Yes" he said simply.

The next few hours passed in a ferment of activity. Some heads had been scratched till they were bleeding and needed doctoring for raw sores. All seemed to be infected. In truth I began to think of myself as some kind of women's pimp, or eunuch as I treated sores, doused heads and rubbed and scrubbed the lavender oil into their scalps. Sir Thomas came to the kitchen door, sniffed and remarked that the stench put him in mind of a House of Profession for Drabs. No doubt he had firsthand experience of such a place. As I had almost finished I closed with him there and then for my reckoning. It transpired he had only 23 shillings. He would give me the florin tomorrow.

His new wife, forty years his junior was a sad simpering wretch, clearly terrified of Sir Thomas and intimidated by her own servants. She was extremely grateful to be free of her "unwelcome visitors" as she called the lice. I wondered how the King had fared last night and if his scalp was itching now. With that in mind I poured the last of the powerful lavender oil into a phial, and placed it in my box of medicines.

It was in fact fear of the bedlinen on the King's bed in the great guest chamber that caused me to make myself comfortable in a large chair where I dozed intermittently. I woke suddenly, convinced I had heard Jupiter neigh. I had not undressed. I snatched up my box and my doublet, ran through the dining room and down the great stairs as quietly as I could. The main doors stood wide open, and sconces were still alight in the hall itself. To my utter astonishment, Jupiter stood at the front door, saddled, bridled, his reins looped over a rail. I had the wit to creep quietly out the door, take the reins, lead him to a saddle block and mount as silent as I could. As I did so I could just make out the outline of Sir Thomas energetically relieving himself, his back to me facing the kitchen wall. As we trotted towards the gate (I could not immediately get my bearings, the night being black as an unswept chimney), I heard a great howl and looked back to see the angry knight, dancing in fury in his own front door, lit from behind by the sconces.

We were through the gate and into open country like a rat up a drain-pipe. I remembered there was a small wood straight ahead and, endangering myself from low boughs went some little way in to observe what might occur. I recalled what the baker's journeyman had kindly told me, "He owns everything round here. Look to your horse." There seemed to be a commotion from the Hall, as if servants were roused unaccustomedly early. I heard instructions issued in the night, and saw two groups of men servants emerge from the gate, carrying torches that flared upwards into the night.

There was a moon of sorts now and my night vision had improved, and clearly none of these grooms were mounted. One group turned north, the other south but then both parties sank down beside the corner lodges, seemingly to wait till dawn. But then a window in one of the gate houses, facing outwards away from the Hall was opened and I heard a low whistle. The group of grooms nearby moved under the window and a makeshift ladder was lowered. The other group doused their torch and moving along under the wall, dashed at full speed across the gate lest a sharp eyed watchman should see them from the entrance of the Hall itself. One held the remaining torch up high to enable them all to swarm up the ladder safely. Then he doused it and climbed up himself. I could hear the sounds of conversation and muffled laughter. Never was there such a half-hearted pursuit and I blessed them for their apathy. The men were clearly more honest than the master and had little enthusiasm for seeking one who had bested him particularly at such an unreasonable hour.

I stayed where I was for another hour but then as the faintest trace of dawn lit a path between the trees, I rode south on it until I heard running water. Jupiter made short work of it and the path joined another that broadened out to a silver ribbon. I could hear other horses on the track both before and behind me. Spurring onwards I came in sight of three Welsh cobs, one ridden by a pleasant looking young fellow in a sheepskin coat who led the other two.

"You're up betimes." I called to him.

"So are you, master, it seems. It begins at seven when it strikes from St Martins."

"What begins?" I asked bemused by his troop of "its".

"The Horsefair. You'll get a fair price for yon. That's a bostin good pad-nag. 'Bout fifteen is he?"

I was amazed. "Yes, three months back. I like your cobs."

"My brother breeds 'em, master, Erdington way. He's sick so he's sent me to sell 'em for 'im. Where you from, master?"

I told him, "Worcester" and then asked, "tell me does Sir Thomas Holte of Aston Hall ever visit this Horsefair?"

He turned his head to one side and spat violently into the bushes. "That greedy old bastard knows better than to set foot anywhere in Brummagem, master. He's the evillest villain in these parts. Sides, the Gild would never let him get up to his mischieves. He'd be drummed out of town, should he come here."

There were more and more horses, donkeys, mules, jennets. If it had four legs and a mane, its representative was that day trotting to the Birmingham Horsefair. We passed by a fine church and some little way beyond was a wide open space where all who had a horse to sell were gathering. I told my new friend of my encounter with Sir Thomas and he wisely commented, "'Tis strange that when a man has everything he still wants more. Better like me to be content with next to nothing."

My new friend's name was Harry Upton. He advised me to ride with him to where stalls could be hired for a few pence, where one could stable ones horse securely well guarded by a trusty fellow who for some reason was known as Gripper .

"Can he be trusted?" I asked Harry.

"Old Gripper?" he replied. "Oh aye! He's sound - sound as a bell."

I gave Jupiter his oats, some water and an apple and left him well content. I helped Harry with the cobs. His buyer was not to arrive till noon so there was a little time for dalliance. I bought each of us an excellent mutton pie, with capers, flavoured with rosemary and mint. The pie woman was one of many traders who were already selling their wares. We wandered round looking at the horses, and also I must confess at the girls, and commenting to each other as to which of them we would find tempting, (and a satisfactory ride!) given the opportunity. I had not felt so at ease with myself and my fellow men, (and women!) as I did in those short hours with Harry. He had the gift of friendship. I insisted that he call me Thomas, to forget Master and suggested that when life was once again on an even keel, he brought his cobs to Worcester where the tradesmen were constantly in need of good work horses and I would find him custom.

I had noticed that there were some few women carrying rich bolts of cloth, which surprised me as I had not thought weaving to be an industry of these parts. They were converging onto a stall in a corner of the market where it seemed their fabrics might be bought. I remembered that I had lost Jupiter's blanket. Perhaps I could buy another. But as we sauntered over behind one plump damsel carrying a rich red damask, I recognised the owner of the stall. It was the pedlar whom I had assisted in the Malvern Hills. But he was in a rare taking.

"And I tell you, no, madam," he was declaiming with vigour. "I care not for the quality. 'Tis stolen! I will not buy or sell stolen goods. I have only one neck and I do not care to have it stretched."

"How stolen?" I asked Harry.

"The King came by yesterday past St. Martins Church and through Deritend," he told me. "I'm afraid his train was robbed by these good ladies."

The women were becoming angry at the pedlar. "Listen, mistresses," he pleaded with them, "Even supposing I would buy stolen goods, I could not. One of these bolts is worth more than I earn in a year. I do not have the coin. There you see, I am an honest dealer."

A comely middle aged matron near me was clutching a most beautiful French pile blue velvet under one arm and a sturdy infant under the other. "Madam," I told her "is there no mercer near here who could make that velvet into a fashionable gown for you? I warrant your Goodman will forsake his cronies and stay within doors when you flaunt yourself in a gown as blue as your lovely eyes!"

I could not believe myself. Where had I learnt to spout such flowery nonsense? But she seemed well pleased. "Why you fancy monger!" she teased, giving me the full benefit of her lovely eyes. "Come on now goodwives. We have gowns and quilts a-plenty to be made from this fine cloth. Leave poor Joseph to his crochets!"

"Are you there again then, young Master?" called the pedlar, "You were ever a help in a dead lift."

The women were shouldering their bolts and clearly resigning themselves to selling elsewhere. Harry and I passed through them. "You remember me then?" I asked the brown pedlar.

"I would be the scurviest ingrate if I did not remember you, young master. You near saved my life!"

"Nay" I told him "I think you saved yourself. One moment there, and then bag and baggage vanished into thin air."

"It seemed expedient," he told us laughing, "Come I must treat you." He led the way to a tavern beside the horse fair. A young man whom I took to be his son was left in charge of the stall.

"So, young Master, tell me what you do here? I can see in your face that there has been a great sadness since I saw you scarce five weeks ago." He bought tankards of the local beer for the three of us, and we sat down comfortably near the window so that the activities of the Fair were clearly visible. Harry echoed the Pedlar's curiosity.

"'T is plain as a pikestaff, Tom, you don't seem to know what you're a- doing. Tell us how you come here and maybe three heads might be better than one."

So I told them everything. New friends, strangers even, but kind and compassionate as if I were their brother. The Pedlar was delighted to hear that Phoebe was now a part of my household. The thought of Phoebe caused me to pipe my eye again. I remembered how she had said when I had asked her to make her home with us, "This is the best, the very best day of my life since..." - since her parents died. Now this morning although there was terrible sadness at the fearful memory of my father's death, and anger and rage at the villainy of Brigstock, there was some relief to be gained by relating my woes and I felt better than I had for some time. Friendship is a blessing indeed.

Harry could not believe or understand that after what amounted to three murders such a villain was still at large. I told him that John Fiennes had promised that he would be brought to justice just as soon as he materialised again for his pay from Luke.

Then the Pedlar told us of himself. He was a Saracen born in Egypt, a follower of Mohammed but he professed to love the peace and tranquility of our English churches and hated to see the desecration that had lately begun by the Parliamentary faction. Our Messiah Jesus was an important prophet to the Musselmen he told us. He gave me information about the two factions. The King had turned south again yesterday and passed through Birmingham, much to the annoyance of the citizens, and seemed to be enroute for London. All he could say for certain of Essex was that he had heard that very morning that he had left Worcester yesterday, the 19th of October, lock, stock and barrel and was travelling towards

Stratford. He and Harry wondered what I would do now. My home town was free again. I could return. I thought awhile and then remembered that I needed a blanket or even two and asked if there was any chance of his being able to sell me one. "Sell, nay. I'll give you two blankets that I bought this morning before I realised where these Brummigem hussies had gained their wares. Return it to the King if you so desire."

Harry had been looking fixedly out of the window to where our horses were guarded. "Seems Gripper can't convince some varlet that your horse is not for sale. Come Tom." I went out with them into the autumn sunshine and saw that Gripper was indeed having trouble persuading someone that he was not empowered to sell Jupiter. I began to fear that perhaps some minion of Sir Thomas Holte had followed me and was bargaining on behalf of his master for I saw that the would-be buyer had a bag of money that he was banging from his right hand into his left palm. Just then Gripper saw the three of us approaching.

"Why here's the young gentleman what's the owner. Here Harry, bring your friend quickly. If he'll sell, here's one would buy at a rattling good price."

By this we were behind the man who wished to buy my horse. He turned to face us. It was William Brigstock.

12

For an endless moment we stared at each other. My hand instinctively grasped Harry's sleeve and then went for my dagger. Brigstock was alone. None the less he first recovered himself before I was able to think what to do. Muttering something about how he had been mistaken, he turned and disappeared up a hill leading west out of the Horsefair.

"That's him I told you - Brigstock the murderer!" I shouted but at that moment Jupiter took it into his head to give one of his ear-splitting neighs, so that only Harry and the Pedlar had any notion of my allegation.

I started after him and looked up the road where he had vanished......Nothing! Harry raced after me. "Listen Tom. I believe, you my friend. But could we convince the yeomen of the Holy Cross? He'd be in the next county before they would sanction the hue and cry. 'Twas as a soldier of Parliament that he committed these crimes. 'Tis for Essex' men to hang the bastard. You said that this commander Fiennes had vowed that vengeance would follow as night follows day. Perhaps you should seek him out now and tell him you saw him lurking here."

We slowly walked back to Joseph's stall. He pressed two blankets of fine wool upon me and told me if he could serve me in anything, he would do so. I had only to ask. But what could I ask? The truth was I did not know what to do. If I sought John Fiennes in the Parliament army, now seemingly hovering around Stratford, I might well encounter Edward Saunders the Lieutenant who held Billiard in such high regard, and who might well remember the resentment he nurtured against the idiot doctor whose fist had made such violent contact with his Cornet's teeth. My knuckles tingled, and I felt ashamed, even now at the memory of my savagery.

I wandered back to the tavern where I had recently enjoyed such good fellowship. Harry's buyers for his cobs had arrived and Joseph had to attend to his stall. I sat head in hands and contemplated my choices. If I followed the King, as I had thought all along that I might, I knew I would be welcomed as there had been little provision made for the medical needs of his army. But my allegiance was at best half-hearted. The old personal grudge reasserted itself in my mind. As a schoolboy of twelve I was old enough to understand something of the shameful reasons why we young scholars had been condemned to learn in the Charnel Chapel rather than in our airy and pleasant College Hall which was to become a library at the command of Archbishop Laud, Charles' ardent supporter. I remember the anger of my father and the other merchants of Worcester, who paid to support the school. "Boys not books," had been their watchword, and earlier this year College Hall had been restored to the scholars. But some of the boys had contracted wasting diseases, it was thought, by being cramped away in the damp, noisome and miserable atmosphere of the monk's charnel house. And this our King had sanctioned. I remembered my father's words "The King no doubt has a Divine Right to Rule - yet how divine and how right was he to allow this?" And then in his period of lone rule he had alienated so many, with his unfair taxes ....Ship Money which had ruined Phoebe's parents. I thought of the poor women today at the Pedlar's stall who clutched the bolts of exquisite cloth in such sharp contrast to the shabby drabness of their dress. Could a man as deeply responsible and moral as Robert Burghill be wrong? But then Essex had hung my father! And so on and so on. My thoughts wandered round and round until I fell into a doze and dreamt I know not what.

In truth the vision of Brigstock had brought back all my doubts and uncertainties. He was as neat, trim and meticulous in his person as when I had first seen him at the Inn at Welland but there was a difference in his expression. It came to me. He seemed hunted. There was the taint of the fugitive in the hollows under his eyes. I could not pity him, would always hate him but perhaps he was no longer to be feared. (Events would prove emphatically what a simpleton I was!)

I went out to retrieve Jupiter from Gripper and learnt what he had gathered about Brigstock.

"Well master! He has plenty of money, not a doubt of that. He wanted a fast mount if you please as he was a trusted scout-master for Sir Samuel Luke and must have the means to hasten from one town to the next in the vanguard of the Parliament army. He told me that three times, master. But he wasn't alone!" Gripper had seen him talking to two fellows who also looked as if they had been accoutred by Parliament, and no, he had not seen which way they went.

By this I was disgusted by my own cowardice. I would ride after the King without further delay. If I did not find him I would follow a scheme that had been fermenting in the back of my mind. I would ride on to London to Southwark and apologise to Ben and his father for my churlish behaviour. There, it was decided. I was resolute.

I bade Farewell to Harry whose company I had greatly enjoyed and who pressed me to remain in Birmingham and thence return safely to Worcester. But now I could not. To go home with my tail between my legs did not appeal. I also sought out Joseph, shook his hand, thanked him for his friendship and rode back to St Martin's church. The King's route I was informed had been through Deritend or Dirty End as some ruder inhabitants seemed to call it, and straight on down the road to Stratford. But that was where Essex had been bound. So in all likelihood the King had gone thither to join battle with him, once and for all. Jupiter had been well rested. Over twenty miles I was told for Stratford .....well, I would make Henley that day at the very least.

And it was about an hour before sundown that I trotted into the courtyard of the White Swan in Henley. Jupiter was tired. I dismounted and looked in vain for an ostler. As none was forthcoming I led him into a fine clean stable, found him some water and gave him an apple. I went into the tap room to find it alike deserted. I waited a moment and then called out "Anyone there?" There was no answer but after listening for a few more minutes I became aware that there was human movement on the floor above. There was a knocking on the floor and I thought perhaps I could hear a woman's voice, in some sort of distress?

I did not wait but bounded up the staircase and found myself in a wide landing, bright with the sun's last rays. A woman lay on the floor, facing me. Her plight was clearly desperate. She was in the throes of childbirth but, alas, all was not well. She had hitched her skirts up round her waist and an infant's foot protruded. If she continued to push and obey the contractions, she would kill both herself and the babe. The floor around was wet and cold. The waters had clearly broken, some time before.

"Help me!" she whispered. "I will try," I promised.

I had not even the time to recover my box of medicines from the stable. This was a process with which I had only recently become familiar. Midwifery was amongst Joan's many talents and she had guided and advised when I had recently delivered twins.

The poor woman convulsed with the pain of a contraction, which due to the child's position must have been even more agonising than I was assured such pain naturally was. I must now try to manoeuvre the child back into the womb and find the head, all between contractions. Mercifully there was as yet little loss of blood. As the tension eased slightly I took the foot gently in my hands and tried to enable it to re-enter. Impossible. I needed grease, oil, fat to facilitate movement. I ran down to the kitchen and found a great vat of goose grease, no doubt set there for cooking. I set a pan of water on the fire, spilling some in the process, snatched up the vat of grease, and ran back upstairs. By this she had had another contraction. I judged from the speed of them that the babe was ready to be born.

I plunged my hands into the grease and tried to gain a hold on the tiny limb. This time I had more success. The leg slipped inside again. There was no help for it but to manipulate the babe through the stomach wall until it was in the birthing position. I remembered Ben's little saying, "Upside down is rightway up." I muttered this to myself. She heard me and smiled faintly. I found the head through the stomach wall and began to push and persuade it downwards, but as there was no fluid in which it could float it seemed to be a hopeless task. She contracted again … and to my joy with that contraction, the child seemed to sense that he must help himself and somersault. With one movement, which must have been exquisitely painful for his mother, he upended himself.

137

Her screams were pitiful to hear. As she was already dilated I was most happy to see that circle of hair appear. With the next contraction it seemed as if only a very few more would be needed. The circle of reddish hair grew ever larger.

"If you could push this time with all your strength? It helps to breathe as deep as you can before the contraction and then gasp as you will," I advised her. She nodded and as the contraction gained in strength, she breathed as I had directed and suddenly on the floor with a roar and a rush and a healthy bawl was the goal of all our efforts. How had I known it was a boy? I knew that mother and son could rest together for a few moments whilst I prepared to cut the cord and deliver the afterbirth. I went into one of the bedrooms and dragged blankets off the bed and edged them round her. I found some linen in which I wrapped the baby, which she tenderly embraced.

"What is his name?" I asked.

"Nay, what is *your* name, sir?" she whispered.

I told her and she smiled. "Then Thomas it is."

I knew now what I had to do. I had often come into a lying in room at this point to help Ben. The baby was snuffling somewhat but breathing heartily none the less. I cleaned his mouth and nose of mucous. Other basic functions, I was pleased to see, were already occurring.

"I must leave you for a moment." I told her. "I must clean a knife and cut the cord. It does not hurt, I give you my word. There is no more pain I promise you."

Ben always insisted that the blades of knives were boiled. I found a good sharp carving knife and placed it in the pan of water I had put to boil over the fire. As I turned from the fire the kitchen was suddenly full of people. A red haired man came straight to me and aimed a vicious blow at my face. Fortunately for my beauty but not my dignity I slipped in the instant in the water I had previously spilt and fell at his boots with a smarting shoulder. My feet somehow tangled with his, and he too was on the floor aiming ineffectual blows at me. "You thieving Parliament bastard!" he roared, "Making away with our pots and knives."

As I staggered to my feet prepared to give as good as I was getting, an older woman screamed at him "Never mind him.

Where is Marion?" For answer the newborn's wails wafted down the stairs. She rushed up the stairs. "What's that?" cried the fiery tempered one, realisation dawning in his face.

"Your son, judging by his hair," I told him, helping him up and he too sped up the stairs like the pox through a brothel.

"I am not a soldier. I am a doctor." I told the assembled company. "I was not stealing your kitchenware, merely preparing a knife to cut the cord." But no-one spoke, but gazed at me open-mouthed, although as the cries grew ever louder and more lusty, they began slowly to grin and congratulate themselves.

"There'll be a drink in this for you," said the young man who was clearly the landlord's younger brother.

I said easily "Surely there'll be a drink for all!" and then the heavy footsteps of the landlord were heard descending the stairs.

"Sir," he said ponderously, "It seems I must be ever in your debt. My wife, tells me, and Her Mother, God bless her, confirms it. If you had not happened upon her, both she and the infant would have perished I am told. He was trying to come, feet first," he told his brother. "Just like his father!" My transformation from thieving villain to guardian angel was somewhat precipitous but none the less welcome.

"It is no matter." I said hoping my bruised shoulder would not affect my riding on the morrow.

"Her Mother, God bless her, asks that you return upstairs to complete the task in hand."

"Willingly," I replied "But may I take this knife?"

He had the grace to look ashamed.

Later as we were dining I asked, "And where was everyone? while your poor wife was in such distress?"

All was explained. It seems that an Alderman of the town wished to toast his neighbours on his birthday. Marian had not believed that her child was due for another fortnight, but feeling cumbersome and with an aching back she had insisted that husband, mother, brother-in-law and their two servants went to the celebrations, leaving her in comfort and quiet to keep all safe at the inn. Suddenly whilst crossing the upper floor, the waters broke and the next landlord of the White Swan forcibly announced his arrival. She had realised after feeling the foot that all was wrong. She had prayed for help and I had arrived.

When all was completed and the afterbirth decently buried at least three feet in earth according to Ben's best advice, I suggested that Walter assisted his wife.

"At this time, you can be most useful to your dear one." I told him like a good old crone of a midwife, "If you would like to go and lie beside your wife and stroke her stomach gently and lovingly downwards, this will help her to recover her figure and restore her vigour."

"I'll do that!" pronounced her mother, making for the stairs.

"No, Mother, God bless you. That is my office. There are lamb collops in the pantry, late beans to cut. Please you set these two to work. We must all eat. Master Doctor Thomas as I learn your name is, you are my guest. No, I'll hear no protestation!"

In fact none had been forthcoming.

So, after the lamb and beans, as we sat over a most pleasing posset, the manservant Nat who had listened carefully to the news in the town, told me of the whereabouts of the two armies. It seemed that Essex had left Stratford this very day, determined to steal a march on the King and reach London before he did. At least that was the rumour. None were quite sure of its veracity for there were still Parliament men a-plenty stealing what they could. As for the King, "Well, master you have gone a deadly deal wrong," he told me kindly but with understandable superiority. "Tis thought that hearing that Essex was for Stratford, instead of hastening to join battle with him, he turned north off this road for Solihull where that mad dog Rupert, joined him. 'Tis said that now he makes for Southam and will thence to Banbury, where he hopes to trounce all sedition and hang all traitors!" He announced this with great satisfaction!

"Are you then for the King?" I asked him.

"Are we for the King today?" he asked Walter.

The Landlord sighed heavily and puffed at his clay pipe, "Aye today and everyday .....perhaps! I tell you something, Thomas, and I have thought long and hard on this vexing matter. This King can no more rule this country than her Mother, God bless her, but come day, go day, he is still the King for all that and unites us if only to complain of him. I have a horror of these longfaced puritan Parliament men telling good English yeomen how to live their lives. I tell you, if the King wins, then all those who have fought against him will choke on a hempen quinsy, and God rot them! But if they win, they will provoke such dissension, 'twere better we *had* all been hanged and in the end, I tell you, I do not know how we shall do without a King."

There were sounds from the kitchen as Marian's mother was giving orders thick and fast to the poor kitchen maid. "In fact you are wrong," I told him.

"How so?" said he with a look of irritation.

"Her Mother, God Bless Her, *could* rule the country better!" I said as the clattering and ordering grew ever louder.

He laughed far in excess of the joke's deserving. A little later I visited my patients, my namesake eagerly refreshing himself at his mother's bosom, "like to drain the Avon," said her Mother, God bless Her, gazing proudly at daughter and grandson. After finally ensuring that Jupiter was resting well and had enjoyed his feed of Warwickshire oats, Walter showed me to a fine room overlooking the street and all now presaged a peaceful night.

It was not to be. I know not at what hour it was that the household was again awake, roused by Nat who had his own reasons for sleeping elsewhere it seems. He came in calling, "Master Walter, look to the horses!" I needed no second warning. Jupiter! On this night foolishly I had undressed myself totally, but managed to pull on my breeches before I threw myself down the stairs with Walter close behind me. The back door was open and Nat hovering on the threshold. "There's two in the stable!" he whispered. Walter snatched up a lantern and Nat handed me a cudgel. I took it in my left hand and had my dagger in my right. But here was a difficulty. I needed a third hand to hold up my breeches. My dagger hand had to perform this necessary and proper function.

Walter went first. There were sounds issuing from the stable, even the clip clop of hooves on the cobbled floor "Surprise them?" I suggested. He nodded and threw open the door shouting at the same time "Was you wanting summat?" The lantern showed Jupiter yet again saddled and bridled by a strange hand, two farm

141

horses similarly prepared, and, cowering from the sudden light, two wretched rogues in their Parliament garments, now no longer new and pristine but ragged and stained by three weeks long contact with the gutters of Worcester.

"The Colonel sent us, Sir," stammered one of them. I knew instantly by his voice that this was a youth from London. It is indeed wonderful how the sight of assailants who appear weak and afraid and at a total disadvantage, inspires courage in the breasts of those who are equally craven.

"Indeed! Did he so?" I snarled "And what colonel might that have been?"

"'Tis my Lord Oliver St. John, even now lodged at Morton Bagot, Sir." the other told us with a hint of pride.

"Oh, *that* Colonel. Well we have just been awoken by one who has ridden in frenzied haste from Morton Bagot. You must return immediately. It seems the King is even now about to march on Henley, and Prince Rupert has vowed vengeance on all London 'prentices. He intends to hang them by their heels from the Market Cross. Get you back to Morton Bagot."

They rushed past us empty-handed, the mention of Prince Rupert curdling their blood. One of them screamed at the other "Have a care to his devil-dog."

"Thank God, it did not come to blows." I turned to Walter and Nat "I would have lost my breeches."

They both roared with laughter. "But if you please I will sit out the night with my horse. I cannot afford his loss." Walter still doubled up with mirth brought out a fine chair which stood at the head of his table, I retrieved my clothes and with my two new blankets contrived to sleep snugly for the rest of the night.

When I came in next morning all had heard the tale. "Get you back to Morton Bagot!" seemed to have become some kind of maxim or motto. Her Mother, God bless her, placed a great plate of gammon before me and laughing heartily repeated the phrase and so did Nat, brother Henry and the kitchen maid.

"Well, I will get me back to Morton Bagot," I announced, pushing back my chair when I had broken my fast most satisfactorily, "or even to Stratford on Avon!"

The entire family insisted on saying Farewell, her Mother first clasping me lovingly in her arms and bussing me soundly on both cheeks.

"Walter, no need to kiss me!" I told him hastily. They all laughed heartily and hand clasps and manly embraces sufficed. I made sure my possessions, food, water, oats, blankets and purse were all in place in my saddle bags, and rode away to their good wishes and hopes for another merry meeting.

Their Farewells were more wholesome and hopeful than my wayfaring. Although the main thrust of Essex' army had travelled on the Worcester road to Stratford, fourteen thousand men will not trudge in single file, directly from one benighted town to the next, but will spill off the track and out over the countryside, looking for food, beds or at the least clean straw. And Essex had dire need of horses. He had ordnances, and men to fire them but how to get the great lumbering guns into position to do most harm to the King? It soon became clear that I must have a care to Jupiter. Small groups of soldiers tramped dismally towards Stratford, their faces twisted with envy as I galloped past them. I realised as I left a village, which I think was Wooton Wawen behind me, that I must have a care to the track ahead and watch for ropes or other traps. Twice dare-devils had launched themselves towards my spurs and twice much against my will I had had to deliver a sharp kick for their pains. Then perhaps two miles from Stratford, a country-woman called to me. She was bent over the body of a trooper.

"Sir, what shall I do? I fear the poor lad is dead."

I looked carefully around. Open country and a clear road in each direction. I dismounted holding the reins ever closely.

The youth was perhaps my age, somewhat smaller. He was most certainly dead. I could see that he had bled to death from a sword thrust to the stomach. Perhaps a passing horseman had had little compassion when this apprentice had made a grab for the reins, I suddenly saw a solution to my difficulty. His buff coat was somewhat too large for him - that and his orange scarf would be a useful disguise for me.

"How much do you need to bury him?"

She named a modest sum. Pence for two strong labourers to carry him to church, shillings for the parson to bury him, "and two crowns for your Christian charity, mistress."

"You are a good boy." She told me, "Your mother is blessed in you."

This brought tears to my eyes. "My mother is dead, alas, but I thank you for the kindness. Mistress, would you permit me to remove his buff coat and sash and replace it with my doublet? I am a King's Man, nay not even that, I am not aligned to either power but ......"

I could not continue. It was all beyond reason. I gathered my powers. "I wish to travel through Stratford. To do so as a Parliament man would ease my passage."

I removed his buff coat from his stiff doll-like body. What had I done except give her money, the easiest of all contingencies? But it was the scarf that would give me unhindered entry and departure from Stratford.

It was soon done. I remounted and left the good soul to the solemn matter of his burial. At least she would not lack for money. As I rode I found there was an inner pocket in the buff coat. I reasoned with myself if I put half my money out of my leather pouch into my pocket, I would decrease by half the chance of losing it all - or rather the mischance of so doing. As I came nearer to the town, the groups of dissatisfied infantry increased somewhat, but my orange scarf gave me free passage.

I rode into Stratford. There were still many Parliament men thronging the streets, shouting, drinking, singing or simply sitting in the gutter, enduring considerable antagonism from the towns-folk. "Soldiers are great eaters and sleepers but poor payers." I could hear my father's voice ringing again in my ear. How blest we had been that Captain Robert Burghill had lodged with us and had controlled his troopers in the barn with fair discipline. Here the results of even one night's enforced accommodation had set the citizens on fire with outrage. If they could be so up in arms against the Military after one short night, how would they have fared if like Worcester they had had to play host to them for three long weeks.

I reined Jupiter in beside a poor woman who was trying to wash sheets in a horse trough at the end of Sheep Street. She was weeping. She told me that this was all she had in the way of bedclothes and the caitiff who had forced his way into her home and fallen drunk upon her bed had soiled all irrevocably. I asked her if there was a baker's that would sell me bread. She told me waspishly if I had coin to pay, the traders in this town would sell anyone anything. The baker's was down the street and indeed I could now smell the fragrance of new bread. I bought two loaves and two apple pies, returned to her and gave her one of each.

I asked her the route to Banbury. She pointed back down Sheep Street and there was ....Brigstock . Was she a witch or an angel trying to warn me? She went on explaining and I saw her mouth moving but my whole person seemed petrified. I forced myself to look again down the street. Mercifully again he had his back to me, and was speaking in an animated manner to two other Parliament men, but surely he had seen me enter and leave the bakers directly across the road from where he stood? I waited for no further instructions. With a swift "Farewell Mistress. God bless you!" I turned Jupiter and galloped back upon myself and found the bridge over the Avon by hastening down the High Street, which was the route I should have followed in the first instance. How terrible it is to look back in retrospect and understand the weighty consequences that rest upon an idle decision. I could have ridden home from Stratford. There was a good road thence to Worcester, though I might not have reached home alive as events will show. Something impelled me forward, pride possibly, the desire to return with something of honour surrounding my actions. Jupiter set off at a good pace down the Banbury road. We soon left behind the straggling knots of Parliament men. My horse seemed in good heart and soon I should surely begin to hear news of the King riding South from Southam.

But as the afternoon wore on, (and for October the sun was bright and strong) I began to doubt my route. In truth as I journeyed I began to fear that I had missed both armies. I found myself trotting through a pleasant village, called Shipston. I dismounted in the inn yard. While Jupiter had a drink and some oats, the straw-chewing ostler told me they had seen nothing of either army. "Many more miles to Banbury?" I asked him.

"Banbury?" he asked, "Nay, this is the road to Oxford."

Any feelings of superiority that I might have been enjoying were swiftly dissipated. I was the bumpkin, not he. It seemed that there were three roads leading south east from Stratford, and I had taken the most southerly in my haste. A carrier had told him that Essex had taken the most northerly road towards Kineton. The middle road of the three was the Banbury road. He even drew the disposition of the routes with the edge of a flint on a flagstone.

Yet again I stood at a loss as to how I should continue. From Oxford the road to London and Ben beckoned, so more slowly I set out again southwards. I pondered on my stupidity. I had been guilty of the sin of prejudging, assuming an ostler was ignorant simply because he was an ostler who liked chewing straws. How blessed I had been in my father who had insisted that I gave respect to all and who had had friends from all stations of life. But I had been guided well in so much by my poor father. His ability to turn pomposity into a jest that set the room aroar, was perhaps my most precious inheritance. The ability to make others laugh was fast becoming as cherished a quality as my doctoring skills. Although it was somehow an exquisite pain to remember his many humorous sayings and quips, the memories brought joy and a kind of gladness, a delight glimpsed through tears.

Thinking on these matters I came to another village. I reined in and asked two children where I was. The boy whose nose was liberally sprinkled with freckles told me, " Long Compton and the Rollrights!" and he pointed directly up the road.

"What might they be?" I asked politely.

"Why, the Rollright Stones, o'course. 'Tis the King and his men. And if she'm naughty," and he poked his small round-eyed sister "The King'll carry 'er off when he comes down for his drink."

I was completely bemused by this. Then his sister compounded my confusion by piping, "and the whippering nights." "Whispering, stupid," her brother told her kindly. I thanked them for their knowledge. A short way on the road was crossed by one of those ancient ridge walks, that often marked boundaries. The sun glistened on the autumn gold of the leaves and the wind whistled in the tall grasses. I decided that since I was now embarked on a holiday journey to London I would discover what were these Rollrights of which I should have known.

I dismounted and led Jupiter along the Ridgeway, with the setting sun behind me. Then I started! Ahead of me there was a great circle of men gathered around, some standing, some sitting, some lying. But there was not a sound. I strained my ears. Someone was speaking to them perhaps. I walked a few more paces and laughed aloud. The child had said "stones," and stone they were. As I walked within the circle, with the sun in my face and saw the clefts and crumbliness of each stone, I had a strange feeling of the passage of years and a glimpse through time of when the stone was young.

Across the track, there was one stone alone, proud and solitary. Was this the King? who came down to the village to drink? Another much smaller group stood further back from the track, leaning together. The "whippering nights" perhaps?

The place seemed a sanctuary in the evening light, no sound save the wind rustling through the wisps of grass. I hooked Jupiter's reins around a branch of a young oak tree that grew conveniently near the track, gave him some oats and decided to eat some of the Warwickshire cheese pressed upon me in Henley. I sat with my back to the King, facing towards the Whisperers some yards up and across the track.

I know not how but somehow the peace of the place of stones overwhelmed me. The heat of the sun seemed to linger there in the stones themselves and lulled me into unconsciousness of a kind. The last unbroken night I had, had been in Wolverhampton. I hoped Bryn's leg would continue to mend and I dropped into a comfortable doze. I dreamed of my father. The King behind me seemed to mould himself into a support and the sound of Jupiter munching the sweet lush grass a comforting awareness that I was not alone.

I awoke suddenly perhaps three hours later, chilled to the bone. The sky was a mass of stars, the moon riding among them like a monarch, surveying her subjects.

Astrologers and priests would no doubt have been able to read justification in this glorious display for the hideous times in which we lived. But as I gazed upwards I could find nothing except a golden frozen indifference. However we might deceive ourselves, God was unmoved by our woes. There were no reasons from the stars.

Jupiter stood near me, dozing on his feet. I must find him some sort of shelter. The night was becoming too cold for us. I cursed myself for my carelessness. And then as I glanced towards the whispering knights, I was stricken with fear. They were moving. Still leaning together the stones were creeping so slowly, crawling at a snail's pace over the grass from their original place, onto the track where they gathered speed and had suddenly surrounded me as I lay helpless with terror, immobile, petrified. There were three of them. Two men, whom I did not know, and Brigstock.

13

When I came to myself, at least I could still smell the grass. In fact there was no way I could avoid it. My face was pressed into the earth. A heavy weight was on my neck. Many miles above me an argument was taking place.

A London voice, wheedling, irritating - "You gave your word you wouldn't kill him till he'd doctored my foot."

"He aint dead. He'll wake up, when I choose." This was Brigstock.

The third man - not a Londoner, spoke after a pause. "What's to do now, then Brigstock?"

"We wait till the dawn. Then we find some place to hide up, up this track. There's a wealth of lonely women in these parts with their men gone to the wars, ripe for the taking...."

"Where will we take them, Brigstock?"

My limbs were tied behind me in some sort of Gordian knot. The pain was indescribable. I had been beaten around the head and kicked unmercifully about the ribs.

"Get the horses, Ferret."

I lapsed again into merciful darkness.

When I lurched again into consciousness, there was a faint greyness about the dark. I did not think I had been beaten again. I judged that my best policy was to seem as close to death as possible, particularly as one member of the group had an interest in my remaining alive. There was movement behind me. Suddenly I was prodded upright, my arms forced backwards, my body in an arc of pain. The small Londoner thrust a rope into my gaping mouth and tied it viciously behind my head. Then he and Brigstock led over a carthorse. There could be no question of my riding, trussed up like a chicken, but when they heaved me up trying to balance me on my stomach with all my limbs in the air, they realised the impossibility of transporting me in this manner. To my relief, my hands and feet were released from each other. I dropped over the bewildered horse, with my head hanging perhaps three feet from the ground, my feet kicking his opposite flank. I heard them all mount, the small Londoner astride Jupiter. His feet must have been well short of the stirrups. Someone clicked the horses forward and the nightmare continued. My stomach voided itself fairly swiftly of the cheese and bread of the previous evening. By now it was full daylight, sunless dull autumnal weather. We trotted north up the causeway for about three miles, my discomfort intense. I had remembered some advice Ben had given me. He had once been captured by bandits in the Alpine mountains of Italy. The outcome had been favourable. He had been rescued but, as always, Ben had advice to impart. Say nothing and do nothing to antagonise your captors. Pretend it is happening to another. I wished with all my heart, the second were true!

As we stopped, I could see that there was a small farm down in a pleasant wooded valley to the east of the track. The sun had broken through and was gilding the shrubs and trees of the farm's garden. There was the soft clucking of hens and the hiss of geese.

"Hide him and the horses in case the men folk are still here." Brigstock dismounted and the horses were led off the track by the other two to a spinney. "Push him off, Ferret!" Lob instructed the small Londoner. As I hit the grass, I contrived to protect my head and neck in a clumsy somersault. They tethered the horses still saddled and bridled and rejoined Brigstock, pacing impatiently on the track. I could not move or shout for help. I raised my head to see if there were some sort of hiding place into which I might roll, but where was the logic of that?

The quiet of the morning was suddenly pierced by a woman's scream. In the stillness that followed I heard the slightest movement beside me. I turned painfully. A boy about twelve was standing very close, his face uncomprehending and afraid. He had three rabbits hanging from a stick, and a small dog at his heels. I beckoned to him with my head thinking he might untie me but then I heard Brigstock shouting out orders over more frenzied screaming. This child was my only hope. There was a patch of mud where a spring had been. I edged and rolled over towards it, thinking perhaps to write in it with my spurs. Perhaps one leg could have achieved it but not two roped together.

There was an ash twig near the mud. I struggled down onto my face and somehow levered the twig into my gaping mouth, forcing my teeth to bite it over the tarry rope gag. The mud was thick and my teeth strained against the sourness of the twig but I wrote Help and beckoned him to look. He did so slowly and then said straight away "Help." Sweet Jesu be praised. He could read!

He made again as if to attempt to untie me. I shook my head violently and the twig still in my mouth contrived to write above the word "Help" the letters G E T. He said "Get Help!" I nodded violently and on the instant heard my captors returning. I turned round to warn him to begone but there was no need. He had disappeared as completely as if he had never lived, the dog with him. I had the wit to roll over and obliterate my message with the back of my head.

My tormentors returned. Brigstock made certain that the horses were not visible from the track, their reins all safely secured. "But how do we get him to the house?" asked Lob. "Nothing easier!" said Brigstock "We drag him."

At first across the grass the discomfort was minimal but when my face came into violent contact with the pebbled paths of the farm, the agony was frightful. I kept trying to lever up my head and twist my face from side to side. I was terrified that my eyelids would be scraped, and my sight damaged. Then came the jolting pain at the front of my skull of three stone steps and then finally a smooth slate floor. I was kicked into a corner.

I know not why horror stays indelibly upon the memory and joy is so elusive. I told myself again, "This is all happening to another!" I was in the kitchen of the farmhouse, I had glimpsed from the road. An old man was hanging from one of the hooks from which hams are usually suspended. Immediately I was back in the East Cheapen in Worcester gazing at my father's slowly rotating body. Like my father he was already dead. I guessed that when the villains had intruded into the farm he had put up some resistance. A sickle lay under the table. Three women, I surmised his daughter and two granddaughters, sat on three chairs opposite me bound around their upper persons to their chairs and gagged as I was. I had some time to absorb this appalling scene. Brigstock and his friends had found the cider and a ham and drank and ate with evil gusto. They even played a hideous game with the old man's feet. As he swung towards one of them, they swung him away again with roars of laughter. They urinated at him, seeing who could launch his stream the highest, like boys in jest behind a wall.

The youngest girl who was perhaps fourteen could take no more. A terrible keening came from her throat. She was in the grip of an uncontrollable hysteria. Her mother I could see, helpless to comfort her daughter, kept darting glances to the door. I knew she must be terrified her son would enter all unknowing. I shook my head at her slightly.

"Time for sport, ladies," said Brigstock, "Lob, get out to the bridleway and keep careful watch. You'll have your turn."

Lob, who seemed something lacking cerebrally, leered and obeyed. Annoyed by the sounds issuing from the younger girl, Brigstock went over to her and beat her once on the cheek. This of course made matters worse. Her sobbing grew louder. He tore her bodice from her and heaved up her skirts. Dropping his breeches he tried to enter her but this could not be as she was seated. Finally they untied her, spreadeagled her limbs upon the floor and Brigstock and then the Ferret deflowered her. The noise she made intensified. Brigstock placed his hand across her mouth to silence her but somehow the rope had slipped a little and she bit him. He looked round as if seeking sympathy and with mock pathos whined "The bitch bit me!" He raised her slightly and with the back of his hand cracked her head to one side. He had broken her neck, just as he did with Sally Beckford.

In one room in less than one hour the most profound horrors lodged in my memory were realised and re-enacted before my eyes. Now all that remained was for Brigstock to stab me and cut off my face as he had tried to do to Philip.

But the Ferret was in pain. "You told me he could mend my foot," he complained.

"And so he will before he joins our old friend up here," he cried jovially. "Go and fetch his box of instruments, Ferret, you sniveller. I have a few scores to settle with this gentleman."

"So did you think, Master Thomas Fletcher, Physician of Worcester, that when we met in Birmingham, I would not follow you and silence you, you bastard? Oh yes, I saw where you stayed in Henley."

I did not think I could have felt worse but the notion of Brigstock's villainy set loose in the White Swan amongst Walter and his household chilled my blood. If he could treat an innocent young girl in the way I had seen what might he not do to a baby? Despair unmanned me. I think I sobbed.

"And then in Stratford, buying bread for the poor. What a great benefactor is here lost to us all! Your unending supply of money? Where is it? Not in your saddle bags. We looked. I don't chose to share it with these dolts. Where? (He beat me about my face and I nodded my head down, indicating my inner pocket. He snatched it out and carefully placed it on the shelf above the fire). "I followed you and saw you take the Oxford road. You are a great simpleton, Fletcher. You never once looked back. Here's a health to your stupidity! I drink to it."

As he downed another tankard of cider, the Ferret returned with the box. "Lob says to say when will you take his watch, Brigstock?"

"All in good time. When I choose! Let him see your foot!"

The stench in the kitchen was already foul and noisome, partly due to the effluent from the poor old man, but also due to the urine of the men which had freely bespattered all the shining kitchen pots and pans. As Lob removed the filthy rags from around his foot, the smell intensified and became the rank odour of decay.

Brigstock came over to me and hauled me up by my collar and pushed me towards the Ferret. "Doctor him!" he ordered. That was not possible. I could not use my hands or speak to enquire about the symptoms. I was hard put to it even to stand. I indicated my helplessness to Brigstock who cut the rope which fastened my hands behind me. Even with that skill returned to me, I could see the case was hopeless. His foot was irrevocably infected. Some filthy sharp object had penetrated between the metatarsal bones, and pus was welling from the point of infection. From this his leg had reddened and was swollen. I pushed aside his shirt. There was a swelling also in his neck with red trails spreading from it down his arms. The Ferret's brow was covered in beads of sweat. Three or four days ago something might have been done for him but now he was too far gone. He was gangrenous. He was a dead man.

I could not treat the illness but perhaps I could use it. The symptoms of gangrene could be, had often been, mistaken for those of plague. I widened my eyes and looked at Brigstock in what I hoped was sudden horror. "What?" he shouted. Realising I could not answer, he roughly untied and tore away the rope gag. I still could not answer, my mouth and tongue dry as dust, but at that moment a diversion in the shape of the small dog I had seen before scuttled into the room. He began to bark at all of us indiscriminately. "Shut him up," Brigstock roared to the Ferret.

Lob came rushing in. "Troopers! About twenty of the bastards. Flags flying. Looks like some of Old Subtleties. On the Ridgeway."

Brigstock glanced at the dead man and the girl. He hurled himself at the cellar trapdoor and heaved it up. He dragged the corpse of the girl over to the gaping void and threw her down. Lob meanwhile had unhooked the grandfather and his frail old body was also flung down the stone steps. Then they turned to their live victims. The gag was replaced in my mouth and my hands tied if anything tighter than ever. The mother's eyes were still alert and darting, but her feet were not tied. Realising this they hurled her, chair and all, after her family and then the elder daughter received the same treatment. I knew now there was no hope for me. I would be impaled on the upturned legs of chairs. I tried to resist my fate attempting to shoulder Brigstock away from myself at the cellar's head, but with a great roar he kicked me down to my almost certain slow death.

But I did not die. Somehow the mother, anticipating this below in the cellar's gloom had with her feet pushed her own and her daughter's chair away from the two corpses. I landed face down on them. A small object was hurled down beside me, there was a great crash above us and all was dark.

An eternity of deafening silence. I tensed in hope again and again waiting for the sound of the troopers above me, wondering how I could alert them to our plight. But there was no sound except the moaning of the elder daughter and the occasional whimpering of the little dog. I waited for what seemed like hours.

154

I think I slept on my macabre resting place. When I woke I realised my eyes were accustomed to the gloom and I could see the vague outlines of my fellow victims. One of the sides of the trapdoor did not fit perfectly and a tiny streak of light pierced the darkness. The elder girl had landed in her chair on her side, her poor mother was upended on her back. As I watched she was trying to right herself by rocking her body forwards and back. I thought she might do more harm to herself if she succeeded, toppling herself sideways and hurting herself upon the floor.

Then the dog who had I think been sleeping beside me, suddenly roused himself. He began to growl and I could sense that he was wagging his tail vigorously. There were at last footsteps above us. We could hear voices.

"Johnny, I told you this is one of your madnesses, you idle boy, bringing me from my work. Your mother of course has gone to Brailes Market as is her wont on a Saturday ......"

The boy shouted, "What is that smell?"

At the sound of his voice, the dog near went mad. He barked and barked, running up and down the cellar steps. "Rags! Where are you?" Johnny called.

And then slowly the boy and the woman pulled up the trapdoor and Rags shot out. We could not speak but I, and the mother mewed and hummed so that they would at the very least hear our distress.

"Christ in Heaven. What is that?" cried the woman, clearly thinking goblins or ghouls were lurking in the cellar.

And then the mother, blest of women, suddenly as loud as she could, began to hum a tune. "If all the world were paper..." I tried to join in and Johnny recognised it. "It's Mother!" he cried and tumbled down the steps, stopping in horror near the bottom. "Knife you stupid woman," he shouted up to the neighbour. "We need a knife!"

And so he and Rags between them rescued us, the neighbour talking non-stop the while. As we emerged unbound into the daylight I stood and gazed dumbly at the mother and daughter. Indeed we could not speak. Our mouths were bruised and broken by the foul penetration of the rope. The mother Mistress Jane went into a dining hall and returned with clean cups into which she

155

poured elderflower wine from a cask. This eased our organs of speech somewhat, but I had cruelly to refuse the family time to mourn or linger. We had to get to safety as I knew Brigstock would be back. The neighbour whom Johnny had brought, was his aunt and lived in a hamlet down the valley less than a mile away.

As I staggered outside I judged by the sun it was early afternoon. All the horses had gone. I had lost Jupiter. Still I was alive. And I must think. I staggered up to the Ridgeway and looked in the dust and mud at the side. The latest horseshoe impressions led north away from Long Compton and the road was empty. Still Brigstock could be anywhere, spying and plotting. I remembered my money and ran back into the stinking kitchen. It was where he had left it on the shelf above the fire. And there was my box of instruments and medicines.

My instinct was to run as far as my legs would carry me and put as much space as I could between myself and Brigstock. Jane and Cecily were now beginning to weep, clinging to each other. Johnny was white-faced and uncomprehending, the neighbour Dame Margery still talking.

"So when Johnny came in crying and asking for help I could do nought, Jane but tell him to wait and indeed he had not to wait more than an hour or so. Was it not so Johnny?... as there were even then twenty or so of troopers come to the village demanding bed and board and I had to apportion them fairly as maybe ...."

"Are there then strong fellows who can protect us from this murderer?" I had to shout to make her cease her prattle.

She looked offended. "There are *now*," she admitted. "With their commander a great gentleman for the Parliament."

"Then in the name of God let us go there and put ourselves under his protection." I was shouting like a madman, my speech broken and uncouth.

I made Johnny lead the way down the valley easterly away from the road, Rags miraculously unhurt rushed about beside him. The chatterer followed. I hated to think of her mindless trivialities grating upon Jane and Cecily who clung to each other, able at last to give voice to their grief and horror.

"And there are sheets on the bushes that the girl will forget about should it rain and indeed the sky was something red this morning so if I do not now return to them, it will be all to do again and I am sure…" It was endless.

Finally I could bear no more "Woman!" I cried, "Know you not that Mistress Jane and Cecily have endured terrible loss and violation. Jane has seen her father and her younger daughter murdered …..and you talk of sheets."

For a moment she was quiet. Then she said, "I saw them lifeless at the foot of the stairs. I hoped to distract."

I felt something of contrition. "Distraction? They can never be distracted, Mistress! What they have seen and endured today will never leave them. This same murderer caused the death of my father and two good friends."

But she was again in full spate. "Ah did you so lose your father, poor soul! And I too lost my father and he a wonder ninety years I swear if a day and I thinking he had dropped into a doze in his chair as was his wont and wishing him to come to table to taste his mutton broth and him sitting there a-smiling and in truth as dead as the mutton itself which I had bought but two days before from Giles Pearcey Shepherd to the squire as he likes to be known, though his father paid many a pound to this King's father to be known as knight……"

And so she brought us into the village. My father spoke inside my head, "a blessed deliverance for the poor old man! The wonder is he endured so long!" So it was with inappropriate hysterical chuckles that I turned the corner of the church with them and found myself among known and trusted friends.

A Parliament soldier leaning against a barn wall was gazing at me. It was Ralph, the contriver. "Why, Thomas!" he shouted "Master Thomas!" He ran to me, and seized my arm. "What a case you are in to be sure! Captain! Captain!"

And there hastening towards me was Robert Burghill, displaying every sign of concern and distress. "Why, my poor Tom!" he cried holding me in his arms "My dear boy! Let me help you!" He led me into the kitchen of the house where he was clearly quartered and indeed suddenly I needed help for I could scarce walk.

This was it transpired the home of Dame Margery, who now bustled in behind us with Jane and Cecily. Johnny sat at the kitchen door stroking Rags. Physically I was the worst of Brigstock's victims but contrived as well as I could to tell the story, praising Johnny for his presence of mind and Jane for her courage and quickness of thought. And Rags? "The best dog that ever lived!" I cried. I was rewarded by Johnny's slow smile. Margery boiled pans of water and I asked for leave to go to an outhouse to clean myself. Margery insisted that I took a great piece of her soap made from woodash, lavender and oatmeal. Ralph kindly came with me carrying my bowl of hot water. More of Robert's troopers came up as I dragged myself across the yard saying they were excessively glad to see me. "Leave him. Can you not see he is spent?" cried Ralph. "Time enough for reunion when he is in his head again."

I could feel that there was painful gravel lodged in my face. Ralph retrieved my box from the kitchen and tenderly as a woman removed the tiny stones embedded in my cheeks. I had mud clogging my hair, long cuts from the kitchen steps on the front of my head, and my ribs and head were bruised black and blue. But I judged I was not mortally hurt and longed simply for food and sleep.

When I returned, clean at last, Robert was even more horrified by the extent of my injuries. Jane and Cecily had been put to bed in Margery's room. Robert had ordered a dozen of his men to scour the country around Kineton where Essex was lodged to find Brigstock and his cronies. They awaited my description of the appearance of the villains. They had all seen Jupiter when they had been in Worcester I explained that one of the criminals was gangrenous but presented no infectious danger to any would-be captor. I calculated that his condition would be worsening by the hour.

Margery, blissfully silent in Robert's presence, placed a bowl of wholesome mutton broth before me. "There, son, her father bequeaths it to you with his blessing!" said my father in my head and I gave a great shout of laughter and addressed myself to my plate like a savage. When I finished I looked up to see them all gazing at me with concern. "Come my boy. Here you are well guarded. No need for further care today. Sleep!" and Robert himself helped me prepare myself for bed.

When I woke after a mercifully dreamless slumber, darkness was almost upon us. Robert had brought up a candle which he placed beside me. Margey followed with roast fowl and boiled cabbage, a dish I loved well. I sat up obedient as a child and was able to thank her like a civilised gentleman for her generous hospitality. Robert was kindness itself. No father could have been more concerned for the safety of his son.

"Well, I have good news for you," he told me sitting on the bench in the window, "We have found Jupiter."

"Wonderful!" I cried. "Is he here?" making to get out of bed.

"Yes but No" said Robert firmly "Yes he is here and in a good state, but No do not get out of bed Thomas. He is well tended I assure you. The other three horses were also stolen and two of the villains apprehended. They rode into Middle Tysoe where Brigstock's old troop, John Fiennes', men under John Carminghell were seeking quarters. It seems this lieutenant Carminghell had personal scores to settle with Brigstock. The troop had reined in at the back of the inn and the three villains walked into the taproom from the front, all unknowing that Essex had moved so swiftly from Stratford. Then as they tried to escape, my fellows arrived, recognised Jupiter and Brigstock's two companions ran straight into their clutches."

"What of him?" I asked.

"He ran through the inn to the back, leapt on a horse and rode off westerly. But our men are everywhere. Essex is at Kineton en route for London."

"Then may I travel with you?" I asked him "I want to see Ben"

"That would indeed be a merry meeting and most gladly you shall go with us. But now, sleep!"

He would not be gainsayed and indeed again I could hardly keep awake. Some time later I was dimly aware of a press bed being set up in the great bed chamber where I was housed. Then once again blissful oblivion!

There was of a sudden a frantic knocking at the bedchamber door. I was instantly awake, my fear of Brigstock convincing me that I was still locked in the cellar and that the fiend had returned to kill me. It was first light on a Sunday morning and there was the comforting presence of Robert in a press bed across the room and ordering whoever had disturbed us to enter.

It was a lieutenant who immediately assumed that I was the Captain as I occupied the large bed.

"Lieutenant Reeve Bayley, sir, and a thousand pardons for this intrusion. Lord Basil's compliments, Captain, but there is a great call to arms. Can you and your men make swiftly for Kineton where my Lord of Essex ....," he faltered, frowning, either at my youth or at my expression which must have been the epitome of incomprehension. .

"I am here Lieutenant," said Robert from across the room. "This is Surgeon Thomas Fletcher, sorely injured, indeed near killed, by the renegade Brigstock. Where do we gather, say you?"

" 'Tis below Edgehill, a great ridge near Kineton. I would advise that you make for Kineton, going up the road for Middle Tysoe. Any direction north and east will deposit you in the King's bosom. He was last night at Edgecote but the churls are drawn up betimes on the ridge of Edgehill. We knew nothing of their proximity. It seems there was a confrontation at Wormleighton, quartermasters searching for billets."

"I am coming, Lieutenant. Haste you down and tell Trooper Ralph Browne to muster the men as you leave. My regards to my Lord Colonel. We will be with him straight in good order."

"Sir ....?" The Lieutenant stammered, looking at me. I scratched my head and tried to appear knowing and adult, attempting to shake off the sleep that still possessed me.

"Well?"

"We need a surgeon. Lord Basil has not allowed for any doctoring. Is this gentleman promised to any other company?"

"Believe me he has endured far more than a young man of his years should be subjected to." Robert announced, pulling on his hose and shirt.

"But I would be safe in the battle, Robert!" I said simplicity personified. "Brigstock now knows for certain he is sought after."

"Aye Brigstock will not be there but Rupert will be and old Jacob Astley, still a great soldier and Heydon with their artillery. A great mathematician who can calculate the fall of cannon and shot to within inches. Tom, you will not be "safe" in any battle."

But I now had "stomach for the fight"! "But I cannot abide to be left behind." I told him "I came to help the wounded. If, as the

Lieutenant says his Lordship has no-one to help with them, then it is my Christian duty to assist." (How did I know then, callow youth that I was, that the words "Christian duty" covered a multitude of sins for the Parliamentarian faction?)

Robert laughed. "The wonderful optimism of the young. Very well Tom. Lieutenant Bayley, would you tell Lord Fielding that Thomas Fletcher will serve as Surgeon for our Regiment but has no skill in arms. Tovey no doubt will find him a station well back behind the lines."

The Lieutenant thanked me profusely and bowed to us both, which in our various undress seemed something ridiculous. I was amazed at how much better I felt. A spasm of conscience afflicted me as I dressed. I had after all planned to assist with the doctoring of troops but had wished to aid those who fought for the King, and here was I aiding the men who had hung my father and despoiled my city. But if Robert and his men needed me ......Robert had dragged himself from his sick bed of pain to plead for me before Essex. By doctoring their wounds when they were too injured to continue to fight, I would not be assisting the King. And if a Royalist came to me injured I would afford him the same charity. I remembered suddenly the reason for my flight from Worcester.

"Robert, what of Thomas Billiard? Did he recover from my blow?"

Robert laughed shortly. "Recover? Aye, that he did. He grievously assaulted an innocent maid at an inn in Inkberrow and lies in Stratford gaol, awaiting the Assizes. He is all brawling and breeches ...Think no more of him. He is known now for a hammer-headed Hector."

I was never happier to obey a command.

When I had pulled on my clothes I ran downstairs to relieve myself and splash water on my face. Mistress Margery had been generosity itself. Robert's troopers were everywhere, rousing themselves from bags of clean straw which she had permitted them to fill from her barn. I greeted her as courteously as I could thanked her for her kind hospitality and asked after Jane and Cecily. I was afraid that they might take it into their heads to return to the farm.

"They will stay here with me, until my brother returns. If your Brigstall varlet shows his face, I will hang him myself." But she had several stout male servants who had been helping with the Squire's cider making yesterday who were due to arrive back within the hour.

"And let us pray they will not be the worse for drink although Old Diggory will preach at them all like as if he was Parson Roberts himself though the good Captain Burghill like a father to you is he not poor soul does not preach I am happy to say but there is tremendous setting up of these Parliament preachers to tell you how to order your soul as well as your body....."

Madam Jabberment would not be gainsayed. I escaped while she was in mid flow.

Jupiter seemed in good fettle when I heaved my bruised and aching person on his back. My saddle was still in place and a swift search revealed that the coins I had hidden in Jupiter's oats had not been disturbed. Robert ever solicitous of my safety insisted that I ride within the group of troopers. I was astonished to see that now there were two women, riding behind their men. One was Martha, the wife of Trooper Thompson, a lively London lady who shouted to me that she would help me, as she had done in Germany. The other was a girl from Worcester, Jenny Harper, whom I recognised as the daughter of the chandler on Bridport Street. Her mother had been a great friend of my mother's and she and I as babes had played together. Now at the sight of me, she hung her head, clinging fast to the trooper behind whom she rode and would not meet my gaze nor answer my greeting.

It seemed the ridge path would lead us close to Middle Tysoe, where we must keep south of Radway. The whole country seemed to be alive with men moving north to the battle. Small groups of troopers rode both behind and before us on the Ridgeway, Parliament men all, by their orange sashes. We had to ride either side of culverins being dragged by great patient carthorses. Robert called out to the gunners "Will you be there in good time?" They laughed and said they hoped to be. But their pace was painful slow. To the north far off, we could hear trumpets blaring out into the Sunday peace. It was a strange journey, five miles at most, but on the air hung the sounds of great unseen bodies of men forming, meeting and settling.

We left the road to Kineton and had to ride through fields, with the ridge of Edgehill rising on our right and now we heard or became aware of a great congregation of men, talking mostly but some singing hymns. As we rode into the valley, a great panorama opened before us. I had never before seen so many gathered in one place. The King's Men had definitely the best of the field. They were in lines and groups below the ridge whence they could survey the whole vista. They had the advantage also that they were in place betimes whilst the men of Parliament were still mustering. And as for the guns....Lumbering, trundling pieces of ordnance were everywhere being coaxed and heaved into position. The shouts of the gunners and the orders of their captains cut across the vast polyphony of background noise.

"How many men are gathered here?" I asked Robert.

He hummed a moment. "'Tis even stevens I hear. Both armies something over fourteen thousand each."

I had another question. "If they are evenly matched why do both sides not agree to forego the guns?"

The foolishness of this made him smile "You might just as easily ask why do not Rupert and our own Lord Basil engage in private mortal combat and resolve the matter between them? Alas, all the questions and injustices would still remain. And besides," he said in an undertone, "Rupert would win! ....hands down!"

"So," I persisted, "if today this great battle is joined, will the questions and injustices be answered?"

He laughed shortly but was saved from answering by the need to greet the Colonel of the Regiment. "Good day my Lord!" he called to the great man, riding up at the head of about eighty men. "My Lord, did Lieutenant Bayley tell you that this young man will doctor for us? I hear we are on the right wing, sir?"

Lord Basil was another of those aristocrats who seem to be so fair and pale as to be almost transparent. His expression was slightly startled, his eyebrows arched above light blue eyes. His moustache was prolific, resembling nothing so much as a gorse bush. He was of that breed of aristocrat who has to have information apportioned out to him in manageable spoonfuls, like pap.

"Oh aye indeed," he said in answer to Robert's questions and stared fixedly at Jupiter. "A hearty welcome to you," he added to the horse. "Tovey!" and like a Jack in a box, a quartermaster materialised. "This is the Sawbones."

"Come Master Fletcher," said Tovey, "We have set you up well and tidy, behind the regiment, and we hope, as I am sure you do, beyond the cannonade. Follow me." I turned to bid Robert Farewell but he and his men insisted on accompanying me.

I protested politely, explaining that although I ached and my mouth was still sore, I was in good shape. Robert laughed.

"Dear Tom, it is not for your comfort but for ours. We need to know where to hobble, hop or crawl once the cannons begin to roar. What did you think of our Colonel?"

"He seemed…. preoccupied as if practical matters were of little moment to him," I observed discreetly.

"As well they might be. This day he takes up arms against his own father, the First Earl of Denbigh, who fights for the King!"

A grim prospect indeed! To use his inheritance or the income from his father's estates to clothe and arm men to fight against the man who gave him life. I began to feel something more of respect for Lord Basil. What a hideous quandary he was in! No wonder his expression was startled …..startled at his own temerity!

"Now, lads take note!" Robert shouted, "Here beside this stricken oak near the hawthorn brake you'll find Master Tom. Mark well!" He turned his horse towards me and clasped my arm "Farewell dear Tom. Let us pray we meet in Heaven."

In fact I found at that moment I could not cry "Amen" to such a pious and saintly wish. I would have found a more mundane meeting place much more to my taste. The dirtiest alehouse in the county would have sufficed.

Trumpets were beginning to blare out what was, I supposed, a call to arms. We were some hundred yards behind Sir Philip Stapleton's regiment, whilst Robert and his men had trotted further along the wing to the right to join Lord Basil. Tovey had found trestles and chairs and Martha who had magically arrived some minutes before me was arranging them so that men might wait for me if not in comfort at least with a minimum of further harm. A young boy touched my elbow.

164

"If you please, sir?"

"Well?" said I, trying to sound more than two years his elder.

"I am come to help you. I have watched my uncle in Stratford. I know how to cleanse a wound and bandage it."

"And your name is?"

"Elijah, sir."

"Well, well Elijah, let us hope we have no need of fiery chariots from heaven."

He grinned in the polite way that boys do when their betters have made a joke that they have heard a thousand times before.

We began to check the contents of my chest of medicaments and tools. I had a pair of callipers, which I suspected we should be using much to withdraw shot and balls. Tovey, excellent man, had placed buckets of clean water for our use, and I directed that we must use it sparingly, pouring it into a supply of bowls that Martha had prudently borrowed from Margery. We began to tear some old clean linen she had also supplied us with to use as bandages. I was down on my aching knees, winding these strips, when I became aware of a pair of boots standing patiently near to me. I stood up and found myself gazing down into the embarrassed face of the man who had directed my father's murder. It was Sir Samuel Luke.

14

I knew not what to say. I could have unsheathed my dagger and "unseamed him from the nave to the chaps" in true Shakespearean style, but he was such a little man. I towered over him as Brigstock had done in Fish Street. Then he said the one thing that I wished to hear him say.

"I fear we have been sadly and tragically duped by the scoundrel Brigstock."

He paused as if waiting for a reply so I said rather waspishly, "So it seems, sir."

He went on with a gesture of his hand, "This is magnanimous indeed, Fletcher, to volunteer as surgeon. I salute you. Burghill has told me of your latest encounter with this devil. Of one thing you may be sure. As soon as he is caught, my Lord Essex had decreed that Brigstock must hang from the nearest tree."

Again he seemed to expect a reply, so I hazarded a question that had been troubling me. "Why? Why does he ...?"

He looked alarmed. "Why? Surely you of all people can be in no doubt as to the justice of such a punishment?"

"No, sir. You misunderstand me. Why does he gain pleasure ....indeed what *has* he gained from his cruelty? He must have known it would all end at the gallows at last."

He sat down on one of the benches we had placed ready for the wounded and sighed. "That has vexed me also. There seems some moral miscarriage in his brain that enables him to pursue a course abhorrent to all natural men and women. And these, our wars and troubles have enabled him to use our loyalties to serve his purpose. We have been his creatures, his muppets in a child's play. For me that is a burning shame, Master Fletcher. John Fiennes sent his Cornet Perron to enquire after his circumstances and found that the day after the Train Bands left London for Northampton, Brigstock's wife and children left their home in Southwark. A neighbour told Perron, Brigstock's departure was a blessed deliverance for her. She and her small children had been beaten and misused far beyond what a woman should endure. It was thought that she would rather beg her bread than stay in that house a day longer, poor soul."

A firm resolution suddenly possessed me. I felt ashamed of the physical weakness that had overtaken me, since I had slept the sleep of ignorance at the Rollright Stones. "Sir Samuel," I told him, "Your rope and gibbet will not be needed. I know not how but tomorrow whenever this battle ends, on my oath, I will find that man and kill him. I will kill him for the two young maidens whom he raped and savagely murdered, I will kill him for Philip Fosdyke who in the short time I knew him was my friend, I will kill him for the poor old man whom he mercilessly slaughtered at the farm where he gave me these bruises. I will kill him for the life he led his wife and little children. And, sir, I will kill him because two poor sick King's men, one mortally wounded, were slaughtered most horribly in cold blood in my father's house who had taken them in at my request for Christian charity. But most of all, Sir Samuel, I will kill him for my father who as you know was unjustly and terribly murdered."

He stood up "Yes" he said simply. "I am sorry. I was deceived. You have my blessing," and he walked away.

My bloody resolution remained hot and fiery in my breast for at least three minutes. Then the cannons began. No-one had prepared me for the noise and it was horrible beyond belief. Elijah unashamedly clung first to Martha and then when she shook him off, to myself. The sight of one even more lily-livered than oneself is a great sinew-stiffener and I contrived to give a good example, though in truth there was never so craven a quake-breeches as I was during that first hour. No-one had prepared me either, for the fact that with the cannons' clamour there would be prodigious quantities of black smoke, billowing out over the field. The closer one was to the ground, the purer the air. The Royalist ordnance in spite of Robert's apprehension of Sir John Heydon's calculations mercifully fell short but were as loud and as noisome as the Parliamentary guns which I learned afterwards found their marks, mostly amongst the ranks of the King's poor foot soldiers. There came a blessed lull in the noise and smoke, during which Martha was kindly able to tell us about her cheerful experiences with her trooper in High Germany, when arms and legs flew through the air like arrows from bows, and men's blood fell like rain, after just such a cannonade. In truth I began to think that from the greenish hue of his face Elijah would be our first casualty.

Then from about a mile away to our left, there came the sound of a series of shots.

"'Tis the left discharging their carbines!" Martha told me confidently. Then came the sound of confused fighting, the clash of weapons, the screaming of horses and the cries of men. Almost as soon as this began, the words "Ramsay's running" were passed along and as I turned to look behind me away from the battlefield where the smoke did not impede ones view, I could see groups of Parliament men, some riding, some on foot, streaming away in the direction of Kineton. As I gazed I could descry their pursuers, the red streaks of Rupert's Lifeguards, pursuing them and forcing them from time to time to turn and fight.

And then I thought that all was over with us. Ahead of us there was again the clash of arms, the terrified screams of wounded men and horses and then as swift as may be, Lord Basil and his regiment were streaming towards us like the great Bore wave on the Severn. "Get down!" they shouted and in the instant I could see they were pursued by mounted King's Men. Martha's benches were again brought into use - even she, hardened veteran that she was, sought cover - as Fielding's regiment streamed and jumped across us. They were pursued by fierce Cavaliers, moustaches bristling, brandishing swords and carbines but at the last instant a great voice shouted "Wheel right" and they passed harmlessly to our left, causing us less upset than their Parliamentary victims had done. Robert I could see was rallying his troop to stand against dragoons on the farthest left of the King's army. This was warfare of method. As the dragoons in one or twos attempted to get close enough to pick off his men, Robert would give the order to make ready and then to fire. As so many were concentrated on so few, this was effective but brutal carnage.

Meanwhile in the centre of the field, the matter had come to "push of pike." These great moving hedgehogs of men had to be most fiercely controlled and must carefully obey commands or there was a terrible chance they would spear their own comrades, like chickens on a spit. They wore armour which I had been told was of great value if all went well but was a terrible encumbrance if its wearer sustained injury. And now we could see under the pall of smoke that still engulfed the battle field, one or two walking wounded who were making their way towards us. The injuries to begin with were minor, splinters in hand or arm, a sword gash to the thigh of a gentleman, an ankle sprained by one of Ramsey's runners when he fell off his horse. Martha proved invaluable. She was experienced in the art of treating small Wounds, often brutally instinctive but once she had removed the splinter, or stemmed the flow of blood she had little interest in her patients. Elijah however, whilst he clearly was not experienced, could soothe and calm those recovering from Martha's ministrations, giving sips of water and kind counsel.

We were distressed to learn that all the poor men who came to us were hungry. There had been little in the way of rations for days, the inhabitants of Warwickshire had taken care to remove all that was edible from the thieving hands and eyes of soldiers, and the sutlers had tried in vain to buy supplies. I was to learn that the King's men were if anything in even worse plight. My store put up so generously by Marian's mother in Henley had been stolen by Brigstock and Margery's fresh matchet rolls were grudgingly donated one each to men that were not merely wounded but starving. I hit on a sort of compromise. If one of the richer sort had food in his snapsack, I would ask for him to give something as a contribution to one of the poor men who waited for my services. They would not then be so perilous weak when they had to endure our treatment, which was in these circumstances, rough and ready in the extreme.

Now the trickle of injured men became a flow. Servants and retainers were at work seeking their masters, and bringing them to us if there seemed a chance of life. I seemed to spend a lifetime probing wounds and binding slashes. Alas, one or two men died under our ministrations, not because of our methods but because perhaps we should not have meddled but let life drain out with such dignity as was possible. As at Powick Bridge one or two men were carried in lifeless and after a while in time spoke and recovered.

Stapleton and Balfours' regiments had long gone forward to engage with the Royalist foot. I could see in the two fields that had originally separated the armies, a few discarded bundles. I wondered - could there be food in these packs. I set off to find out, as hostilities had moved over to the centre and Martha and Elijah had matters in hand.

To my horror, I discovered that what I had thought were bundles were in fact corpses, often left in grotesque positions. When I saw one or two of them moving, I felt that I must help. They were the detritus of the ordnances. There were perhaps ten or twelve men so sorely wounded that no surgery, no medical treatment was possible. One poor fellow had had both legs blown away. Mercifully he died as I watched him. But one man, a Royalist had lost the contents of his stomach on a pikehead. To my eternal horror he was still alive and conscious and spoke to me.

"Sir, sir, would you end it for me?"

I could not reply. I stood and gazed at him. He clutched feebly at my leg. If only I had some draught, some hemlock that I could gently give him to sip. Finally I shook my head. "I cannot," I told him like some green girl. His eyes flickered away from me. I turned. Martha had followed me. She took in the plight of the sufferer and asked me for my dagger. I gave it to her, said stupidly, "I was looking for food." She nodded and pointed back to our station, saying quietly, "You are needed." I left her then amongst the dying and the dead and hurried back noticing as I did so that women from the edges of the field were moving between the corpses.

As I came towards our sad makeshift surgery, I could hear the sound of terrible sobbing. A Royalist, a Life Guard by his scarlet doublet, sat beside the humble men awaiting treatment for cuts and bruises ....and hunger. Elijah raised his eyebrows as I came near and looked meaningfully at the man who wept so pitifully. I ascertained that none would die if I delayed for a short while. I led the King's Man some short distance so that his cries no longer distressed the others.

"Are you hurt?" He shook his head. "In pain?"

"Do you know what I have done?" he asked me, "Alas no. You could not know. I have killed Mitchum."

"Who was Mitchum?" I asked.

"Our steward." He broke forth a–crying again. "The best man in Hampshire. He used to shield me from my father's wrath when I was a child."

"Did you know he was for the Parliament?" I asked him.

"Oh, aye. He was dismissed last year.... He would not have been brought to this pass if my father had allowed him to keep his position and his views. And I cut him down. And he knew me. In the instant of his death, he knew me."

I could not think how to help him. It was growing dark. "Could you not find him tomorrow and arrange for his burial? Who was his commander?"

"Ramsay. I will do what you say. And I will make shift to assist his wife and children. I heard that he joined to get bread for them. Oh God! He was no soldier! He was the best man alive. He used to chide my bothers for cruelly mistreating me. He cared for me more than my own father. And now I have killed him."

He broke out crying again. I thought to tell him briefly of my own plight but then thought me of William Brindley's words. "When all this is over, have as little on your conscience as is possible." All that I could do was decide for myself, what was best for me. If that meant havering on the fence than so be it. I could not now help reflecting if this poor man had had less certainty in right and wrong, he might have resisted the call to arms and not be in this terrible torment. And then another thought intruded. So cowardice or uncertainty and a clear conscience might be judged as horses from the same stable? But was "a fierce neutrality" another word for cowardice?

"Did you have divine guidance in choosing to fight?" I asked him.

"No, just threats from my father. Believe me there is nothing of the divine about him."

"For me there is as much bravery in refusing to kill my innocent fellows when all men might revile me for a coward."

He was lost in thought at my words and I too was surprised at what I had said. I was not a coward. My fist had met Master Billiard's chin with no thought of heroism. If only I had killed Brigstock, when I attacked him in defence of Sally at Martin's inn. Tomorrow I would kill him.

"I follow a course of fierce neutrality. I do not think I am a coward. The cowardice lies in allowing others to make up your mind for you. Now you are a brave man because you will not kill others any more, simply because your father bids you. If the King's cause seems just in your heart, then you will continue. If not just enough, then you will cease. Live for Mitchum now. He cannot live for himself. He was a good man. Love his memory and live."

I amazed myself by my words. Did I really believe this or did the occasion call forth the response? Was I preaching? I hoped not. I had begun to lose faith in a benign Almighty. I knew that although my father had loved the Cathedral, which his ancestors had built, he had little faith in either Puritan preachers or Anglican bishops. I remembered a conversation we had had a year ago, some weeks after Bishop Thornborough had licensed me to practice surgery. We had heard he had died peacefully in his bed - he was an old man - and my father after he had spoken conventional pious sorrow, had turned to me and said: "Now, son Tom, believe me the dear bishop did not despair and die because he realised he had recently made you a doctor. He was taken to Abram's bosom, without that notion vexing him!" The three of us had laughed inordinately. I remember Ben getting up for more ale and clapping my father on the shoulder as he passed him and telling him, "Amyas, I pray you, never change!"

I began to laugh myself. Then I recollected where I was. The Royalist had gone. I shook myself mentally and knew I had to play the man as the memory of my laughing father so vivid, of such loving fellowship had brought me close to tears. The night was closing in. We had perhaps twenty or so invalids who if they rested well this night might survive our treatments, but not if they were exposed to frost and cold. Then I noticed that the sounds of battle had died away.

"What has happened?" I asked Martha, looking round.

"Both sides are spent. No light, no warmth, no drink, no food, precious little spirit for the fray." She seemed disappointed. I praised her efforts in her search for food. She had it seemed been successful. "The men I took it from no longer needed it," she said shortly, sniffing derisively at my weakness. I made up my mind to dispense with her services. She was effective but depressing to ones spirits.

"Could you return to Captain Burghill and see how they all have fared? Your husband will be concerned about you. Would you tell the Captain I have borne up well?"

She sniffed again, but collected her belongings and said she would see us at first light.

"Elijah!" I called out, "We must have fire. These men must be kept warm at all cost, else we shall lose them all. Who has a tinder-box?"

One man pointed to his snapsack. There was a copse nearby which we had used as a place of easement. I went to the far side and to my delight made out the pale ends of a stack of logs. I called Elijah and we heaved them over to our station, together with some handfuls of brushwood that caught easily. We soon had a fine fire burning - if not merrily - at least vigorously. There was an immediate lifting of the spirits of those patients as were conscious. They began to talk softly and those whose hands were free helped their fellows to gain a little more comfort. I kept returning to the two who I knew still lived but who were unconscious. One moaned when I kept chafing his wrist and calling to him. There was still a degree of cold felt by those furthest from the fire. There was nothing for it. I would have to remove the buff coats from corpses and use them to protect the living. I left Elijah in charge of the fire and managed to fashion a burning brand so that I could see. I made my way cautiously to the centre of the battlefield. To my surprise there were others there before me, flitting from body to body stripping the dead. They were women.

I went over to them and thanked them for their thoughtfulness and took the coats two of them were collecting. They seemed astonished by my actions. I had the impression that they did not wish to give up their bundles.

173

Then a very large lady blocked my way. "And who are you to steal our rightful pickings?" she demanded, arms akimbo.

"I am a surgeon, madam, trying to save the lives of those who are like to die of cold. Did you think I was a tailor or a mercer, selling again what are not mine to sell? Come to the fire there for your coats in the morning when I hope that the friends or captains of the men I am trying to help will have found them....alive."

The women murmured amongst themselves. Like Martha these were veterans. I did not dare enquire if the men whose coats I held had been living or dead when these angels of mercy had removed their garments. I confess I felt impatient at being delayed by a group of ignorant women but it was perhaps expedient to leave them as friends rather than enemies.

A well known voice spoke out of the darkness. "Thomas, is that you?" I peered behind me. The good Captain had again come to my aid. "Captain Burghill!" I said, "I am delighted you are safe. I am asking these ladies to lend me these buff coats for my patients who may recover if they do not die of cold."

There was a groan at my feet. It was as I suspected. The harpies had been stealing from the living as well as the dead. I raised my torch but they were hastening away. I turned to the Captain. He shrugged and offered to help me carry the coats. He had a matchet roll with ham for me, which tasted like ambrosia. I stuffed half of it into my mouth and put the rest in my snapsack.

"Could your men go to these places where the dead lie and bring to me any that live?"

"Alas Tom. They would be at that sad work all night. You are asking too that they assist those who have even now been trying to kill them. But I will see what can be done. Ralph, I am sure will help you."

As we came in sight of the fire I could see that there were men standing at the edge of the group, two of whom were holding up torches hastily fashioned like mine. They had the mien of servants, showing great reverence for the men standing near them. They had clearly brought an injured man for treatment. The Captain beside me stiffened. Abruptly he pushed the coats he was carrying into my arms and saying he would see me later went back without explanation to his troop. Elijah I was pleased to see had placed the invalid on a chair and was gently cutting away the cloth which surrounded a bloody wound in the man's thigh.

I was well pleased with Elijah, and gave him the remaining half of my matchet roll. In a few short hours he had become used to dealing with my problems. I told him I was delighted with his resource and asked him to tuck the coats under and around the men lying suffering on the cold ground.

As I examined the new patient's injury, I was able to tell him that if he could sustain the great pain that I would cause him in a few moments, there was a chance, a good chance of some kind of recovery. The musket ball had sheered across his flesh and lodged perhaps three inches deep inside the great muscles that assist the femur to maintain our upright posture. There was much bleeding and torn flesh but if we could extract the ball cleanly and avoid infection, there was a chance he might yet live to mount his horse.

Blessed Master Tovey. We still had three buckets of clean water. I poured some into a bowl and yet again washed my hands with Margery's soap, bidding Elijah do the same. I cleaned the whole area of the wound with Pares Lotion and asked when he had received the injury. He told me shortly after the onset of hostilities.

"But good sir, you should have sought help before this. Why did you postpone it?"

"Misguided loyalty," said someone behind me.

"Loyalty to who or what?" I said waspishly, Master Doctor to the life. "No-one and no creed is worth the loss of a leg. Elijah, I need you beside me."

I tut-tutted at the stiffness of the leg, the blood beginning to encrust. Ben had reflected at Powick Bridge, the sooner the treatment, the better the chance. This was in a way the most serious of the wounds I had seen because it had been neglected for so long. There is a slim chance that the body will adapt to foreign matter, healing over it and allowing the alien, safe harbourage till natural death, but in this case I could not take the risk. Besides which the foreigner might cause the muscles to knit together crookedly. I instructed Elijah to hold back the great flap of skin while I probed for the ball. The firelight gave me good vision and I carefully extracted it between my callipers and laid it on the bench beside me. The patient lost consciousness as was normal. I told Elijah to spoon water between his lips.

"Now for shreds of cloth from britches or hose," I told him. "They can cause as much distress as the musket ball itself. To it again Elijah!" and he again held back the flap.

There they were! Shreds of burnt cloth embedded in the sinews behind the area where the ball had entered. I picked them out meticulously like a whore killing fleas and laid them out beside the musket ball. I ordered Elijah to try to fold them out if he could and piece them together so that I could be sure I had removed all. My probings caused more bleeding - a healthy sign I thought. I cleaned the gaping chasm as best I could. Yet the body itself does this better than any surgeon. I pressed the flap of skin back in place, and held it for some time wishing I could stitch it or sew it perhaps. I could only hope it would knit together. I cleaned the area with the essence of lavender, I had removed from Lady Holte's still room.

"Elijah, bandages!" I snapped out. He had them ready. I bandaged the thigh and then and only then looked again at the patient's face. Drops of sweat trickled down his face but he smiled at me and raised his hand in salute. He had made no sound at all. When had he regained consciousness? All through my excavations he had kept his leg still and perhaps watched my progress.

"You are a brave man, sir." I told him.

"Nay, you are a brave surgeon, sir" he replied.

"Well, whatever," I said reverting to the testy doctor, "All will go for nought if you now break open the wound for foolish exertion. You must rest. Here," and I turned to the man who had been standing behind me patiently all this while. "Cover him with your cloak, and stay here with him by this fire. By daylight we shall know if we have cheated infection."

"And if not?" the patient asked.

"I cut out the infected part and we dress the wound again." I told him, matter of fact and honest.

"And will I walk again?"

"You walked here with it in, did you not? Nothing surer, provided the gash heals. You are the lighter by all this ironmongery and mercer's goods. You will walk all the more carefree, I think, when the sinews knit."

It was a heavy jest but he and his companion behind me laughed. I have often noted how men and women will smile at their physician's humour, be it never so ponderous. Perhaps they think laughter will placate their malady if they are pleasant with the man that they think can cure it.

"'Tis true," said the patient, "I did walk here. But I had right royal assistance." He gestured at the man behind me. I looked again. Sweet Jesu, it was the king.

My jaw near hit my navel. I gawped for a few seconds then remembered some vestige of my manners and bowed. "Elijah!" I hissed. He seeing me bent double thought I was looking for something on the floor. He crouched at my feet. "What is it? What is it? Tom?" he gibbered, scrabbling about under my nose. "'Tis the King you yokel!" I told him. "For God's sake, bow!"

But the King was laughing heartily. "I never thought to have such courtesy from a Parliament surgeon."

"No, no," I said my voice somewhere in my stomach. "I am fiercely neutral in these matters! and my lord King I have two blankets that are yours."

"How so?" he asked me.

"A dear friend, an honest brown pedlar bought them in error from a poor Birmingham woman. They were taken from your baggage as you passed through that town. When he found I was coming here to tend the sick, he gave them to me to return." I was burbling like a lunatic brook, scattering the contents of my saddle bags. At last I found them, folded them and presented them as best I could.

"They are yours, Master Doctor," he told me still laughing at my antics. "Is there aught else you need?"

"No, no" said I. "Yes, yes" said Elijah, more in his head than I was, speaking to me in a sort of embarrassed stage whisper. "We have tended King's men here as well round this fire and all need *food*."

"I will send such food as I can command, but as to your earlier instruction, I fear I cannot stay longer with Edward here. I will send a litter for him in the morn."

And he left us, his servants carefully seeming to note the exact location. I stood looking after him for a moment stupidly clutching the blankets. As a man among men who loved him, he was clearly compassionate.

The new patient - Edward - he was named suddenly coughed and said, "I have a question for you, Master Doctor."

I came to myself. "Pray, ask," I told him.

"Why did you mention my mother when you cleaned my wound?"

"Your mother?"

"Yes. You said clearly, 'Lady Holte's still-room.' They were strange words to hear but wondrous comforting, as if she had sent you to me."

"I confess I took the lavender essence that cleans and makes sterile skin, from her still room. I was in Aston Hall a few days ago, a day after you and the King had left it. Your father spoke to me of you."

He smiled. "He would not speak well of his spendthrift ne'er-do-well. I have never attracted money nor laboured to make it, unlike my revered progenitor! To tell you the truth - Tom - may I so call you? - my father and I hate each other."

I said carefully, "I did not find him a lovable man. He tried to steal my horse."

He repeated what Isaac had said, "Only your horse?"

I told him something of the strange happenings of that night and of how his servants had deceived their master, by not pursuing me at all. I pleased him well by this account.

"Is it not strange," I spoke my thoughts aloud. "You dislike your father who lives. I loved and love my father above all other men and yet he is dead one month ago, hung by Essex Lifeguards in Worcester."

"And you are how old?"

I had to think for a moment. "I am nineteen."

He seemed distressed. "Only nineteen! The grief and sadness you have suffered is etched in your face which shows clearly this most recent terrible loss."

For some reason my control departed. Compassion from a companion such as Edward Holte had the effect of turning me again into my father's child, overwhelmed by his loss. Perhaps also the stresses of the night and my weariness compounded with his sympathy. I turned my face away from the warmth and good cheer of the group around the fire and stared at the cruel darkness of the battlefield and wept. Poor Elijah seeing my distress thought I grieved for the dying who were still out there. He timidly approached me and kindly laid his hand upon my shoulder. His goodness of heart increased my sorrow. He had had nothing from me all day but sharp words and hasty orders. I sat down heavily on the freezing ground and thought I would weep my heart away.

The King's servants returned with another courtier. He went straight to Edward, obviously concerned that his friend had found himself under the care of a dangerous howling madman.

"No, no Lucius, all is well. I have provoked this grief by speaking ill of my father. This poor gentleman surgeon lost his father, hung in error by Essex but one short month ago in Worcester."

"And yet you tend both Parliament rebels and true subjects here?" asked the newcomer.

I sniffed and composed myself. "Blood flows, the same rate, the same colour, whatever the thoughts and opinions of he who bleeds. I made a pact with a good old man that I would have as little on my conscience as was possible when all these troubles are at an end. So dear sir, whom I do not know, I pursue a fierce neutrality."

He looked at me for a moment. "And who knows, dear young doctor whom I should like to know better, but that you are not in the right of it there!" He turned to Edward. "The King instructs me that tomorrow I am to accompany you by litter to Great Tew to Eliza and Letty. The first will kill you with love, the second with philosophy."

He stood closer to Edward so that I might not hear their discourse, and finding myself so dismissed, I turned to helping poor Elijah. The King had sent us the remains of a roast goose, some pork chitterlings, bread and pears. My father said inside my head, "This King has sent us excellent Commons." Again my great lunatick snort of laughter. Elijah turned to me in alarm and the man called Lucius together with Edward turned to look. Edward said so pleasantly, "Tom, please tell us your jest." I did so explaining that my father spoke in this merry way inside my head from time to time, that it was my joy to hear his wit, alive still. They both laughed at my drollery as did some of the men who were still awake and Lucius said, "Your father's son is plainly a man of infinite wit also."

I went to my two patients who had been brought in, alive but unconscious. Sadly one had regained his mind but for a few seconds before giving up the ghost. We had no notion what internal injuries he might have sustained. The other groaned again when I tried to encourage life to return and then opened his eyes and demanded to be helped to his bed. I wrapped him in one of the King's blankets and that seemed to suffice for the rest of the night. I listened often to his breathing and all seemed to go well with him.

This was the strangest of times. Elijah and I took turnabout to guard the fire and ensure it did not fail us. I blessed the good farm worker who had all unknowingly supplied us with so ample a supply of kindling, and had saved so many lives. As the night progressed, men who could walk, stagger or crawl came to our circle and sat waiting for me to treat them, which I did as well as I could although now my supplies were pitifully small. My heart went out to the poor souls who could not now be reached on the battlefield, dying perhaps of loss of blood, loneliness and cold.

The man named Lucius stayed with us and tried to help me. Finally I made him chief fire mender - he did least harm in that persona. Edward called me over to him when Lucius had gone in search of more logs.

"Viscount Falkland wishes you to accompany us to Great Tew tomorrow. Shall you come? You need rest."

I thanked him courteously and told him nothing would give me greater pleasure but that I had to attend to certain matters. I indicated the invalids I had tried to help. "Also..." I paused. I could not tell him of my resolve to kill Brigstock. He was so pleasant I could not bring myself to speak of such bloody matters. "Also I must bid farewell to Captain Burghill," I told him. He frowned at the mention of a Parliament officer but respected my obligation.

"What is the nature of your duties for the King?" I asked him.

"I am one of the Grooms of the Bedchamber. An excellent post in that the King is the kindest of men to those whom he loves but alas there is little remuneration. For that I have had to look to my father but so far have had little generosity and even less money. He hates my wife who is the loveliest and merriest of her sex, because she brought only a small dowry to the Holte coffers. Even the King cannot move Sir Thomas to be a good father to us, though he has persuaded, cajoled and even threatened him. All to no avail. How blest you are Thomas. To think of your father brings you joy. To think of mine is gall and wormwood!"

Grey fingers of light stroked the Eastern sky. What a long, long night it had been! The Viscount, who was of small stature, pushed one of the last logs on the fire and told me he would seek the King's litter and would return for Edward. Suddenly Tovey bustled up. He frowned at the sight of King's Men round the fire but when I told him saucily, "All cats are grey in the dark, Master Tovey. Have you not found it so?" he laughed and clapped me on the shoulder, and paid me for my pains. He clearly wanted a gossip.

"What thought you of my Lord Bazil when he and his men rode over you so soon after the cannonade?"

"What thought I? I thought perhaps he had remembered an urgent message he and his troop had to carry elsewhere for the King."

He laughed again and confided in me, "'Tis thought when his father, the Earl who fights for the King as you know caught sight of him, he shouted that he would lambast his son's arse for him! Our young gentleman could not risk that indignity and took to his heels."

There must have been about a hundred men sitting quietly around the fire, hungry and thirsty but at least they had not died of cold. Ralph came walking over and told me he had fed Jupiter who was well. The King true to his promise sent his litter for Edward.

"Come to Great Tew Tom," he bade me. "I will see you there later today. Go back to the Rollrights and strike east across country. Cross the road to Banbury and ride down into one of the prettiest vales in England. Do not fail me. The Viscount expects you." He was carried away, still shouting directions.

Commanders from both armies came and claimed their men, thanking us for our care of them. A few men remained but two or three good women from Kineton came with a cart and offered them beds and sustenance ......for money of course. For those who had none, I dug deep into my pocket and found the crowns, my money that I had retrieved from Brigstock.

Brigstock! I looked at Elijah, innocence personified. "Get back to Stratford to your dear mother," I told him, "Cherish her well. Come to me in Worcester next year if you still wish to be a sawbones." I paused. "And if I am still alive."

Tovey bustling around with his chairs and benches told us, "No Master Fletcher you will live long and plague some good woman into marrying you, no doubt of it. We are finished here. Essex has gone towards Warwick, and its thought the King is for Banbury."

I looked round our makeshift surgery, the grass trampled, the fire dying. The women from Kineton were helping the few remaining foot soldiers into their cart. It was almost as if there had been a great Play here in a theatre and now all the characters were dispersing. "We must pack up our pipes and begone." So said the musicians when it seemed there would be no wedding. Was I the only auditor who found Romeo and his Juliet, the most stupid pair of lovers to draw breath?

Elijah shook my hand and thanked me yet again for teaching him so much in so short a time. I told him 'twas not I but the battle that had been his teacher and thanked him for helping me so efficiently. I felt as if we were about to flounder and drown in all our courtesy and good wishes so I told him, "Oh for God's sake, off with you." He grinned and was gone.

I could see Robert and his troop about half a mile away. Jupiter was safely tethered in among their horses. I wandered over, my bags and blankets slung over my shoulders. I saddled up and mounted.

Then I stopped. Two men were bound hand and foot in a cart under some elms. It was the Ferret and Lob. I could see that the Ferret was as near death as a man could get, his eyes rolling in his head. But Lob screamed curses and imprecations vowing that Brigstock would avenge their deaths. When he saw me astride Jupiter contemplating him he fell silent. Robert who was supervising the cleaning of weapons seeing me gazing in horror at my torturers told me, "They are to hang at noon. Don't look so stricken, man. There is a trail of terror that this Brigstock blazed.

Even in Northampton his outrages began. My Lord Essex has a list a yard long. 'Tis not merely you who seek redress, I assure you Tom."

"But are these two guilty of Brigstock's crimes?" I asked

"Oh, be sure they played their part, believe me. They were his creatures ever ready to assist. Brigstock was the source and root of the evil but Robin Payne and Ludovico Ferris here were ever ready to embellish and support his villainy - murderers both, Tom. In one instance the killers of helpless children, I assure you. Will you wait with us till then? Brigstock may have joined them by then. Sir Samuel had many of his company seeking the scoundrel in the country round about."

I shuddered. "Thank you, no. The whole notion of hanging, innocent or guilty, is anathema to me. And Robert I have thought again as to the wisdom of accompanying you to London. Perhaps I should return home to Worcester. Six people there depend on me, two in my father's shop and four in the doctor's. I have been told that I may stay near here and rest for a day or two, by two men whom I suppose I may count as friends."

He looked hurt. I went on - "as I count you Robert. The best friend I ever had since the death of my father."

"They are for the king, I take it, these two 'friends'?" he asked coldly as if 'friends' and 'fiends' were the same and Edward and Lucius were Beelzebub and Lucifer."

"Yes, Robert," I told him, "but that is as naught to me. They are good people as you are. I care for none of it. There are no reasons for these wars, nor no solace nor forgiveness either from a benevolent Almighty. All must come from a man's own heart and brain. It is our own will. There is nothing else. Nothing!"

He gazed at me and smiled sadly. "No reasons you say. Well, you are a good youth notwithstanding, and I would wish you should not be contaminated by the worldy viciousness of Kings."

I had to leave him. I did not want ever to fight for the King and knew I never would, but now I knew him, I could not for my life listen to treachery.

"Robert," I cried turning Jupiter eastwards, "I must go. If I find Brigstock I will bring him to you, or kill him myself," and before he could speak again to plead with me to stay and accompany him, I had clicked Jupiter forward into the rest of my life.

15

I was swiftly away from the battlefield. There were signs every-where of the terrible events of the previous day. A few wounded men had made their way from the scene of the conflict and collapsed on the cold ground to bleed their lives away. I dismounted once or twice to be certain that life had departed. Frightful also was the sight of dying horses. I remembered Rupert riding about the field at Powick, putting them out of their misery with his flintlock and wished I had the means of doing the same.

I began to regret my abrupt parting from Robert and yet where would have been the sense of lingering? Yet I wished we had not bade farewell on such a sour note. Robert was an intensely good man, totally determined on his perception of the right way of life. Perhaps his Puritan-like morality *was* the virtuous route through this vale of tears - he certainly believed it to be! And, after all, he did not preach and could laugh as heartily as the next man. There was always however, this certainty lurking below his undoubted good fellowship that his approach to life was the righteous path and somehow holier than any other man's.

I knew too that I was perhaps cast in something of the same mould. I did have difficulty laughing at myself. My father had balanced this trait in me. If I spoke of some matter something too ponderously, Amyas would always show me the humour lurking behind heavy and serious conclusions, when the topic merited a light-hearted touch. I remembered him saying once after I had complained that one of his customers seemed to find in me a cause for mirth: "Son, do not take yourself or your life too seriously. Avoid pomposity. The man who cannot laugh at himself will find many who will do it for him."

Someone had told me during the course of the night that the Ridgeway was the county division between Warwickshire and Oxfordshire. The Cotswolds stretched around me, high broad hills in every direction with long views, interspersed with the prettiest valleys, in which hidden tree-shaded villages lurked. It seemed that Lucius Carey lived in just such an enviable place. I longed to see it and realised that by now, as it was close on noon he and Edward would have reached their destination.

I turned right onto this strange old path and realised I would be again passing close to the farm where I, Jane and Cecily had suffered so much. My brain refused to dwell on these atrocities. Would Brigstock return there? I thought that he would but was for shrugging away the responsibility now of any kind of confrontation with him. Robert knew all the circumstances, knew that Brigstock might well go back for my money he had forgotten, and had promised to patrol the farm en route to Warwick in the march after the Earl of Essex. In truth I needed respite. I slumped in the saddle, suddenly bone weary. Ahead of me far away was a group of mounted men - no doubt some other Parliament group bound for the Earl's muster. But less than half a mile away was a lone figure, steadfastly plodding along, raising a slight flurry of fallen sycamore leaves, with a stick, twirled more for dalliance than use. It was Elijah. My conscience gnawed at me. He had had nothing from me but swift harsh words through the endless night and then had been summarily dismissed and told to go and find his mother. He had firm but gentle hands and had seen and done more useful work during and after the battle, in the midst of horror than most young lads would perform in a lifetime. I was an ungrateful scoundrel and he, a patient uncomplaining scholar.

I reined up beside him and dismounted.

"Come then. Up with you!" I threw at his startled face. "Your turn to ride, numbskull."

He grinned delighted, as any sixteen year old would be and heaved himself into the saddle, looking down at me, now the poor peasant, our roles reversed.

"But there is room for us both up here," and made to shuffle forwards out of the saddle. I stopped him. "Don't you know the story of the father, his boy and the donkey?" He shook his head, and clicked Jupiter into a slow walk. "A father and his young son had a fine donkey to sell at a market." I continued, ambling alongside. "Father rides the ass, son runs beside. They meet a farmer. "Shame on you, Sir, to ride while your poor boy runs to keep up. He is young and small. Shame on you!" So Father dismounts and puts son on the beast. A little further and they pass a marketwoman jangling along in her cart. "Why, young Sir!" she cries out to the boy, "You ride and your tired old father must trudge alongside, his old bones aching and his poor feet, sore with blisters!" So Father climbs up on the poor donkey, alongside the boy. They travel a little further and meet a grand lord out alone for the chase. "Look at that poor creature, weighed down by the pair of you!" he shouts. "Have you no brains that you treat your dumb beasts so ill! The ass will die before his time, the victim of such usage!" They dismount and scratch their heads wondering what's to be done. The answer comes to them like a flash of lightning and there they go, staggering and tottering into the market, carrying the donkey between them."

I confess I had never so appreciative an audience. Elijah had to rein in Jupiter and fell over his mane, laughing so heartily I had fears for the horse. However Jupiter simply looked back at us with large reproachful eyes, as if to say "What fools these young humans are!" Perhaps it was his equine air of superiority or perhaps the strains of the night, or perhaps the infectiousness of Elijah's delight in the tale, that caused me too to bury my head in Jupiter's flank and give way to unbridled mirth. We stood so for a few moments one of us pausing, to be set off again by the other.

But suddenly there were four of us. Nipping and barking round my ankles was Rags, Johnny's dog. Where Rags was, Johnny was never far away. I looked round for him and saw we were at the place where the track ran from the Ridgeway down to the farm that I wished never to see again. I realised I had dreaded passing the place and with sinking spirits knew now that I could not do so. Johnny and Rags had saved my life. There was something in the dog's agitation that alarmed me greatly.

"Stay here! "I told Elijah. "The dog's owner, a young lad, may be in mortal danger. I must go to this farm to see." I gazed up and down the empty road as I had done but two scant days before.

"Any troopers for the King or Essex, it matters not, if they ride down for sweet Jesu's sake, send them after me." Then as he gazed open-mouthed, "There is a madman down there I think who caused my father's hanging." He made to turn Jupiter to follow me. I told him: "No! Stay here! One of us must stay free and he will carry you to safety if troopers do not come."

The farm looked calm and peaceful as I followed Rags down the track. Hens still scratched and clucked gently and the cock sent up his fanfare as if all were well. Perhaps it was and all would be as we had left it. Soiled and stinking, with Jane's careful housewifery set at naught, but all safe, nonetheless, as we had hurried away, shocked and bruised by Brigstock's villainy and somewhat drunk with Joan's elderflower wine.

The kitchen door was ajar. I pushed it open and looked straight into Johnny's terrified eyes.

To my everlasting horror the child was seated between his dead relatives. Someone had retrieved them from the cellar. The grandfather lolled over the table face downwards whilst the young girl seemed to have been forced back in her chair, her face still taut in the rictus of death.

Johnny screamed: "Tom!" His eyes were on the unseen space behind the door. I threw myself down and forwards, shouldering the door back on its hinges as I did so. This gave me the second I needed to be on my feet.

Brigstock, his sword drawn, stepped from behind the door. This was a different man from the sleek Quartermaster who had dogged my steps from Welland. His once chestnut hair, now greasy and tangled, hung in rats tails over his shoulders. His eyes were red and glazed over, remnants of his orange sash hung in tatters. He came towards me his sword pointed towards my throat.

No matter. I knew a trick worth two of that. Get under his guard with your dagger and dispatch him, I told myself and my right hand went across me for my weapon. Nothing! Of course! Martha, curse her, still had it. Brigstock came on, his mouth open in an ugly sneer. In that instant Rags who had been cowering and whimpering near the door, at a word from Johnny, suddenly lurched forward between us, barking and growling. Brigstock's eyes left mine and he sliced at the dog, but as he did so, my left

188

hand fell on and grasped what I thought was a thick stick lying on the table. It was a joint stool, one leg still rough and jagged, longer than the other three legs, the subject of Johnny's crude carpentry. The seat held in both hands over my chest made a rough sort of shield and perhaps the legs could deflect the sword away.

There was an anguished yelp. Brigstock had sliced at Rags' tail and wounded him grievously. The brave dog slunk away, I knew not where, for my attention was again focussed on the madman who thirsted for my death. I clasped the stool to my chest, aware that the area the seat protected was pitifully small. An upward thrust through my ribs would be my ending.

I was afraid. Taller than Brigstock, had I had any kind of weapon I knew we would be evenly matched. He came towards me now grinning, panting, saliva gathered at the corner of his mouth and lowered his sword arm for a killing stroke up through my abdomen. I backed away clutching my makeshift shield, and as he circled me, turned ever to face him, hateful though it was to look at his bloodlust. He began to stab at me, and I moved the stool to deflect his thrusts. He slashed upwards again, and again I jerked the stool against the blade. But at a cost! One of the even legs clattered to the floor, displaced by the sword's violence. We circled again, I knowing now I must at all costs, not lose the eye contact I had with him, even though I could see my death in his fatal gaze. He slashed at me again, catching my sleeve, above the stool's seat. He had forced me round the kitchen and now I felt the table's edge, pressing into my back. He thrust at me now in earnest, right, left, pinning me against the table until I was arched backwards over it. Then he seized one of the remaining even legs and tried to pull the stool from me in order to inflict the final blow.

I closed my eyes, not wishing my last sight on earth to be his frightful face. I found at the last I could not look upon my murderer and see the manner of my death. Something rushed between us at our feet, and suddenly a terrible pressure was on my arms and a great stream of water gushed onto my face. Only it was not water. It was blood.

I could only open one eye. The longest unfinished leg of the joint stool was protruding from Brigstock's mouth. It had pierced the great blood vessel which carries blood from the head. He had tripped over the dog and impaled himself.

He stood for a moment, frowning slightly, and then crashed backwards on the filthy floor, blood still flowing from his gaping mouth. The stool, which I had dropped, lay on him, the leg still forcing his mouth wide open.

I remember standing for a moment, relishing my life. Then Johnny leapt onto the table, jumped down and hugged me as if he could never let me go. In the same moment a small angry man like a hornet came rushing in, pushed Johnny aside and with his fist, buffeted me on the chin. The blow alone would not have done for me. T'was only enough to rattle my teeth and knock me backwards. I staggered, lurched, grasped at nothing and fell, cracking my head on the wooden fender.

I recovered for a moment as they were bundling me onto a trestle, to hear Johnny, weeping and crying and a buzzing voice like a hornet in truth declaiming, that in such a charnel house as his home had become, how was he to know villain from saviour.

And so for the second time in two days, I was laid to rest in Dame Margery's best bed. However on this, the second occasion, I was slower to recover myself, thanks to my encounter with the fender. Captain Simon Croker, Jane's husband and Johnny's father who had thought I was Brigstock, intent on molesting his child, could not apologise enough.

I became aware on the second day, when the October sun pierced through the casement, making a criss-cross pattern on my counterpane, that a great many persons seemed to be concerned for my recovery. Elijah sat beside me, refusing to vacate his chair, except to relieve himself. Robert, finding Brigstock, stone dead, in that ill fated kitchen, had left wheeled with his troop once again for Margery's farm, and blamed himself repeatedly for allowing me to ride off alone from the battlefield. His men were once again eating Dame Margery out of house and home, although Ralph, enterprising poacher that he was, seeing one of her fields alive with rabbits, snared enough for several pies.

I was not (now) vainglorious enough to suppose that all this kind attention rose from the attraction of my nineteen year old person. I had gained a firm awareness of my value as a surgeon, battlefield, hedgerow makeshift, or quietly professional in bed-chamber or shop. A messenger had been sent by Robert to Samuel Luke, explaining Brigstock's death, and had returned with orders that my every comfort was to be supplied. I wanted nothing but insisted that Elijah was to be paid for his night's work on the battlefield, and requested a pen and paper that he might record his actions. It seemed he had been to the King's School in Stratford whilst his father was alive and could write well enough so between us as I lay there, wrestling with my headache, we composed a record of our doctoring for that fearsome night of Sunday 23rd October.

By Thursday I could heave myself from Margery's best bed and stagger to the outside privy. On Friday I insisted on standing, naked beneath the pump, to erase from myself, with the help of Margery's best oatmeal and lavender soap, all trace of Brigstock's blood. Captain Simon Croker who had been borne a farmer and who took clumsily to soldiery stood beside me holding a napkin, still apologising as did Dame Margery, his elder sister, still talking. I was wearing a linen nightshirt, which they had dressed me in. It seemed my clothes had been burned. Simon offered to give me clothing and helped by Elijah, we returned to his bedchamber where he found me stockings, breeches and bequeathed me his second best doublet.

I asked Simon as I dressed what action he had seen on Sunday last. He told me testily: "None at all, sir. Lord Saye and Sele declared himself too old to fight and sent his sons instead. I wielded the pen, not the sword. In fact the only blow I struck......." I begged him to forget his understandable mistake, thanked him for his kindness and care and told him Elijah and myself would take our leave on the morrow.

"But, dear sir," I told him, "have a care to your son. He has endured much and his ordeal with Brigstock could scar his mind. Keep him with you and his lady mother and sister, who have also suffered terrible sights. After such horrors, the mind must take time to heal itself gently and patiently. I grieve for your terrible losses, but implore you to have a care for their state of mind."

I was afraid that he would take offence at my advice as he was an irascible little man, who thought all at fault but himself. He was silent for a moment, whilst I waited for his wrath. But thankfully he took my words in good part, wrung my hand and asked me to come later that day to the burial of his daughter and father-in-law.

The Burghill troop was bound that day for Warwick, Robert having satisfied himself that I was well on the mend. In truth although my head hammered like a busy smithy, I could not wait to be on the road. I could return home. The knave Billiard was discredited and imprisoned. There was no longer need for my self-inflicted exile.

Early next morning I saw Martha scurrying across the yard, clearly anxious to avoid my company. But I gave her no choice in the matter. "My dagger, if you please, Mistress Martha!" I commanded, in a manner unusual for me. I was determined to be no longer a Worcester hobbledehoy, but a Master Physician. She retrieved it with a shamefaced air from the pocket of her apron and returned it, without a word.

I bought a mount for Elijah from Robert, that had been ridden by one of his seasoned troopers, who had been grievously wounded by Lord Wilmot's cavaliers. Perhaps I paid more than the nag was worth. No matter, for our farewell, on this occasion was cordiality itself. He clasped me to him lovingly, too lovingly perhaps for my comfort, bade me put not my trust in princes - again - mounted, and galloped his troop back to the Ridgeway. Elijah and I stood at the roadside and shouted Godspeed to them all. I was sorry indeed to see Ralph ride off to war. Poacher or not, I knew not his equal for contrivance.

The morrow brought a prolonged and tearful farewell from the Crokers. They owned much of the land hereabouts, and were yet another household who had been taxed beyond their capacity. "Ship money!" cried Dame Margery. "Ship money! I ask you, Master Tom, how many ships have you seen hereabouts or on the Ridge? 'Tis an idle feckless King, who will ruin his subjects and one day himself, no question."

As we rode yet again along the ill-fated Ridgeway, Elijah asked me: "What think you of the King, Tom? Is he indeed so evil?"

I remembered an old uncle of my father's who had told me of the stench of burning human flesh, when heretics had been burnt at the whim of Mary Tudor, even in Worcester corn market. "And we are all heretics, now nephew," he told me. "'Tis a strange world."

"At least he doesn't burn us for what we think," I said finally to Elijah, and we trotted on in silence.

We came to the road back to Stratford but although I knew Elijah wished to make haste homewards to his mother, I had a fancy to see the Rollright Stones again. It was about noon when we turned aside to dismount and sit in the soft grasses that sighed in the light wind. To my relief today they were nothing more or less than a collection of boulders and rocks. I did not tell Elijah of my shameful capture there, as it was pleasant to bask in his unquestioning admiration for a little longer. It was pleasant also to bask in the October sun and to unwrap Dame Margery's matchet bread. Her cooking skills far exceeded her powers of conversation. As we munched, a shepherd, a young fellow with cheeks burned from the sun on these heights came by to count his flock. I think he had heard our laughter and came to join our chat. I offered him bread and in return he pulled out russet apples from his sheepskin bag.

"You be a soldier then?" he asked me. "Warm work up there at Kineton," and he jerked his thumb northwards in the direction from which we had come.

"Not soldiers. We try to help the wounded," I told him.

He sat upright. "Are you the doctor then?" he asked his blue eyes widening. "Would you be Doctor Tom? They sent me to look out for you. Three, four days back I been on the Ridgeway, asking all they chaps coming from up there."

"Who sent you?" and as he told me I remembered my half promise to Edward Holte.

"The gentry, at the big house in Great Tew. Lord Carey come back with Mr Edward on a trestle. Come you there with me now, masters and Lady Letty'll give me a crown and a new smock."

Elijah was already on his feet, his nose twitching and his eyes shining with expectation at the prospect of hobnobbing with the gentry. I rose more slowly.

"You are sure you want to go?" I asked Elijah. "What about your mother?"

"Mother will wait," he said somewhat callously. "But what about your mother?"

"Nay my poor mother will wait out eternity. She died long ago. I have no-one," I told him.

Was that true, I pondered as we retraced our steps and were again on the Stratford Road. Was I totally alone? There was Joan of course and dear Robert who had so kindly made their home with me, and Roger. And then of course there was Phoebe......

"This road goes all the way to Oxford," said our guide. But we goes up now and over the Glyme and across the wold down to Great Tew. The sheep I tend are Lord Carey's."

"Is he a good man to work for?" I asked.

He answered simply: "The best."

And so we came to one of the loveliest villages in England. But far from being a Great house for Great people as the name suggested, it was the homeliest of mansions, the front door close to the path, and the whole house, seeming to nestle into the folds of the Oxfordshire hills, like a child in his mother's arms.

The shepherd went round the back, leading our horses, bidding us wait on the path to the front door. A moment later it flew open and the Viscount himself came out.

"Doctor Tom! What a case you are in to be sure! That head of genius!" for I still sported a sorry bandage. "Was the battle unfinished? Did I abscond betimes? I am overjoyed to see you and you too, good, sir." this to Elijah. "Pray you, come in come in, dear sirs. Your patient longs to see you. Letty!" he called, "Come dearest one. Here is Edward's doctor!"

He pushed us into a fine room where we stood for a moment bemused at the splendour of the furniture. A servant proffered wine in silver goblets and a lady came in with a gracious smile, which faded as she stared at me in disbelief.

"This is Edward's doctor?"

And indeed, I must have been a sorry sight! My wound had bled slightly from the jolting of the ride and I was aware that my bandage was hanging down my back. The sleeves of Simon's second best doublet came just below my elbows and his breeches whilst wide were painfully short. His hose scarce covered my knee. Only my boots were my own and they were scratched and worn through in the sole, like a beggar's at the town gate. Elijah was in better fig, but we were neither of us fit for courtly company.

Well, we would brave it out and go! "Madam," I cried, "Forgive me! My clothes were burnt, for I was attacked by a madman. Too long and tedious a tale for a lady. But Madam, be sure!" and I broke into lusty song. 'What though my back go bare, I'm ragged and torn and true!' and I bowed long and low, with a gallant flourish of an imaginary hat.

At the sound of my voice, a recorder in a nearby room took up the melody. Lucius Carey laughed with delight and Letty seemed to soften.

"Come then, master doctor, to your patient. I protest I could not know his mind until now, he was so anxious and determined on seeing you again. You are - what can I say? - A Doctor with a Difference. His wound is mending, we have tended him as best we may."

And so began two months of my life that were to me both university and holiday. No day passed without interesting discourse. Poor Lucius, and he insisted that I called him by his given name, was torn in two by his beliefs. He was the King's true servant, having accepted the post of Secretary of State, no less, at the outbreak of war. To the notion and idea of Kingship he was ever faithful, but he had serious doubts and misgivings as to Charles' capability as a leader of men.

"He mistakes deviousness for intelligence," he moaned after one trying day he had spent in Oxford where Charles had his court. "He listens to and is guided by that silly French Hussy, who writes him foolish advice from the Low Countries."

At this his wife would bridle and pout for she shared Henrietta Maria's religion. To sweeten her temper he would assure her: "Ah dearest love, if only you had charge of the heart and hand of our sovereign, then we would have Peace indeed."

Great men came weekly to stay and talk. Indeed I never knew that one could talk so much on matters that had always seemed to me to be immutable. Lucius and Edward spoke much on the duties of fatherhood. The Viscount, like Edward had fallen foul of his father, the first Lord Carey for similar reasons. He had married for love not money, but unlike poor Edward had inherited excellent Oxfordshire estates from his mother's family. Like Edward, he tried to be reconciled with his father, but to no avail. Both men spoke of their envy towards me, because my relationship with my father had been so easy and loving, and laced with humour.

From our personal stances we spoke often of the duty of the King to be a father to his people and both my mentors despaired of Charles ever attaining this role. "He is a father, yes a good, kind and patient father to his own children, and to his servants but as for his subjects, he is blinded in his attitude to them by his assumption of his Divine Right. If they do not also assume it, in his eyes they are damned."

"And yet," Lucius would cry "Silence, friends! for our King is no tyrant."

"And yet," Elizabeth would echo, "silence indeed is what followed the death of Strafford, and say what you will of Black Tom he was ever the King's faithful servant. How came Charles to sign the death warrant of his viceroy in the North?"

"Yes, Charles signed, for others wished it," said Letty, sighing, and reaching out for her husband's hand. "Dearest love, have a care."

Somehow the weeks flew past in pleasant mirth and action and Edward's leg mended apace. I supervised his first few steps, Elijah having made a willow frame for him to lean on when he must needs attempt to walk.

I think I fell a little in love with Elizabeth or Eliza as Edward called her. She never failed to thank me for my skill, wondering much on what would have happened if I had not been at Edgehill to dress Edward's wound. I managed perhaps the most courtly compliment of my young years.

"Madam in one way, I cannot help but rejoice that events transpired as they did, for it has brought me the valued acquaintance of the loveliest of ladies - and of her husband too." I added for good measure, lest she should think me saucy.

We were walking in the garden on a rare fine day, the first day of the New Year. She was not a beautiful woman for all my fancy speeches but she had an air of prettiness and could converse, with both sense and humour. Edward supported by Lucius walked ahead and suddenly she asked me: "But Tom, what of your life? Are there not family members in Worcester who know nothing of your health or whereabouts?"

196

I had paid a messenger to take news of my survival and good entertainment to Worcester at the end of November, but he had returned with the message undelivered having had the contents of his pockets removed by a thief as he slept in an inn in Stratford. Elijah in December had resisted all invitations to stay for the Christmas festival and had returned at last to his mother promising that he would send word to Fish Street that I was well. I gave him several guineas to cover that expense, and to bring good Christmas cheer to his mother. Now fair Eliza's question awoke a sleeping guard dog, my conscience. I had been so taken up with thoughts and arguments, so willingly seduced by good living and conversation and merry-making, I had neglected my duties and responsibilities.

"Yes, lady I have two concerns in Worcester and you are right. I must return."

"What are they, these 'concerns' of yours?" she asked with a wide smile, "I would not have you leave us for 'concerns'."

"And yet they lie upon my conscience," I told her "You are right. I must be gone. One is a butcher's shop, my father's legacy and the other - is my life, my future, my heart's desire."

She stopped and looked at me, her arched eyebrows raised slightly and her lips smiling quizzically.

"So this second concern. Is it a doctoring enterprise or a woman?"

I could make no reply. I only knew that I must return at once. I sought out Lady Letty with her maids, feeling as if I had suddenly awoken into life from a most pleasant dream. And yet life must be faced and accepted, relished even - not pushed aside.

"I must take my leave now dear madam and I thank you for your kind hospitality and the excellent good fellowship I have enjoyed here with you. You have taught me much. I have changed from boy to - well if not to man - to something approaching that maturer state."

She laughed and told me "Dear Tom, you are a man indeed. So, go tomorrow. Let us hear you sing once more, "Ragged and Torn and True." I will never hear that again without remembering your visit."

There were great arguments and discussion that evening as to my best road back to Worcester. Eliza wished me to go through Stratford as she wished to know how Elijah fared but Lucius was adamant.

"My dear Tom," he almost shouted, "'tis quite clear. Drop South to the Evesham Road and make your way through Moreton in Marsh and Chipping Camden to Evesham. Your road is clear west from there. Indeed you may see the Cathedral from Broadway Hill."

At this Edward intervened. "But Tom you have said that you made a good friend of a Birmingham horse-trader. Would you not wish to see if you can further that friendship and perhaps make some financial gain for yourself?"

I felt guilty that I had never told them that for my sort of middling person, I was rich. It seemed so strange to myself. As it was I said:

"One may be sure that when three or more persons discuss the most convenient way in England, from one place to another, all three will ever disagree as to the best. But certain sure it is that I must be up betimes to use the daylight."

I asked at least could I pay for Jupiter's stabling. But they would have none of it.

They crowded outside next day to bid me Farewell. I could hardly speak for grief at our parting but muttered some sort of blessing. I turned at the top of the ride and saw my four friends clustered in the path outside the house and thought that I had never thought to enjoy myself so much, just three short months from my father's terrible death. I waved and wept a little although perhaps that was the cruel wind that had arisen in the night, afflicting my eyes. I murmured again, "God bless you all," and turned my horse towards Enstone and Chipping Norton, and thence north west for Worcester.